Praise for the novels of Amber Garza

"Propulsive.... Combining high drama with issues—aging, sibling rivalry, the shadow of past mistakes—to which most readers can relate, Garza keeps the fast-paced plot twists going into the book's final pages. Fans of smart, female-centered thrillers will love this."
—*Publishers Weekly*, starred review, on *A Mother Would Know*

"Garza deftly explores family dynamics and mental illness in this twisty, fast-paced mystery. Perfect for fans of B. A. Paris's and Camilla Way's psychological suspense." —*Library Journal*

"Books like *Where I Left Her* by Amber Garza are a reminder of why thrillers are my favourite genre. This is a tale that's dark and twisted, one where everybody has secrets galore, and the characters will have you shifting allegiances multiple times over. And that ending! It'll blow your mind. More, please!"
—Hannah Mary McKinnon

"*When I Was You* doles out twists and turns at the perfect pace, leading up to a fantastic conclusion. A gripping psychological barnburner."
—*Shelf Awareness*

"Exhilarating, page-turning, shocking, this is one of those rare psychological thrillers that really is the whole package. An electric, raw, emotional story that will leave you breathless."
—Christina McDonald on *When I Was You*

"*When I Was You* is a fast-paced, beautifully plotted book that will keep you reading until the last page. You won't want to put this one down."
—Samantha Downing

Also by Amber Garza

When I Was You
Where I Left Her
A Mother Would Know

IN A QUIET TOWN

AMBER GARZA

mira

Recycling programs for this product may not exist in your area.

ISBN-13: 978-0-7783-3425-5

In a Quiet Town

For questions and comments about the quality of this book, please contact us at CustomerService@Harlequin.com.

Mira
22 Adelaide St. West, 41st Floor
Toronto, Ontario M5H 4E3, Canada
BookClubbish.com

Printed in U.S.A.

For Libby, who made Tatum's character come alive for me.

IN A QUIET TOWN

PROLOGUE

His hands were in her hair, fingers threaded through the silky strands. I knew what it felt like. My fingers had been buried in her hair many times, including last night. When their lips met I sat up straighter, leaning forward. It didn't feel real. I worked my jaw. It popped and clicked. My own mouth buzzed with the memory of how her lips felt on mine.

The kiss was long. Too long.

She liked it.

My shoulder muscles pulled tight, a rubber band being stretched beyond its limits. I thought they might snap.

The two of them drew back. She smiled. Smiled with the same lips that had smiled at me. Kissed me. Told me they loved me. Clearly, a lie.

She brushed back her hair, and the diamond on her finger sparkled.

Her ring. The one I'd given her. She was wearing it.

It felt like a punch to the gut. Like a big "fuck you" to me. It wasn't like she knew I'd followed her. But still... Shouldn't she take her engagement ring off before she hooked up with another dude?

Throwing her head back, her neck exposed, she giggled.

Imagining my hands wrapping around that tender flesh, I squeezed the steering wheel. It gave under the pressure, and I squeezed harder. It felt good. Therapeutic. I pictured her terrified. Pleading. Mouth tight, eyes bulging. I squeezed and squeezed, my teeth grinding, the vein in my forehead throbbing. My muscles ached by the time I released my grip.

Their hands clasped. My breathing was labored as I watched them walk off together, around the side of the building, out of sight.

I'd loved her. Given her so much.

How dare she?

No one made a fool out of me.

She wouldn't get away with this. Not by a long shot.

PART ONE

1

THE MOTHER

Present

I am a liar.

For the past three months, every Wednesday evening, I kiss my husband on the cheek, smile sweetly and then proceed to lie straight to his face.

Kiss. Smile. Lie. Repeat.

Kiss. Smile. Lie. Repeat.

Every. Single. Week.

Which brings us to tonight: another Wednesday evening.

Shane leans over the back of the couch, his face cleanly shaven, his salt-and-pepper hair slicked to the side. The sun sets outside the open window, and it casts a dim glow in the room that makes Shane's face appear almost eerie.

I kiss his cheek and force a smile. The scent of his cheap hair gel is cloying. "Have a good time tonight."

"You, too." He glances down to the book lying open in my lap. "Gonna do some reading?"

"Mmm-hmm."

"Great. Sounds nice." He stands up straight, adjusting his

collar. "I might be home a little late. Reid's gonna be there tonight."

I nod and laugh, needing no other explanation. It's the shared knowledge of twenty-seven years of marriage. I used to envy couples who had made it this far. I saw longevity of marriage as success. As something to aspire to.

Now all I saw were the sacrifices I'd made. The one-sided compromises. The pieces of myself I'd lost along the way.

"Tell him I said hi," I say.

"Will do."

Listening to his footfalls behind me, I stare down at the book in my lap. My eyes blur, the words swimming on the page as I zone out. The front door opens and closes. I angle my head toward the window and listen. Outside, a car door slams, and then the engine turns on. I wait. Tires on the driveway; next, the gravel, then silence. I shove the book off my lap, stand up and go over to the window, where I peer out. The street is quiet, and our driveway is empty, Shane's car nowhere to be seen.

The clock is ticking.

I spin around and hurry into our bedroom. Since the blinds are closed, it's dark in here. I flick on the wall switch. Our room is done in muted grays and blues, Shane's preference. The bed is neatly made, the top of our dresser shiny from being dusted this afternoon. The scent of Pine-Sol still lingers.

The hardwood floors are cool against my bare feet as I open my closet and yank down a black top and jeans. Once changed, I slip my feet into a pair of black sandals and head into the bathroom where I brush through my shoulder-length hair. My purse hangs on a hook by the front door, and I snatch it up on my way out.

The air is comfortable, not too warm and not too cold, typical of a spring night in Northern California. The town of Rio Villa sits along the Russian River, so it's often cooler here than in the valley. But this evening it's perfect.

I take the long route, not wanting to pass Grace Community Church. Shane and the other men will most likely be inside the sanctuary, but I can't be certain. I have no idea what "Men's Ministry Night" looks like. Shane has been the senior pastor of Grace Community for twenty years, but only recently started the "Men's Nights" once a month on Wednesdays, the same evening as the youth meet.

The Float Down is a good fifteen-minute drive from our house, hovering right at the edge of town. When I reach it, I pull into the lot and park as close to the entrance as I can. I'm nearer to the water now, and a breeze circles me as I step out of the car. I tug my jacket tightly around my body as I walk across the uneven asphalt of the lot toward the front doors. When I get inside, I'm careful to keep my head ducked, chin locked against my chest. I can't chance anyone I know seeing me. Shane doesn't know I frequent this place, and he has eyes everywhere in Rio Villa.

There aren't many people in here tonight, one of the many reasons I like coming on Wednesdays. It may have been out of necessity, but it worked to my advantage. Most of the local men were at Grace Community. Since this bar is on the periphery, it attracted more out-of-towners than most of the establishments here in Rio Villa. At any of the other restaurants or bars, I'd be sure to run into someone we know. Not only is Shane the pastor of Grace Community, but he also runs the local foodbank and serves on city council. *Quite the prince among men, my husband.*

Jazzy is behind the bar, making a drink, but I don't see Adrienne. Maybe she's in the back. I climb onto a bar stool, resting my purse in my lap. I glance toward the restrooms, the side door.

"What can I get you?" Jazzy asks, wearing a polite, if not

slightly hard-edged smile. That's typical of her, though. The first time I'd met her, I'd asked Adrienne if she was a musician.

"No. Her name's Jasmine. Jazzy's her nickname," Adrienne had explained.

But it wasn't her name that made me ask. It was her vibe. She's got that starving-artist toughness about her. Jazzy's makeup is slightly smeared, mascara gathering under her right eye, and the edge of her bangs are damp. I know the girls work hard, and it is a little warm in here.

"Um...is Adrienne in the back?"

Jazzy shakes her head, stabs her bangs with long, claw-like fingernails, neon pink. "She's not here tonight."

"But she always works on Wednesdays," I say as if her co-worker doesn't know that. It's like when Adrienne was a child and Shane would try to feed her something she didn't like. *Adrienne never eats that*, I'd think, wondering why he bothered trying to cajole her.

Back then I knew her best. Knew her better than anyone else.

That's no longer the case.

Jazzy probably knows more about her than I do. It would be easy to blame Shane for our distant relationship, and I did for years. He'd been pushing Adrienne away with his off-the-charts expectations and controlling nature since she was a child. And when he kicked her out two years ago, I wondered if I'd ever be able to repair the damage he'd done.

After she moved out, I hardly saw her. Christmas and Thanksgiving, the occasional awkward family dinner—honestly, I was shocked she even came to those. She was still living in Rio Villa, and I knew she worked at the Float Down, but she'd never invited me to her apartment, and Shane didn't think it would be appropriate for us to go to a bar. He had a reputation to uphold, after all.

I always thought it was more than that, though.

Shane rarely talked about Adrienne. It was like after he kicked her out, she ceased to exist to him. Like she was nothing more than a word written in pencil that could be erased with one hard swipe. I didn't understand how he could do that. She was our daughter. Our flesh and blood. And he was keeping her from me.

But on a Wednesday night a few months ago, while Shane was out of town attending a Christian Education Conference in Tahoe, it hit me. Shane wasn't the one keeping me from my daughter. I was.

I thought of all the fights Adrienne and I had gotten into over the years, and the theme was always the same. Why had I not fought for her? Stuck up for her?

I had no spine; that was why.

But I was working hard to gain one, and I was determined not to let Shane dictate my relationship with Adrienne any longer. So that Wednesday night I put my book down, dumped my tea into the sink, changed out of my sweats and, under the blanket of night with only the moon watching, I drove to the Float Down.

I'd never been inside a bar before. Not an actual one. I'd been in restaurants that had bars, that kind of thing. But not a place where drinks were the main thing being served. It looked about like I'd expected it to, though. Plush, scarlet-red bar stools were pushed up against a slick mahogany bar. Bright yellow light shone on the shelves displaying the liquor. Circular tables were scattered throughout the room. In the back corner a dartboard had been tacked to the wall, and two gentlemen around my age with long hair reminiscent of my high school days tried unsuccessfully to hit their darts directly into the center dot. A country song played lightly in the background.

So far I hadn't recognized anyone, and a sense of relief flowed through me. I spotted Adrienne behind the bar, scooting a precariously tippy glass across the wood surface toward a woman in a little black dress, blond hair skating down her spine. Adrienne walked away to replace the bottle on the rack while the gal carried her drink to a circular table surrounded by other young ladies in little dresses. I took the spot she vacated, climbing up onto the bar stool.

"Mom?" Adrienne's eyebrows shot up when she saw me.

"Hi." I waved and smiled as she made her way over to me.

"What are you doing here?" She wiped the counter in front of me with a wet rag.

"A mom can't visit her daughter at work?"

"A mom can, but this mom never has." After looking around, she leaned toward me. "Does Dad know you're here?"

I played with the purse in my lap, fastening and unfastening the clasp. "No, he's out of town. But I don't need his permission. I can be in a bar if I want."

Adrienne didn't respond to that, but her lips scrunched. We both knew I was lying.

I was grateful she humored me. "All right. Well, do you want to order something? A soda? A sparkling water?"

"What was that?" I bobbed my head toward the girl in the black dress. "The drink in the pretty glass you just made for that lady."

"You want a Manhattan?" she said, her tone incredulous.

I lifted my chin. "Maybe."

Adrienne held my gaze a moment, as if challenging me. I didn't waver. Finally, she shrugged. "Okay, fine."

As the shaker rattled in her hands, I felt a shiver of anticipation run through me. A couple made out in a corner. A table of young ladies laughed loudly. The men playing darts high-fived one another. They must've finally gotten one in the center. My friend Gillian would've been so proud if she could've seen me then, and I made a mental note to call her tomorrow. Adrienne carefully set the caramel-colored drink in front of me, a cherry sitting at the bottom.

"Thank you." Smiling, I lifted the glass to my lips and took a hesitant sip. It burned a little going down, but the aftertaste was nice. Orange, yet not sweet. Oakey, but not bitter.

Adrienne watched expectantly.

"It's good," I said, and she kind of laughed.

"I have to go help those guys over there," she said, "but then I get to go on break. Wait for me?"

"Of course." I raised my glass and tipped it toward her. "I have to finish my drink."

Nodding, her smile deepened.

As I took a few more sips, my body warmed. I thought about how my evening had begun with me on the couch, reading a mystery novel and sipping a cup of tea. I looked around the room, at the people laughing and talking loudly, and I felt something stir inside me. Something foreign and a little scary.

But I liked it.

When I left that night, Adrienne placed a hand on my arm. "Dad's gonna be pretty mad if he finds out you were here, isn't he?"

I was going to respond in my usual way, assuring her that her dad would be fine. That we'd be fine. But Adrienne was no longer a child. She was twenty-four years old, and she deserved the truth. "I don't think I'll tell him. It'll be our little secret."

"Mom, you rebel, you," she teased, but she was looking at me in a new way, as if seeing me for the first time.

It was supposed to be a onetime thing, but the following Wednesday I found myself back at the Float Down, and again the week after that. I'd never missed a Wednesday, except for a few weeks ago when Shane wasn't feeling well and stayed home.

And even then, I'd texted Adrienne to let her know. Wouldn't she have the same consideration for me?

Now Jazzy clucks her tongue, shrugs her shoulders. "Yeah, I know she works every Wednesday, but tonight she didn't come in."

"She sick?"

"No idea. Didn't call, didn't show." Jazzy sounds annoyed.

"Has she ever done this before?"

"Not that I know of," Jazzy says. "Anyway, are ya gonna order or what? I've got a lot to do."

I shake my head and slide off the stool. "No, I'm good. Thanks." Clutching my purse, I hurry out of the bar.

2

THE MOTHER

Present

I've been knocking for several minutes, but there's been no answer.

"Adrienne," I call through the door. My mind flies to all the worst-case scenarios. I picture her sick and lying on the floor in distress, unable to move. Or hurt. Or, worse, dead. "Adrienne!" I holler louder, still pounding.

The door to my right springs open, a woman's head poking out. "What the hell?" She looks at me with narrowed eyes, mouth tight. By her leg stands a toddler, sticky, jelly-stained hand wrapped around her thigh.

"Sorry," I say. "I'm Adrienne's mom."

"I know who you are," she says, and that's when I realize she looks somewhat familiar. "I go to Grace Community… on, like, holidays and stuff."

There are a lot of people in town like that. Don't attend regularly, but enough to be associated. "Have you seen Adrienne at all tonight?"

She shakes her head. "Heard her earlier today, I think."

"Do you remember what time that was? Did you hear her leave?" I move toward her.

She backs away, her hand falling to her child's shoulders. "Maybe. I don't know. I can't be sure. Could've been one of the other neighbors, I guess. Kinda got my hands full over here. And she's usually pretty quiet. So quiet it's like she's rarely home." She throws me a pointed look.

Glancing into the woman's apartment, I see another child seated on the couch watching cartoons, a little older than the one by her leg. Diapers sit on the kitchen counter. Does she have three?

Curtis and Adrienne were enough for me.

"She didn't show up to work tonight, and she's not answering her door," I say. "That's unlike her and so I'm worried."

Admittedly, I don't know my daughter as well as I'd like, but in the few months that I'd been visiting her on Wednesday nights, she'd never been a no-call, no-show. Jazzy's comment seemed to confirm that it was abnormal for her as well.

I check my phone again.

Still, no texts.

She knows I come by on Wednesdays. Why wouldn't she contact me?

Because she can't.

Because something is wrong.

"You wouldn't happen to have a key to her place, do you?" It's a long shot, but I have to ask.

"No. Sorry." The woman's fingers play with her daughter's fine, curly hair.

"That's okay," I say. "Thanks for your help."

When she ducks back into her apartment, I check my phone again. Still nothing.

I dial Adrienne's number the same way I had several times on my way over here.

"Hi, you've reached Adrienne…"

Blowing out a breath, I end the call.

I don't know how to reach Adrienne's friends. The only ones I even know about are Jazzy, Ted and Sienna from the Float Down. But I don't have any of their numbers. From what I gather, they don't hang out much outside of work, anyway.

I miss the days when I knew all her friends, had all their numbers.

Wait. I do have one number still. Mara's. They may not hang out all the time like they used to—as kids they were inseparable—but they've always been connected, like sisters. They have the kind of bond that will last forever. I know they still talk.

I click on Mara's name in my contacts.

It rings several times.

Come on, pick up.

I tap my foot on the frayed hallway carpeting. The smell of mildew lingers in the air.

"Mrs. Murphy?" she answers. It's funny that she still insists on calling me *Mrs. Murphy*, same way she's done since the first time Adrienne invited her over in seventh grade. Most of the kids who grew up with Adrienne and Curtis called me Tatum now. But not Mara.

"Adrienne isn't with you, is she?" I ask.

"No. Why?" A sense of déjà vu hits me. I've had this exact conversation with her many times before. Adrienne was always sneaking off with some boy when she was younger, using Mara as her scapegoat.

"I'm at her place, and she's not here."

"She's probably at work."

I doubt Adrienne told Mara about me visiting her at the Float Down, so I stick to the facts to be safe. "I checked there. She was a no-call, no-show tonight."

A baby's wail bursts into my ears. Wincing, I draw the phone away.

Away from the receiver I hear Mara whispering soothing words to her baby. When the child's cries soften, she says, "Hmm…that's weird."

"I've been calling and texting and she's not responding."

"Here, let me text her real quick, see if she answers," Mara mutters into the phone.

It stings a little that she thinks Adrienne will respond to her and not me, but it shouldn't. It's probably accurate. And at this point I don't care who she texts back as long as it's someone.

"I'm sure she's fine, though," Mara says. "She's probably out with a guy. I think she has a boyfriend. Maybe she's with him."

"A boyfriend? Really? I didn't know that." She'd never mentioned it to me—or Mara, it sounded like.

"Um… I could be wrong. I know she was dating someone a few months back, and since then she's been acting like she does when she's in a relationship," Mara says. "I haven't really asked her about it because I've had my hands full with Lainey and her colic, and Isaac's been working long hours. Honestly, Adrienne and I have barely talked. But that's the thing. She's usually really good at reaching out and staying in touch with me…unless she has a boyfriend. Whenever she's in a relationship that completely takes over for her."

Odd that Adrienne would never mention that to me. Then again, our conversations on Wednesdays were often shallow and surface. We're still trying to feel each other out and I can tell Adrienne doesn't fully trust me yet. We also get interrupted a lot, and there are always other people around, so it doesn't lend itself well to sharing private information.

We have plans to get lunch and mani/pedis together this Friday while Shane's at the church writing his sermon, and I've been looking forward to some time alone with her.

"Has she texted you back yet?" I ask, hopeful.

"No, not yet."

"Maybe I should call the police, have them do a wellness check."

"Do you think that's wise?" Mara asks. "If she is just out, can you imagine how upset she'll be if she finds out the police were in her apartment? It'll be even worse if she's, like, in there with a guy."

I hadn't thought of that.

Chewing my bottom lip, I press my ear to her door. No detectable sound or movement.

The neighbor's words drift through my mind.

She's so quiet, it's like she's rarely home.

Is that true? Is she rarely home?

There's so much I don't know about her. If I have any hope of us getting closer, of getting to a place where she shares things with me—important or private things—I can't afford to mess this up.

But what if she's not out? What if something bad's happened?

"I think it's best to wait until morning," Mara says. "I'm sure she'll be in touch by then, but if not, then we can call the police."

"Okay, yeah, that sounds good," I say with some hesitation. "But call me right away if you hear from her."

"I will, and you do the same."

"Okay," I say robotically. "I'll talk to you soon."

It's logical. Smart. The right thing to do.

So then, why does it feel so wrong?

I beat Shane home. When he walks through the door, he finds me right where he left me—on the couch with my book. The only difference was the mug of chamomile tea steaming on the table, in an effort to steady my nerves.

"Have a good night?" He peels off his jacket and hangs it on the coat rack.

No, nothing went according to plan, and I have no idea where our daughter is, I want to say, but I swallow the words. There's no way to tell him without confessing where I went tonight. Going to Adrienne's apartment when she isn't expecting me and is supposed to be at work doesn't make any sense. It makes even less sense that this would freak me out, rather than feel like a given. I'm not ready to tell him the truth. If Mara's right, then Adrienne will be home safe and sound tomorrow and I will have ruined all the momentum I've gained these past few months.

So I close my book and answer, "Mmm-hmm. What about you?"

"Yeah, I did. Exhausting, though. And I have an early day tomorrow, so I'm gonna hit the hay." He walks over to the couch and kisses me on the forehead.

"I'll be in in a few."

I reach for my tea while he walks to the back of the house. Wrapping my fingers around it, warmth seeps into my palms. The floral scent reaches my nose. I breathe it in and pray that Adrienne will text me back.

Minutes pass and she doesn't.

Finally, I take a bath and get ready for bed. I don't sleep, though. I flip around and incessantly check my phone, panic mounting with each hour that passes. By morning, with still no word from Adrienne, I hate myself for not calling the police last night. For waiting. I've wasted precious time.

Shane rattles around in the kitchen, opening drawers and pulling out dishes. Mugs clink together. I smell eggs and coffee, and it turns my stomach.

Swinging my legs off the side of the bed, I extract my phone from the charger and text Mara.

I haven't heard from her. Have you?

Several minutes pass before little bubbles appear on the screen.

Please let her say yes. Please let her say yes.

I hold my breath, anxiously waiting for the bubbles to transform into words.

No. Getting ready now, then I'll drop Lainey off with my mom and meet you at Terrace Grove.

Adrenaline surging, my fingers seem to have lost the ability to type something intelligible. After several tries, my thumbs type: Sounds good. See you soon.

3

THE DAUGHTER

Past

Growing up, we went to church every Sunday morning. When Mom would come into my room at the crack of dawn to wake me up, I envied the few nonreligious friends I had at school who had told me they spent their Sunday mornings sleeping in, watching cartoons and eating sugary cereal.

There was a strict dress code for our family, and there was no wiggle room. As a little girl, Mom would lay out my clothes on Saturday night when she tucked me in. Always a ruffly dress, itchy tights and patent leather shoes. On Sunday morning she'd braid my hair or roughly comb it into two pigtails, complete with big pink bows. Once I hit middle school, I could at least forgo the ruffles and pigtails, but not the dress and tights. I fought Dad on it in high school, begging him to let me wear jeans or even slacks like some of the other kids at church, but I lost the battle.

With Dad, I lost every battle.

Mom always dressed up as well in tasteful, and, in my opinion, boring, outfits. No fun colors or patterns or stylish cuts. Mostly, she wore shift dresses or empire waist skirts with blouses, and often in black, khaki or navy blue.

The three of us sat right up front, the row directly in front of the podium, Mom and I in our dresses and Curtis in his collared shirt and slacks, hair slicked to the side, save for the cowlick he had in the back that stuck straight up despite the copious amounts of hair gel he used. I loved to tease him that he looked like Alfalfa, and since it was a source of great embarrassment for him—which, like, really? It's just hair—he would get so angry with me. Obviously, that only made me say it more often.

Anyway, I had a difficult time getting comfortable on the wooden pew. I'd shift around, trying to alleviate pressure from my tailbone, and the pew would creak beneath me. Dad would glance over from where he stood at the podium. Mom would gently place a hand on my leg, a silent admonishment.

I'd get so bored during Dad's sermon that I'd count the beams in the ceiling, or the scuffs in the floor. When I got a little older, I'd sometimes make a game out of Dad's message, counting how many times he said "um" or "sin" or "Jesus."

Grace has always fielded a full choir and I liked that, especially when Rebecca Mains first came to town. She was a young single mom, and she had a great singing voice. But more than that, she had a cool, edgy style that was rare around here. No bland khaki and modest pearls for her. Not Rebecca. She wore short dresses with knee-high boots or jumpsuits with high heels or skinny jeans with floral shirts and strappy sandals. She frequently changed her hair color, from platinum blond to a glossy red and everything in between. Once, she even had pastel pink streaks. I thought she was the coolest grown-up ever.

I'd stand in front of the full-length mirror, knot the bottom of my shirt and roll the waist of my skirt to shorten it. Then I'd sway my hips the way she did while singing and imagine looking like her one day.

But not everyone was as impressed as I was. The other women in the church didn't seem to like her, and sometimes I heard people whispering about her. Within six months of her joining, they started wearing choir robes. Thick and black. Everyone knew it was because of Rebecca. I eavesdropped on my mom and her friends one afternoon and heard Julie Wise say that Rebecca and her revealing outfits were causing the men in the church to sin with their eyes.

It confused me.

When Curtis and I fought, I tried to blame it on him all the time.

"He made me do it," I'd say.

"No one can make you do anything," Dad used to say.

If that were true, then how come Rebecca was being blamed for the men in the church sinning?

I believed it, though. I saw the way the men looked at Rebecca, even the married ones. Different from how they looked at their wives, that was for sure. We were all in awe of her, I guess.

"I wanna be just like Rebecca when I grow up," I told Mara once.

"No, you don't," Mara said, frowning. "My mom said she lives in those low-income apartments across town. You know the ones by the little bar on the river? The scary ones? Anyway, she's all alone with her son. No husband or anything."

To me, all alone meant freedom. No one to tell you to cook dinner or clean the house or iron clothes. It sounded like Rebecca had a better life than my mom. She got to do whatever she wanted when she wanted, and she could *make* men sin with their eyes. My mom couldn't even *make* my dad help her with dishes.

I'd always thought witches were the only women with power. But maybe I didn't need to know magic. Maybe there were other ways to be powerful.

4

THE MOTHER

Present

"Everything looks to be in order. No signs of forced entry or a struggle," Tony, or in this case Officer Delucchi, says. It's hard for me to think of him as anything other than Tony, affable and friendly, always quick with a smile and a joke at the church picnics.

His partner, Officer Plunkett, a younger guy with an unfortunate handlebar mustache and perpetually red cheeks that make him look more like a cartoon character than a person, marches in and heads straight for him. I've met him a couple of times before, and I think he's a Robert. "Her car isn't in the lot, sir."

"I understand you're worried, Tatum, but it really looks like Adrienne skipped town, maybe went on a trip for a couple of days. Every sign points to her leaving on her own volition," Tony says.

I know he's right. Mara and I looked around as well and couldn't find anything out of the ordinary. A few dishes in the sink, which at my house would mean I wasn't going out of town. I always clean my house from top to bottom before a trip. Nothing worse than coming home from vacation and having to clean a messy house. But considering how messy Adrienne's room was growing up, she probably doesn't have the same compulsion as I do. I'm actually a little surprised at how tidy her apartment is. She even has a vase of fresh flowers sitting on top of her kitchen counter.

"Do you have any family out of town? Maybe she's with them." He snaps his fingers as if having an epiphany. "What about Curtis?"

There's no way Adrienne's in Arizona visiting Curtis. He'd been living there for a year now with his wife, Sarah. They met at college and after getting married, she wanted to live near her parents, in the town she'd grown up in. That's how they'd ended up in Glendale. It's a nice city. Shane and I visited once. It's hard having him so far away, but he's happy there.

He and Shane talk most days, and I call him at least once a week to check in. But as far as I know, he and Adrienne rarely talk. They were never close. Polar opposites since they were born.

Still, it doesn't hurt to try.

I find Curtis in my contacts and click on his name. It rings several times before going to voice mail. I'm about to leave one when a text comes through from him.

In a meeting, it reads. Everything okay?

Of course. It's the middle of a workday.

I text back: Have you heard from Adrienne?

The reply comes quickly: Not in the past month.

Ok, I text back.

What's she done now?

I frown at his response. It solidifies my thought that she'd never go to him. Like his dad, he always thinks the worst of his sister.

Nothing, I say. I'll call you later.

"She's not with him," I relay to them.

"Any other family member she might be with?" Officer Plunkett asks.

"No, our parents are in assisted-living homes. She couldn't stay with them even if she wanted." Which I'm certain she doesn't.

"Probably off with friends, then," Officer Plunkett says. "Or a boyfriend. Is she seeing any—"

"She's not responding to our calls or texts," Mara interrupts him.

Tony's mouth pulls to one side. Then he shrugs. "Maybe she's vacationing in a spot without cell service."

I hadn't thought of that, but it is possible. The campgrounds around Rio Villa have poor cell service. If she was enjoying any kind of wilderness retreat, near or farther afield, maybe she'd have no service there. Adrienne loved summer camp in the woods every year growing up—maybe she grew up to be outdoorsier than the rest of our family, explored it more in her two years on her own. I don't know.

Still, a thought nags at me. "But what about her being a no-call, no-show at work?"

Tony and his partner exchange glances, and then Tony crosses his arms over his chest, offers me a tight smile. "We'll talk to her boss and coworkers. See what we can find out."

I nod, appeased.

"I'm not seeing anything that points to criminal activity. My hunch is she took off for a bit." Tony offers me a conspiratorial smile. "It wouldn't be the first time, right?"

So that's what this is about. The real reason he's not taking this seriously. I open my mouth to defend my daughter, a frequent occurrence in this town that only sees the worst in her. That only remembers her sins.

But then Mara speaks before I can. "Normally, I'd agree

with you, but the timing of it is odd, don't you think?" I note a quiver under her words. It makes me turn. Her face is pale. "For Adrienne to just vanish like this, and only two weeks after what happened to Jane Dekker."

The floor tilts beneath me. I grip the couch in front of me to keep from toppling over. How had I not even though of that?

I'd found out about what happened to Jane Dekker at a church picnic. Shane and I don't watch the news and we're not on social media, but it's not like we're in the dark about what's happening in our town. The rumor mill in our congregation keeps us well informed.

The picnic was on a Sunday afternoon. Brightly colored blankets and black fold-up chairs sprinkled the lawn to the right of the auditorium. Shane clutched my hand as we smiled and greeted the guests.

"Tatum," Kristen called, waving me over. She and a few of the ladies from my former bible study stood in a cluster, wearing flowy sundresses, strappy sandals and large, fake smiles. My stomach churned.

"You can go join them." Shane released my hand as if he was my dad, encouraging me to go off with my friends.

I forced a smile and stepped in their direction. The closer I got, the more my stomach hurt. A year ago I would've wanted to hang out with Kristen and the others.

But that was before I'd met Gillian. Before my eyes had been opened.

I'd changed a lot since then.

"Hey, girl," Kristen squealed like we were teenagers, not empty-nesters. I used to like when she called me *girl*. Now it made me feel ridiculous. Her hair was big and bouncy, curls framing her heavily made-up face. "How are you? It's been forever."

I saw her every Sunday morning, but I knew what she was

getting at. I'd dropped out of the choir, I no longer attended her bible study and I hadn't accepted any of her lunch invitations lately. Shane wasn't pleased, and I'd had to justify my actions to him many times. *They're nice ladies, Tatum. It would do you good to get out of the house a little, socialize, make the rounds. Scott says Kristen is concerned about you.* I was weary of explaining myself, and I owed no such explanation to Kristen.

I simply nodded and said, "I'm well. You?"

"Good." She smiled.

"Hi, Alice. Hi, Mindy." I greeted the other two ladies and they responded with hellos and smiles.

The four of us exchanged small talk for what felt like a painfully long amount of time, but was probably only ten minutes or so when Kristen asked, "How is Adrienne doing?"

"She's fine," I said.

"I was wondering about her…because of—" she lowered her voice "—what happened to Jane Dekker."

The Dekkers don't attend Grace, but they own the only hardware store in town. Jane had been in the same grade as Curtis and they'd had some classes together over the years. I don't think he knew her very well, though. They didn't run in the same circles.

"What happened to her?" I asked.

Blinking, Kristen looked around and scooted even closer to me. My instinct had been to pull away, but curiosity kept me rooted in place. "She was murdered."

"What?" My body went hot. "How have I not heard about this?" Murders are rare in Rio Villa.

"It's not really common knowledge yet. Her body was found this morning. I found out from Felicity Delucchi. Tony was called in at 4:00 a.m. He—"

"But wait, what does this have to do with Adrienne?" I asked, confused.

"Well, aren't they friends?" She fidgeted with the strand of pearls around her neck.

"Not that I know of," I say. "Jane was Curtis's age."

"Right, but Jane's kind of a wild child…" As if realizing that came across judgmental, she adds, "Or, rather, a free spirit, like Adrienne. So I figured…"

It was flimsy at best, and felt more like a dig than a drawn conclusion.

"Well, as far as I know they weren't friends. And if this isn't common knowledge yet, there'd be no way for Adrienne to even know, so your concern for her is a little misplaced," I say, more sharply than intended.

Straightening up, she wriggled her shoulders. "I was only trying to be helpful. Jane had been out with friends when she went missing a few days ago. I thought maybe Adrienne was one of those friends, so I thought this might be a hard time for her." She'd wrapped her pearls so tightly around her finger, her skin was now bright red.

If it was someone else, I might have believed them. But I knew Kristen too well. We'd been friends for years. Gossip was her favorite pastime, followed by criticism and judgment.

"They weren't friends, so maybe just save your concern for Jane's family," I said before whirling around, weaving through picnic blankets and people spread over the lawn. Once I reached the building I slipped into Shane's office where I'd left my purse. It was cool inside, and goose bumps rose on my flesh. I snatched out my phone and dialed Adrienne. Despite the confidence I displayed in front of Kristen, I didn't know with one hundred percent certainty that Adrienne and Jane weren't friends. She'd never mentioned her, but I suppose they could've run in the same circle. Adrienne normally worked on Sundays, but not until evening. I prayed she'd answer.

After four rings, she finally did.

"Hi." Her voice was groggy as if I'd woken her up, which

was odd since it was afternoon. Then again, she worked late nights.

"Hey," I said. "It's Mom."

She let out an amused laugh. "I know."

"Right." I looped my hand around my opposite arm, hugging them both to my body, and leaned my back against Shane's desk. "Um…have you heard anything about Jane Dekker?"

"I heard some guys talking about it at the bar…that she's been missing. Was she found?"

"Um, yeah…she was."

"Oh, good. I figured she'd just run off for a few days. She's about to get married. Maybe she was gettin' cold feet."

"Oh, no, I'm sorry," I interrupted. "They…um…they found her body."

She gasped. "Shit. Are you serious?"

"Yeah," I said quietly. "But don't say anything. I don't think I'm supposed to know yet."

"Gossip chain's working hard at church this morning, huh?" she joked, but her tone had an edge to it that it didn't have when I first called. Was it grief? Fear?

"I'm so sorry." It was all I could think to say. "You two… you were friends?"

"No, she was older. Curtis's age, I think," she said. "But she came into the bar sometimes and we'd make small talk. Always ordered a glass of the house white. I can't believe she's dead. Do they know who did it?"

"I don't know."

"It's probably the fiancé. Isn't that what they say?"

"Who is he?"

"Never met the guy. He's not from here. Just got a job in the Bay Area. I think they met at college there or something. She was going to move as soon as he landed somewhere, she said. Maybe that should have been a clue," she added. "Girl waits and pines for Guy. Girl lets Guy dictate where she's going to live and when they're going to be together. Guy turns out to be controlling psychopath."

I ignored the acid in her voice, distracted by a wave of relief. It made me feel better to indulge in this narrative, even though I knew it was awful. For all of Rio Villa's flaws, it was a safe place to raise a family. At least, physically so. Crime was ridiculously low. Then again, the population was a little less than two thousand. It would be hard to get away with a lot here.

I liked thinking that the murder had been carried out by someone on the outside. It was way too scary to think there was a murderer living among us.

"This is nothing like the situation with Jane Dekker." Tony stands with his legs apart, bouncing on the balls of his feet as if he can't stand still. "Jane was out with her friends, a night of drinking and partying. They separated and she never came home. That's not what happened here. Adrienne left her house on her own. She took her car, her keys, her purse, her phone. She's an adult. She can do that."

"I know. I get that, but something isn't sitting right with me about this, Tony," I say, speaking to him not as Officer Delucchi, but as my friend. As a long-time member of our congregation. "She didn't tell me she was going out of town. She didn't tell anyone. It doesn't make sense."

"We don't know that she didn't tell anyone," Tony says, his tone less gruff as if trying to soften the blow. "She just didn't tell you."

"Or her work…" I glance over my shoulder. "Or Mara."

"Look at this, sir," Officer Plunkett calls out. He's holding a small square card. Probably came with the flowers.

I follow behind Tony as he walks toward him. Tony takes the card in his hand, reads it then hands it to me.

Thanks again for last night. N. S.

My cheeks heat up. *Thanks for last night?*

Sounds like a hookup.

"Is Adrienne seeing someone?" Tony asks the same question that had been dismissed by Officer Plunkett earlier.

"I think so," Mara answers from the other room. "And I think this might be him."

My mouth dries out as she comes toward me with a picture in her hand. It's of Adrienne with a man. A very good-looking man with dark hair and eyes, a crooked smile and a dusting of stubble along his sharp jawline.

"We need to talk to this guy," I say, thrusting the photo toward Tony.

5

THE FIANCÉ

Past

Fucking joke.

Those were the last two words my father spoke to me.

And, okay, yeah, he wasn't calling *me* a *fucking joke*. But I knew that was how he saw me. As a fucking joke.

It was how he'd always seen me. I was a disappointment to my family. The one child of my father who didn't go to college. Technically, I was his only child. But my dad didn't see it that way. He was more than happy to claim my stepsisters as his own. I think he'd trade me in for them in a heartbeat.

Many families would be happy with their son learning a trade. A skill is a skill, right? I make an honest living. But when your oldest stepsister is in her first year of residency, and your other stepsister is in law school, trade school to be a plumber doesn't stack up. My family worships at the altar of education. As a toddler, my room was lined with books and educational toys. I was more familiar with flash cards than action figures. I spent hours upon hours at the doctor's while my mom tried to figure out what was wrong with me. Why wasn't I moving at the same pace as the other children my age?

To me, the words on the page were jumbled. Scattered. Unreadable.

"Try again," Mom would demand. "Sound. It. Out. It's not that hard."

But it *was* that hard.

When I finally got the diagnosis—dyslexia—I thought things would get better. Now my parents would understand. It wasn't my fault.

But things only got worse.

I was damaged goods. Their one son, and I'd never be what they'd hoped I could be.

When Dad left Mom for a younger woman—one I'd caught him making out with one afternoon when I was supposed to be playing in my room—she blamed me. She'd pinch my skin and whisper in my ear, "He left because of you."

Funny the things you believe as a child. Things as stupid as your dad leaving your mom because of your learning disability, rather than the fact that he was horny and selfish, and his new wife was young enough to still have perky tits.

When I told my dad I was moving here for a job, I thought he'd be happy for me. Instead, he was confused. "Why do you need to move that far away for a plumbing job? You can get those anywhere."

But the far-away part was what intrigued me. What made me want to go. It was far away from my family. Far enough that maybe I'd learn to like myself. Learn to be okay with who I was.

As I'd packed up my car, my dad had shaken his head. "This must be a fucking joke."

But it wasn't.

Now here I was. Hundreds of miles away from my family, making a life for myself, and it felt damn good.

Smiling to myself, I rolled over in bed. It was late. I should've been asleep, but I was too amped. I'd always been like this. When something good happened, it kick-started my adrenaline as if I'd downed a dozen energy drinks.

And my night with her had been more than good, I thought, staring at the woman lying beside me. Her hair was splayed over the pillow like long fingers stretching out, touching my shoulder. She slept with her face upturned as if staring at the ceiling. Her eyelids twitched, and her lips pursed. It made me wonder what she was dreaming about. The comforter lay across her chest, the swell of her breasts exposed. In the moonlight her skin was pale, almost translucent. It had contained a golden glow under the yellow lights in the bar when I'd met her a few nights back.

I'd seen her almost immediately after sitting down on a rickety bar stool. Even before ordering a beer. She was hard to miss. She was the hottest girl in the place, and, if the subtle and not-so-subtle glances from many of the other guys in the bar were any indication, I wasn't the only one who thought that.

As I watched her, I remember thinking that no one would call her a fucking joke.

It was that thought that loosened my tongue, that gave me the courage to talk to her. I'd expected her to shoot me down. She was way out of my league. Anyone could see that. But when the conversation started flowing, I realized that I'd misjudged her the same way my family had misjudged me. Not only was she hot, but she was also cool, fun to talk with. Usually, that would make her even more out of my league, but that night I was matching her, witty comment for witty comment. It surprised the shit out of me. But it shouldn't have, because of her eyes. Those beautiful light eyes of hers held an aching sadness. One that I knew all too well.

She may have been the hottest girl in the room, but she didn't know it. She didn't feel it. Maybe she didn't even want it. To me, it seemed like what she really wanted was to disappear, and that was something I understood.

We talked for hours—about families, about loneliness, about escaping. I wanted her in my bed that night, but I didn't want to blow my chance by coming on too strong, like I did the other times.

You're seriously scaring me.

God, what are you, like, obsessed?

You've gotta back off, bruh.

Sitting on the bar stool, my eyelid twitched at the memories. I blinked. Took a breath. I needed a win.

So I went old-school. Asked for her phone number. And, thankfully, it worked.

Now, two days later, she's in my bed. Not a fucking joke now, huh?

You always jump in too fast. You've gotta take things slow, my mom said to me at the beginning of my last relationship.

I should've listened. Then maybe things would've worked out.

I won't make the same mistakes this time. I can try harder. Do things better. In the moonlight my gaze skates over her bare skin. I drag my fingertips along the side of her neck, resting my hand at the base of it, the steady rise and fall of her breathing pulsing against my flesh.

6

THE MOTHER

Present

Tony doesn't take the photo of Adrienne and the strange man from me. Instead, he smiles in a relaxed and slightly triumphant way. "Well, I think we've solved this mystery. She went on a romantic getaway with her boyfriend. I see this kind of thing all the time. She'll be back soon. I'm sure of it."

He isn't taking this seriously at all. I throw a desperate look to Mara, but it's clear in her expression that she believes him. So does Officer Plunkett. They're all looking at me like they can't understand why I don't.

"Tony," I say, pleading with my eyes.

"I promised you I'd talk with her coworkers, and I will. And we'll check the local hospitals and shelters and check some of the surveillance videos in the area to see if we can figure out where she went."

"But sir," Officer Plunkett interrupts.

Tony holds up his palm. "For Tatum, we'll do this." He places a hand on my shoulder. "I know you've been going through a tough time."

This causes me to bristle. Their Friday morning bible study at Mel's Diner. Apparently, Shane had been doing more than talking about the Bible. No wonder Tony isn't taking me seriously.

I fight back a biting remark, keeping my lips locked as I breathe through my nostrils.

He continues, "But that's all we can do. I can't put any more man hours into this until more time has passed or the circumstances change. Understand?"

I nod. I guess I should be relieved that he's doing anything at all. I know what everyone in this town thinks about Adrienne. After the incident with Kim, they all villainized her. They didn't just cast the first stone; they threw handfuls at her.

And Shane didn't stop them.

In fact, he joined in.

Tony, too.

When his hand slips from my shoulder, I mutter, "Thanks, Tony."

You'll catch more bees with honey, my mom used to say. It's something I've always lived by. I'm friendly. Polite. Sweet, even.

To a fault.

What happens when you catch all the bees, and you want to smash them? Crush them under your fingers? Drown them in the sticky substance?

What then?

"I'll be in touch," Tony says, and I blink.

After saying goodbye, Mara and I walk out to the parking lot together.

"Do you think they're right?" The sun is warm today and it beats down on my face. The scent of asphalt and damp grass wafts under my nose.

"Yeah," she says. "I do. When I was looking around, I didn't see a suitcase. Not in any of the closets."

"Maybe she doesn't have one." As a kid, she had a bright pink one. When she was a teenager, she refused to use it, so she'd take one of ours. I have no idea if she has her own now.

"Or maybe it means she has it with her," Mara says.

As we approach my car, sunlight glints off the rearview mirror, hitting me square in the eye. It disorients me, and I squeeze my eyes shut for a moment. My body sways. Mara's hand collides with my shoulder, steadying me.

"You okay?"

I open my eyes, stamping down the panic that was beginning to rise inside me. Other than the spots that fill my vision, I'm okay. It's not happening again. Not right now, anyway. It was just the sunlight piercing my eyes. Nothing more. The last thing I need is for my health problems to surface again, giving people more reason to think I'm not credible.

"I'm fine," I say with more confidence than I feel.

Mara smiles, easily satisfied, and then says, "Remember that time Adrienne and Kim took off, following those guys from the…" She scrunches up her nose, tucks a strand of hair behind her ear. "Were they from the circus?"

"No. Traveling carnival. Remember, they came through one year and set up kids' rides in the church parking lot?"

"Oh. Right." Mara nodded.

I haven't thought about this in forever. It wasn't one of Adrienne's finer moments. But that's not why. Mostly it's because I don't like to think about any memory that involves Kim. It's too painful.

But now it's all coming back to me. Adrienne and Kim had met two young men who worked the carnival, and, Mara's right, they skipped town with them. I guess in their eighteen-year-old brains they thought the carnival was their perfect escape from this town. Neither girl told their families until after they were long gone. But they did come back a week later, out of money and disenchanted with the vagabond lifestyle. I don't think working at a carnival was as fun as they thought it would be.

"That was right after graduation, though," I say. "She was going through a rebellious stage. She's different now."

"But there was also the time she flaked on our girls' night to go on an overnight trip with some guy she'd just hooked up with."

I'd never heard about this before. I hoped Shane hadn't, either. "When was this?"

"Like right after she started working at the Float Down. I don't even think she called me until after she left. I'd been waiting for her."

"But she called you," I say. "Both times she called. After the fact, yes, but eventually." I pull out my phone. "She still hasn't this time."

"True," she said. "My point is that Adrienne is impulsive. She's a romantic. It really looks to me like she took off for some whirlwind weekend."

Gnawing on my lower lip, I nod. I know it's logical. Rational, even.

But it doesn't feel right.

It doesn't feel like the truth.

Mother's intuition has never steered me wrong before, and my gut's telling me something's wrong. I pat the photo I'd tucked into my pocket. The one of Adrienne and the mysterious man.

The strange boyfriend she's never told me about.

I spot the pointed steeple, the long, dark brown building, and I cut across the lawn, passing the small two-bedroom house that used to be used as the parsonage. Twenty years ago we'd briefly lived in that house. It was the main reason Shane took the job at Grace Community. A job that came with a home seemed like a dream come true.

It wasn't.

Hugging myself, I hurry past the house, the windows following my every movement like a pair of curious eyes.

We moved out of the parsonage less than two years after we'd moved in. Our house is only a couple of blocks away, but enough to give us some space. Distance. Privacy. Now the old parsonage is where the youth group meets on Wednesday nights. I've been inside many times, seen the tables and chairs set around the room, the bulletin board on the wall, papers tacked to it, the guitar and keyboard set in the corner. And yet, as I pass it tonight, I can still see our old, tattered couch, the oak coffee table, our box TV with the bunny ears sticking out on top.

I round the corner to the narrow walkway between the parsonage and the main auditorium. My pulse quickens. I walk faster. When I reach the front doors, I grip the large ornate handle and muscle it open. Inside, I'm struck with the familiar smell of wooden pews and dusty Bibles. It's drafty and cool. Cooler than it is outside. I glance up at the high, vaulted ceilings as I step forward. In the early days, when Shane first took over this church, I used to love the acoustics in this room during worship. The way the voices of the congregation fused together, swelling up into the rafters, echoing throughout the spacious room. It comforted me like a cup of tea before bed, warming my insides. But over time that warm feeling faded, the sound echoing through the chapel becoming darker and more dissonant to my ears.

The front pew to my right—the one directly across from the pulpit—is where my kids and I sat together while they were growing up.

I picture Adrienne, pigtails sticking out on both sides of her head, the pastel bows I'd affixed rising like little fairy wings. She was always so wiggly during church, tugging on her knee-high tights or fiddling with the edge of her skirt.

Often, she'd pump her legs up and down like she thought she was on a swing. She'd get so rambunctious the heel of her patent leather shoes would hit the underside of the pew, causing a loud bang. Shane would pause from his sermon, throw her a stern look. Curtis would frown and shake his head. He knew better. He never made a scene during church.

I still sit on that pew on Sunday mornings.

Only now I'm alone.

I rub my hands up and down my upper arms. The cross looms overhead. There was a time when I would've come here to feel peace. I might have dropped to my knees and prayed or sang. Maybe opened the large Bible displayed at the front, flipping to one of my favorite stories. One that would offer hope.

But today I just want out of here.

I cut across the auditorium and head out the side door to my left. Down a short hallway is the door leading to the offices. After taking a deep breath, I hold my head high and step through it.

"Oh, hi, Mrs. Murphy," Leah, the receptionist, greets me with a large smile. I haven't known her long. She's newer to the congregation. She and her husband have only been attending for about a year. But she seems sweet, and has a friendly disposition, perfect for her role.

"Hi, Leah," I say. "Shane in his office?"

"Yeah. You want me to let him know you're here?"

"No." I wave away the suggestion. It always feels weird to announce my presence to him like he's the king, but I know she's only doing her job. "I'll just head back. Thanks."

Past Leah's desk is a conference room, long table in the center, surrounded by chairs. To my left are a few cubicles for the administrative staff. I keep my head down, not wishing to make small talk right now. *Tap, tap, tap* go their fingers on their keyboards. When I reach Shane's office in the back, his assistant, Darcy, is on the phone. She shrugs and points to the receiver as way of apology, but I'm relieved.

I knock twice on Shane's door and then pop it open.

"Hey," I say, poking my head in.

"Tatum? Well, this is a surprise." He looks up from his computer, his hands sliding from the keyboard. A large smile sweeps his face. "Going to prayer group?"

My stomach knots. I'd forgotten that's this morning.

"Um...no." I walk inside and close the door behind me. Tugging at the edge of my sleeve, my fingernails scrape the tender skin on the under part of my wrist. Claustrophobia closes in. Religious books line the bookshelf hugging the back wall like saints judging me. "I just...um... I need to talk to you."

"What's going on?" His eyebrows draw together, two caterpillars kissing.

My mouth is so dry it's like I haven't drunk anything in days. I swallow thickly and then blurt it out, "Adrienne's missing."

"What do you mean, *missing*?"

"I mean that no one knows where she is. She didn't show up for work last night, and she's not returning my or Mara's texts or calls. She's not at her place. She's just...gone."

"Well, you know Adrienne."

"What's that supposed to mean?" I fire back.

He sighs. "Come on, we both know she's not our responsible one."

He always does this. Compares her to Curtis. It's not fair. "When it comes to her job, she is. She doesn't miss work. She's never been a no-call, no-show."

"How could you possibly know that?"

"Her coworker told me." I perch on the edge of one of the chairs that sit across from his desk.

"They called you? When she didn't show? Hmm. I wouldn't think she'd use us as her emergency contact."

She never would. That isn't believable, so it's not the lie I use. "No. Mara is."

"Ahh, okay." He tents his fingers. "Well, I'm sure she's fine. Just give it a couple of days and she'll be back. Probably here…asking me to smooth things over for her with her boss."

I want to wipe that stupid smug smile off his face. He likes to think he has pull with everyone in this town, but not with Hollis Hendricks. I met Adrienne's boss behind the bar when he covered a shift or two, and he was never shy about his aversion to church. Besides, there's no way Adrienne would go to her dad for anything at this point. He overestimates the importance he holds in her life. Always has. Like he's entitled to her respect simply by being her dad.

But this isn't the time to get into all that. I lean forward, placing my hands on his cherrywood desk, files piled on one side, a stack of old books on the other. "Shane, I have a bad feeling…like something is really wrong. But the police…well, they don't think so. They think she left on her own, but I just know she didn't. So I was hoping that you could—"

"You called the police?" His gaze flew to the ceiling as if hoping God could intervene. "Tatum, why would you do that?"

"Because our daughter is missing and I'm worried. Mara was, too." No need to admit she isn't anymore. "Can you please talk to Tony? Just nudge him a little. I think he'll listen to you. Maybe then they'll take this more seriously and really look for her."

He lowers his head, dragging his thumb and index finger across his forehead. "No, Tatum. I'm not gonna do that. If the police don't think something's wrong, then it probably isn't."

"But I think—"

He cuts me off. "Tatum, you always think something's wrong, even when everyone is telling you it's not."

The words hang between us, smoke from shots fired. I gather composure as the plumes clear.

"That's not fair." My leg bounces up and down, my muscles reacting to my pent-up frustration. Why does he always bring this up? "And, also, it has nothing to do with this."

"I disagree." *Of course he does.* When does he not disagree with me these days? "It's the exact same thing. You're making something out of nothing."

"Something out of nothing?" I raise my arms from the desk and grip my head. "How can you say that?"

His gaze flits uneasily toward his office door. "Okay, calm down. You know what I mean."

"I don't, actually. My health is a big deal. Our daughter being missing is a big deal."

He vacates his chair, the seat swiveling. He makes his way over to me, lowering down onto the edge of his desk in front of me. Then he lowers his voice, clearly cognizant of how thin the walls are in this place, and of his office staff being within earshot. "You're healthy and our daughter is not missing. Those are the facts. I know you feel like they're something different, but feeling something doesn't make it truth. The prayer group is probably just getting started." He places his hand on my shoulder. "You should join them. I think it would be really good for you."

Prayer.

It's been Shane's answer for everything since we first met back in young adult group at the church I'd grown up in. I knew all the boys in the group, had dated some and been rejected by others. But then one day Shane showed up with his kind eyes and charismatic smile. He was shiny and new and caught the interest of a lot of the girls in the group.

But for some reason, he had his sights set on me.

I felt so lucky.

Or, rather, blessed. Luck wasn't something I was supposed to believe in.

Even my dad liked Shane, and he never liked any boy I dated. It must have been the minister-in-the-making thing. The minute Shane said he was applying to seminary, a smile had lit up my dad's face so bright it would rival a Christmas tree.

I'd dated guys who were handsy and pushy, who clearly only wanted one thing. But Shane was a true gentleman. He'd waited to kiss me until we'd been dating for two months.

That night we'd spent the evening playing miniature golf with some friends. Afterward, Shane had driven me home and walked me up to the door as usual. His hand had slipped into mine as we made our way up the front walk. He'd first held my hand a few weeks back and since then it had become a regular occurrence, his hand finding mine frequently. But that night something felt different. Charged. Electric.

When we reached the front door, I smiled at him. "I had fun tonight."

"I did, too," he said and then winked. "Even if you did beat me."

I laughed at that. "What can I say? I'm a master at mini golf."

"You play a lot, do you?" He raised one brow.

"Well, I have grown up in church," I said, meaning it as a joke.

But Shane's face turned serious, his hand reaching out to temper a strand of hair that had been kicked up by the breeze. "You're the perfect girl, aren't you?"

For a second I felt a deep and startling desire to run. I wasn't perfect. Was that what he expected of me? It was too much.

He stepped closer and I froze, the urge to flee disappearing as he merged the gap between us.

"Is it okay if I kiss you?" he asked, and I was stunned. I thought guys only did that in movies.

I wiped my clammy hands on my pants and licked my lips, then nodded right before his lips pressed to mine. The kiss wasn't passionate or earth-shattering, but it was nice. And at the time, nice was enough.

Shane's hand on my shoulder now feels like a vise holding me in place. I'm relieved when he draws back.

"No, I don't wanna go," I say, keeping my voice steady and strong, determined not to let him strong-arm me into joining the prayer group.

He pushes off the desk and pumps his jaw. "I don't know why you can't see how this journey you're on is hurting you," he says, punctuating the word *journey* to indicate how silly he thinks I'm being. "You were getting better for a time, but now you're right back where you started. Letting your anxiety get the better of you."

"That's not what this is. This is mother's intuition, and you and I both know that my mother's intuition was right before. If I had listened to you all those years ago, our daughter would be dead. So why can't you listen to me now?"

"You always wanna bring up things from the past, don't you?"

"How is that any different from what you're doing?"

"It's very different. You're talking about something that happened when Adrienne was a child. I'm bringing up something we've been dealing with for the past two years."

"*I've* been dealing with." I say the words I'd wanted to say for so long but haven't had the courage to. "It's me. I've been dealing with it. Not you. You have no idea how hard these past two years have been for me, because it's not happening to you. It's happening to me. And I'm so sick of arguing about it or having to justify myself. Something is wrong. With me. With my body. And with our daughter, and if you're not going to help me, I'm going to find someone who will!" Trembling with anger, I shoot from my chair and burst out of his office.

Darcy gawks at me as I walk past. Normally, I would be mortified about causing a scene. I can't count on all my fingers and toes how many times I'd swallowed my words and bit my tongue so hard it bled at church events, trying not to have an outburst. But today I don't care. Let her stare. Let her think what she wants.

Let them all think what they want.

I know the truth.

7

THE DAUGHTER

Past

It all started with a slight tummy ache in the morning before school. I'd ignored it then. At thirteen years old, I often had a stomachache before school. I chalked it up to how hard math was, how mean Ashley and her little group were to me and how most of the kids at school called me PK—Pastor's Kid. It wasn't original, but it was annoying. I hated only being known as Pastor Shane's daughter. Everyone made assumptions about me based on that one thing. A thing that didn't have a lot of bearing on who I was as a person. As an individual.

The tummy ache progressed over the course of the day but didn't come to a head until the middle of the night. I rolled over in my bed, switching from my back to my stomach to my side to try to find relief. But nothing worked. The pains were so intense, I couldn't fall back asleep. I sat up, clutching my belly for a few minutes, before sliding to the edge of the bed.

As I headed out of my bedroom, moisture filled my mouth. Gagging, I thought I might throw up—the flu again? I'd missed a week of school less than a month earlier.

Then again, several days off from school, lying on the couch watching daytime television and drinking Sprite, did sound kind of nice. I usually didn't get to watch more than an hour of television a day, and we rarely had soda in the house.

As the nausea intensified, I bolted into the bathroom and fell to my knees in front of the toilet. Leaning over, I retched but couldn't get anything up. After a few minutes I clutched the edge of the toilet seat and hoisted myself up to a standing position. My teeth chattered and my body felt a little achy.

Yeah, it was the flu all right.

I shuffled through the dark hallway toward my parents' room at the end of the hall. Dad popped up from his pillow the minute I pushed the door open and stepped inside.

"Adrienne?" Rubbing his eyes, he swung his legs over the side of the bed and stood up. "You okay?"

I'd been hoping for Mom, but she didn't even stir, her body facing the opposite wall, light snores rising from her pillow.

"My stomach hurts," I said, rubbing it for emphasis.

"Okay, let's get you some medicine." His hand fell to my back, and he guided me out of the room.

In the medicine cabinet Dad found a bottle of Pepto-Bismol. He filled the little clear cup with the bright bubblegum pink liquid and handed it to me. I downed it, grateful for the way the chalky substance coated my stomach. For a moment I felt slightly better.

"Come on." Dad ushered me into my room.

After I'd climbed back into bed, he laid his hand over mine and prayed for me. Then he leaned over and kissed my forehead before leaving the room. I wiggled and rolled uncomfortably around in my bed. Eventually, I fell back asleep.

But when I woke up in the morning I felt worse, the stomach pains almost unbearable.

Mom came in and placed a cool hand on my forehead. "Oh,

Adrienne." She drew her hand back. "You're burning up." Scurrying from the room, she returned with some Tylenol.

"My stomach hurts really bad." Sitting up, I doubled over, pressing my arms into my stomach.

Mom's eyebrows pulled together like they did when she was worried. "I'm gonna run to the store and get some soup and Sprite. How does that sound?"

Just last night that had sounded appealing, but now that my insides were knifing their way to the outside, it didn't.

Still, I nodded, hopeful that maybe Sprite could do the trick.

It didn't.

I couldn't keep the soda or the soup down, and I was too sick to enjoy any of the house-flipping happening on TV. I only wanted to sleep until this was all over. I wafted in and out of consciousness, my head fuzzy, my body hot, stabbing pains in my stomach.

"I really think I should take her to the ER," I overheard my mom whispering in the hall.

"For the flu?" Dad responded.

"I'm not sure it is the flu."

"Dr. Bradley said it was."

"No, he didn't. He said it sounded like the flu, but if it got worse to call again. It's getting worse," Mom said. "I'm gonna call again."

"It's a stomach bug. It'll pass."

"She says she's having cramping and pain. That doesn't sound like the flu to me," Mom said.

"Maybe PMS?"

"No, it's not PMS." There was a quiet venom in Mom's tone.

"I'll go in and pray with her," Dad said, and I slammed my eyes closed, pretending to sleep. The last thing I wanted was to have to pray with him. I felt his cool hand on my head, heard him whispering a prayer of healing over me.

Footsteps sounded near my door. "I can't get through. I left a message."

"It's not like the ER's going to do anything." Dad stood and my bed creaked. "They'll probably just say the same thing, only you'll have sat there for four hours and paid an insane copay for the pleasure. Here's your Advil. That'll be five hundred dollars please."

Without acknowledging him, she lowered down onto my bed, placing the back of her hand on my forehead. "Feeling any better? Your fever seems to have gone down a little." I peeked out of one eye. Hope blossomed over Mom's face, and I didn't want to take that away, so I nodded slowly, painfully.

"Yeah, maybe a little."

Her eyes flickered to the glass of fizzy Sprite on my nightstand. She picked it up and handed it to me. "Drink up. You don't want to get dehydrated."

I pushed myself up, squishing my back against the pillows propped up behind me. Then I took a few sips, bubbles meeting my mouth. The sugar tasted unbearably sweet on my tongue.

Mom's fingers pushed my hair back and I savored the coolness of her skin. "I'm gonna go make you some more soup, okay?"

I nodded dutifully, the idea of any more chicken noodle absolutely nauseating, and forced down a few more sips of soda for her sake.

Half an hour later I was hunched over the toilet bowl again as she rubbed my back. "Mom," I croaked. She helped me sit back against the bathroom wall, one hand steadying my shoulder as the other pressed ever so gently, accidentally on my abdomen. I gasped and hugged myself.

She studied me a minute. Then she nodded in that no-

nonsense way as if she'd just made a decision. "Okay, let's go get on your shoes and coat. I'm taking you to the hospital." She helped me off the floor, collected my things, tied my sneakers on my feet as if I were three again. Then she whirled off to find her purse and keys.

Shivering in my coat, I walked down the hallway.

"You don't think it can wait until morning?" Dad's voice asked as I shuffled toward the front door. He and Mom stood together in the entryway, unaware of my presence.

"No, I really don't."

He shook his head and muttered something under his breath about money and overreacting.

"Let's go." Mom's arm came around my shoulders and together we walked into the crisp night air.

The ER was busy, but we didn't wait for four hours like Dad said. Once they brought us back to triage to take my vitals and hear my symptoms, things moved quickly. Mom's first instinct had been right.

It wasn't the flu.

It was my appendix.

The doctors caught it just in time. I overheard them telling Mom that if she'd waited to bring me in, it would've ruptured. In that moment I realized that everything I'd been taught by my parents had been a lie. From the time I was little, they were always telling me to pray.

Pray when I was sad, sick, scared, in danger.

They said that God would comfort me, heal me, protect me, rescue me. But when I'd needed to be healed, it was the doctors who healed me, not God. If I'd stayed home praying, the way Dad wanted me to, I might have died.

8

THE MOTHER

Present

As I stomp across the church parking lot, hot tears sting my eyes. I don't even know why I came here. Why I thought he might help me. He never has. I'll handle this the same way I've handled everything. All of Adrienne's health scares. All her heartbreak and difficult times.

He wasn't there for her then.

I was.

Nearing my car, I fish in my purse for my keys. Once I find them, I sniff and wipe the tears from my face. As I unlock the car, a funny sensation brushes over the back of my neck. Like I'm being watched.

My neck swivels to look.

I don't see anyone. But that doesn't mean no one's there. Probably some church busybodies.

But then I catch movement behind a tree at the other end of the lot. A flash of something black. A man wearing a hood, sunglasses over his eyes and hands tucked in his pockets is standing on the church lawn staring at me. A chill skitters down my spine. He doesn't resemble anyone I know. At least, from what I can tell by his build and stance. With my keys in hand, I take a few steps forward, and then he springs into action, whirling around and running the opposite way.

Well, that's suspicious.

I hop into my car, then peel out of the lot, heading in the same direction as the man. I slow down and stare hard at the trees lining the road. But I can't find him.

I'm certain he was there, though.

And he had to have been watching me, or else why run away?

Does it have anything to do with Adrienne?

I turn, drive down the street slowly again. Nothing. I groan in frustration, smacking my hand down on the steering wheel. A few women, standing in a cluster in front of the church, peer over curiously.

I want to circle back, drive down the road again, but I don't dare. Shane already thinks I'm making things up. I don't need to add to that.

It was two years ago on a regular Tuesday in January when my world began to spin out of control. *Literally.*

I'd woken up at eight, like usual. The house was quiet, Shane already at work. Adrienne was working and Curtis was away at college. I made coffee, then took a shower and got ready. The sky was a deep gray, almost charcoal-colored when I stepped outside, clouds covering the sun. There was a chill in the air, and I tugged my jacket tight around my body.

Frank, from across the street, headed toward his car in the driveway, briefcase in hand. He and his wife had been attending Grace Chapel for years. I lifted a hand to wave as I did every Tuesday.

"Good morning," he called as he unlocked his car door.

We both hopped into our vehicles and headed in opposite

directions, him to his office across town, me to the hiking trail. It was a routine we'd both been doing for years. Most mornings I took a walk by the river.

Tuesday was my errand day, so after my walk I'd hit the stores. They were usually quiet on Tuesdays since most people were at work.

I parked and then made my way to the trail. On the weekends, when I had more time, I'd walk the mile and a half from our house to the trail, but during the week I always drove to it. Not many people were out this morning, so I had it mostly to myself. I breathed in the river-soaked air. Took in the gray, cloudy sky. Listened to the water rushing over the rocks. Spotted the ducks, a splash of white on the bluish-black surface of the water.

When I reached the halfway point, I turned and looped back around to my car.

The aisles at Safeway were scarce, nineties music spilling through the speakers. I considered it a good sign that my cart had smooth wheels, no squeaking, rattling or catching. Familiar with the layout of the store, I made my way through it with ease, ending at John's register like always.

"How are you this morning?" he asked as he scanned my items.

"Great, and you?"

"Pretty good. It's my Friday." He smiled.

That I did know. Tuesday was always his Friday, but I found comfort in our routine, our common conversation. "Any fun plans for your weekend?"

"Just catching up on my shows."

John and I had very different interests when it came to TV. Well, when it came to everything, really. But that was what I found refreshing about him.

Afterward, I made a quick trip to the bakery. I was in charge of treats for bible study on Wednesday night.

Clouds had rolled in, thick and ominous by the time I got back home, but I didn't mind. I liked the cold and rain. It was one of the reasons I wanted to live near the water. There was nothing better than cozying up inside with a fire and a warm, fuzzy blanket, or on nicer days, sitting at the edge of the riverbank, a cool breeze at my back.

I didn't want the groceries to get wet, though, so I carried them in as fast as I could and ended up beating the rain. The first drop didn't hit until I'd put everything away and had just put a kettle of water on the stove for tea.

From the hutch, I picked out my favorite mug—navy blue with swirls of teal reminding me of the river, the place I'm happiest and most at peace. The kettle whistled, becoming a screeching wail by the time I plucked it off the burner.

Sipping my tea, I sat at the kitchen table and looked over my daily planner. The week was chock-full with church activities. I'd always helped Shane with things at the church but had taken on more volunteer responsibilities once the kids moved out. It beat sitting around the house, listening to the floorboards creak.

I called the families who had missed three Sundays in a row to check on them; I organized the meal train for families who had had a baby, surgery, or trauma recently; I pretty much ran the women's ministry, and I helped out with the children's ministry as much as I could.

When I stood up to refill my mug, the room spun around me. Reaching out, I clutched the edge of the table to keep from falling over. When the spinning refused to stop, I squeezed my eyes shut. Lowering myself back into my chair, I took a few deep, cleansing breaths. Moisture filled my mouth, and my skin was a little clammy. Was I getting sick?

With the back of my hand, I touched my forehead. Not feverish.

I attempted to stand once more, but it happened a second

time. The dizziness. The spinning. Like I was on a tilt-a-whirl at the fair. I plopped back down. My vision swam, the pictures on the walls bouncing like beach balls in the waves. What was happening? I gulped in a few breaths of air, hoping to steady myself. When it didn't work, I pushed myself up to a standing position again. Reaching out, I placed my palms on the wall to guide me down the hallway and to my room. Once inside, I flung myself down on the bed and pressed my face into my pillow.

"Tatum?"

My eyelids fluttered open, staring into the white of my pillowcase. My mouth tasted like cotton, my nostrils stuck to the silky fabric. I rolled my head toward Shane's voice and peered up. The sun had gone down, the room dimly lit.

"Are you okay?" Shane lowered himself onto the bed beside me.

The mattress sloped down, and one side of my body slipped toward him, my arm brushing his thigh. My gaze fixed on the mirror hanging on the opposite wall. It moved up and down slowly. Squeezing my eyes shut, I blew out a frustrated breath. "Something's wrong with me," I groaned.

"Are you sick?" Shane's hand gently touched the back of my head, his fingers caressing my hair.

"I don't know," I spoke into my pillow. "Everything is spinning."

"Maybe you have vertigo. Ethel had that recently, remember?"

I did. She wrangled me at the dessert table at our last potluck and talked about it ad-nauseam. Then again, at eighty years old, health problems seemed to be all she talked about.

Leaning down, he kissed the crown of my head. Or, at least, he attempted to. Instead, he kissed the air right before my forehead, his lips never even grazing my skin. I'd like to think it was because I was sick, but it was a common occurrence. A goodbye kiss before work was often an air kiss in front of my lips, as if he couldn't be bothered to make sure he reached my mouth.

When we were dating his caresses were slow and lingering, full of aching and longing. Sometimes I felt like I would combust when he'd draw away.

After his fake kiss now, he straightened up and backed away from the bed.

"Try to get some rest. I'll bring you some water and soup, okay?"

Days turned into weeks and weeks, but the spinning continued. Doctors had no idea what was going on. They'd run blood tests, an MRI, a CT scan, a VNG test, an EKG, but all were normal. There was a theory that it might have to do with Eustachian tube damage, but it was all conjecture with no fix.

There was, as far as they could tell, nothing wrong with me.

And yet, there was. The episodes would come on suddenly and last several minutes at a time, and occasionally multiple days. Sometimes they stacked, one following swiftly behind the next. They made me anxious to cook, to drive, to socialize. What if I was holding a pot of boiling pasta water or behind the wheel and lost control? I worried. What if something deeper was wrong with me? Something they'd find during my autopsy and only then think, "Oh, yeah, that explains it. If only we'd guessed sooner... Woulda been highly treatable."

One night at dinner I suggested that Shane be the one to pick up the dry-cleaning in the morning. I had felt twinges of vertigo all day and felt certain that a real attack was imminent.

"When are you going to let this go?" Shane asked one night at dinner.

My head jerked up, my fork suspended over my plate of spaghetti. "Excuse me?"

"The doctors can't find anything wrong. You're perfectly healthy."

"Nothing's resolved," I said, dumbfounded. "I'm still having symptoms."

He cleared his throat and stared at the noodles on his plate. Twirling his fork in them, he worked his jaw. Clearly, he wanted to say something. I sat still, waiting. When his gaze met mine, he leaned into me slightly and said, "Do you ever think that maybe it's in your head?"

My fork clattered against the table. "You think I'm making this up?"

"No." He shook his head vehemently. "I know you believe you have these symptoms."

"I believe I have these symptoms?" I stood up, my chair scraping the linoleum. "Trust me, I wish I was making all this up. I hate feeling like this and having no idea what's wrong with me."

"Medically speaking," Shane said, "there's nothing wrong."

"Then how do you explain the dizziness, Shane?"

"The doctors told you their theory. Eustachian tube damage. Your ongoing sinus issues. It makes perfect sense to me."

"Oh, really? So, if this was happening to you, you'd just chalk it up to sinus issues and move on?"

"If the doctors ran all the tests and told me I was fine, then I would, yes."

Frustration burned through me. "Well, it's not happening to you."

"I mean, it kinda is," he muttered. "I definitely have to deal with it."

I let out a bitter laugh and backed away from the table. "Fine. You know what? You don't have to deal with it anymore." After storming down the hallway, I went into my room and slammed our bedroom door. An angry sob tore from my throat as I made my way across the room.

If only I was brave enough to express all my worries to his face, instead of running off and hiding in my room like a child. I thought of marching back out there and saying those words, but then the rest of the scenario played in my mind. I pictured his condescending tone and pitying eyes as he argued back, probably quoting scripture, words about not succumbing to despair, and pointing out how I'm not living by the Word. And I withered, exhausted at the prospect. I wouldn't win. I never did.

Perching on the edge of my bed, I pulled out my phone and dialed Kristen. She was my best friend. She'd understand.

After she answered, I heatedly relayed the dinner conversation between Shane and me, emotion coating my throat like acid. When I finished, it was silent for a moment. I thought I'd lost her.

"Kristen?"

"Yeah, I'm here." Her tone was hesitant. My insides knotted. "It's just... I mean, do you want to hear what I really think?"

"Of course I do." I put my free hand's fingers to my temple.

"I kinda think Pastor Shane has a point."

I hated when she called him Pastor Shane. It made him sound like the ultimate authority. Of course she'd side with him.

"You think I'm making this up, too?"

"No," she said. "But you have to admit, you do have a lot of medical anxiety. You have ever since Adrienne's surgery."

"Do you blame me?"

Silence again. I waited, sitting forward until my elbows hit my knees. "God saved her, Adrienne."

No, I saved her. Me. Not God. Not "Pastor Shane." Not even the doctors. Me.

"I feel like that should've been the takeaway for you, but it wasn't," she continued. "Look, I wasn't sure I should say this, but I'm feeling led to you now." Nothing good ever came after that phrase. I should have stopped her then. Call it morbid curiosity, but I held my breath and listened. "The other night when I was praying for you, I very clearly heard the Holy Spirit say that you don't have enough faith. So I don't think the issue is your health, Tatum. I think it's your lack of faith."

9

THE DAUGHTER

Past

For as long as I could remember, I'd been "boy crazy" as my mom called it. In kindergarten I had a crush on a boy named Nicky, who proposed using a Ring Pop at the spring carnival. And in third grade I played almost every recess with Max Price, the boy every girl agreed was the cutest in our class. But it wasn't until I was fourteen that I knew what it felt like to legitimately like a boy and have him like me back.

I met him at Sunday night youth group. His family was neighbors with the Carter family, and Daniel had brought him. I saw him the minute I plunked down in my usual seat, because he was directly behind me. He was impossible to miss. Not only because he was new, but also because he was seriously cute with eyes so blue it was like looking at the sky on a sunny day. A few minutes into Pastor Jon's message, the boy whispered something to Dan that made him chuckle. Mara threw him a sharp look. I smiled. When the program was over that night, I'd been standing on the lawn with a group of friends when he approached me.

"Hey." He pushed his toe along the grass.

"Hey," I answered back shyly.

"I'm Adam," he said, making no attempt to shake my hand. It was tucked securely in his pocket.

I liked it. So often, people were overly polite around me, as if I was going to tell on them to the pastor if they didn't mind their manners. It annoyed me.

"Adrienne," I said, glad that he didn't already know who I was. That he wouldn't treat me like the pastor's kid.

"Do you come here every week?" he asked, surprising me.

"Um…yeah, usually," I said, rolling my eyes. "It's lame, but my parents make me."

"It wasn't that bad." He smiled.

"Really?"

"Beats staying home with my parents having them ride me about homework."

My best friend, Mara, caught my eye from where she was still huddled with the other girls, their conversation coming out in puffs of cold air. She threw me a look of approval. It was a big deal, having this boy talk to me. All summer we'd fantasized about what high school and youth group would be like. Talking with a cute boy was high on that list of fantasies. I'd been the unofficial leader in our friendship, paving the way for most of our firsts. I had my period first. I got us into our first party. But I'd secretly worried that Mara would surpass me this year. She'd finally come out of her awkward, skinny, braces phase and with her new straight teeth and C-cup, I figured she was the one the boys would be into.

As I chewed on the inside of my cheek, I tried to think of something, anything, to say. But my mind was blank. Well, maybe not completely, but enough that no words were forthcoming. None that were worth saying, anyway.

"Hey." Mara stepped up, cutting into our conversation.

"We're about to leave." Then she turned her attention to Adam. "I'm Mara. Adrienne's best friend."

"Hi, Mara, Adrienne's best friend," he parroted, and I giggled.

"Are you coming with us?" Every Sunday night after youth, some of us went out for ice cream. Daniel was part of that group, so I figured Adam would be coming, I'd hoped he would be.

"To ice cream?" he asked, his gaze finding Daniel's from where he stood with some other guys a few feet away. "I think so. Daniel had mentioned it."

"Cool." God, there was that word again. Did I know any others?

Adam did end up coming to ice cream. We talked the entire time over our dripping cones. We learned that we had so much in common. We both loved Rocky Road, the color blue and the show *New Girl*, even though my parents didn't approve. We both thought Pastor Jon was so lame, his message so cheesy, and we both hated math.

He came to youth group the following week and then every week after that for a month. And every time he came with us to ice cream afterward. By the third time, we started to hold hands under the table as we ate our ice cream. A week later my dad came to the dinner table on Monday night visibly upset.

"Adrienne, is there something you want to tell me?" he asked as I swallowed down a bite of rubbery chicken.

"Um…" I looked at my mom, hoping for some help. A hint. A clue. Something. But her face was a blank slate. "I—I don't think so."

"It's been brought to my attention that you have a boyfriend."

Curtis had stopped eating and was gawking from across the table, but not in a concerned brotherly way. His lips were twitching and his eyes dancing as if he was thoroughly enjoying this.

Mom sat perfectly still, hands in her lap, lips tight.

"Boyfriend? No, I don't."

Dad slammed his fork down, and I jumped. Mom imperceptibly flinched, but then breathed in and resumed her trance-like stare.

"Don't lie to me, young lady."

"I'm not," I said softly.

"You haven't been holding some boy's hand at the ice cream shop?"

Oh, that.

How did he find out?

Curtis was full-on smiling now. But I knew he didn't tell on me. He didn't go with us to ice cream. So who did?

"Well, yeah, it doesn't—we just like each other," I tried to explain.

"You know the rules. No dating until you're sixteen," Dad said.

"But—" I started.

"No buts," he interrupted. "You're grounded for the next two weeks. You can go to school and church and back. And after that, your mom will chaperone you if you join the group for ice cream."

"What? But that's not fair. Curtis goes to ice cream with Laura!" I shouted, pointing.

"Curtis is sixteen," Dad pointed out, and it sounded logical. But I knew Curtis had hung out with girls before he was sixteen. Dad and Mom knew it, too.

They didn't care. The double standards in this house were maddening.

Angry, I shoved away from the table, ran to my bedroom and slammed the door as hard as I could. So hard my window rattled from the force. If I could have, I would have slammed it so hard the whole stupid house would've fallen around me. Then maybe it would've been as messy and broken as the people living in it.

For the next two years I had crushes from afar, but never acted on them. I didn't think I could take the humiliation or heartache of Dad getting involved again. As my sixteenth birthday approached, I was giddy with excitement. But I should've known better than to think that my patience would pay off. That I'd have any control over my dating life.

"Why are you in such a bad mood?" Mara asked the day after my sixteenth birthday. "I would think you'd be over the moon. You can finally date Dylan."

"Goodie," I said sarcastically, scrunching my nose up.

"What? Dylan is so cute and he's totally into you."

"Yeah, I know. He's already asked my dad for permission."

"Aww." Mara rolled over, clutching her chest. "That is so romantic."

"I don't want romantic. I want passionate. I want impulsive. I want…" My nerve endings tingled at the image of the boy who popped into my mind. The boy I had a huge crush on. The boy I'd been secretly talking to at lunch on the days Mara went to Bible club.

I'd bowed out of joining Mara by saying, "I already go to Bible club, every night at my house. I don't wanna go at school."

Mara had understood. She'd spent enough dinners at my house to know that my dad lived and breathed scripture speak.

"You want *what*?" Mara rolled back onto her stomach.

Hesitating, I picked at the comforter by my feet. I'd always told Mara everything. She was my best friend. I could tell her this, right?

"Parker," I whispered.

Her eyes widened. "Parker Sebold?"

Nodding, I smiled.

Mara's gaze shot to my closed bedroom door. She leaned forward. "There's no way your parents will let you date him."

I frowned, knowing she was right.

Parker Sebold was by far the hottest guy at our school. Maybe the hottest guy I'd ever seen. He was also a senior and notorious for getting in trouble and skipping school. He spent most afternoons in detention. I overheard Lindsey Lloyd in the bathroom speculating that he was a pothead, too stoned at any given time to be a functioning human. But none of that was true. The Sebolds owned a farm in the rural part of town, and Parker had a lot of duties to help his family run it. That was why he was late to school so often or fell asleep in class. And *that* was why he got detention every once in a while. Not every afternoon, as had been exaggerated by the other students.

It wasn't just the detentions and the fact that he was older, though. The Sebolds didn't attend church. They weren't religious at all.

And that was what made him off-limits for me.

Dad had made the rules of dating clear:

1. I had to be sixteen.

2. And it had to be someone he approved of.

Dad only approved of boys who went to church. Preferably Grace Community, although he'd never explicitly say that.

It didn't matter that Parker was sweet. That he'd told me I was the most beautiful girl he'd ever seen. That he helped his parents on the farm every single day rain or shine, weekend or weekday. What would matter was his religion and his reputation.

Neither would look good to my parents.

"I know," I finally said with a groan. "God, why do my parents have to be so weird?"

"They're not weird. They're just…" She shrugged. "Parents."

This got a tiny smile out of me.

She tapped my shin. "Look on the bright side, though. You'll finally get to date, and you can go on them with me and Wyatt."

Mara had recently started talking to Wyatt Bell, Dylan's best friend. All she had talked about for weeks was how cool it would be when the four of us could go on double dates. I thought it sounded like fun, too. Double dating with my BFF. I just wanted it to be Parker beside me, not Dylan.

But she was right. My parents would never go for it.

10

THE MOTHER

Present

When I get home from the church, I immediately call the only person I can trust right now.

Gillian answers on the second ring, and at the sound of her voice I burst into tears.

"Tatum? What's going on?"

"I'm sorry." I sniff, wiping at my face. "It's...Adrienne. She's missing."

"What do you mean?"

I start the story back at the beginning, relieved that I don't have to leave any parts out. Gillian knows about my visits with Adrienne on Wednesdays. She'd gone with me a couple of times before. I tell her about last night and then end with my disastrous conversation with Shane at the church moments ago.

When I finish, a heavy breath floats through the line. "Shit, Tatum."

"Yeah." I run a hand through my hair.

"What do you need? Want me to come over?"

I smile. That's Gillian. Always there for me.

"No, not right now, but wanna come with me to the Float Down tonight? I'd like to see if I can get a little more information out of Jazzy and her other coworkers. And who knows, maybe Adrienne will show up and I've been worrying for nothing."

"A night out at the bar. You know I'm down."

"Thanks, Gill," I say. "Pick you up at six?"

"I'll be there with bells on."

I laugh. Gillian's a lesson in contradictions. In some ways she's the coolest person I've ever met, but other times she says things like this, reminding me of the deep bond she had with her mother and the fact that she's an old soul at heart. "And if you need anything in the meantime, don't hesitate to call."

"I won't."

"How'd you bypass the warden?" Gillian asks as we climb up onto our respective bar stools. Ted is mixing a drink for a man sitting a few feet to our right. Jazzy's talking to a group in the corner.

"He had a late counseling session, so he wasn't home when I left."

"I'm glad he's getting the help he needs," she jokes, and I laugh.

Her quips about Shane used to make me uncomfortable, like if I laughed it would be an unforgivable betrayal. I think he and my mom would both agree with that. My mom never said one bad thing about my dad, that I can remember. Then again, my dad isn't anything like Shane. But being married to a pastor means I do have to be careful about what I say and do, particularly when it comes to how it relates to him.

"When you're out and about in town, your behavior reflects on this family," he used to say to the kids. "You're representing God and the Murphy name."

I took the mantra seriously for many years. Still do, to some degree.

But I know Gillian's merely being a good friend. She's maybe the only person in this town who has my back over Shane's.

"What can I get you ladies?" Ted heads over to us, dropping two napkins on the counter. He pushes his black-rimmed glasses up his nose and blinks his large eyes. With his flannel top, skinny jeans and black boots, he's what Adrienne calls a hipster. He's also the youngest bartender here—only twenty-three.

"Um, we actually just—"

Gillian interrupts me. "I'll have your Pilsner on tap, and she'll have a Manhattan."

"Oh, Gill, I don't know…" I start to say, but Ted speaks over me.

"Comin' right up." Then he's gone.

"I don't know if I should be drinking," I say once he's out of earshot.

"Trust me, you should." She wags her hands around in the air. "This energy you're carrying, it's a bit much. This will relax you. And…you need that."

It would anger me coming from Shane, but from Gillian, it doesn't bother me for some reason.

When Ted returns with our drinks, I touch the glass and say, "Thanks. Hey, do you remember me? Tatum, Adrienne's mom."

"Oh, yeah." He glances around and then leans forward. "Where is she, by the way?"

"I don't know."

He rolls his eyes and says, "Well, she better be sick or dead or else Jazzy's gonna kill her."

My eyes widen and an involuntary gasp leaps from my throat. Gillian pats my hand. "We're actually here because no one knows where Adrienne is. No one's seen her since Wednesday."

"Oh, fuck." Now both hands are around his face. "I'm sorry. God, I… I had no idea. I just thought… Oh, man."

"It's okay," I say, finding my voice again. "I wonder if there's anything you can think of, anything she said or did in the last week or so, that might help us find her."

"Um…" He rubs his chin, thinking. "I worked with her last weekend. Sunday night. And she got a phone call. I overheard her saying she was excited about something. I said something like, 'Big plans?' And she said, 'Something like that.'" He shrugs. "I don't know if that helps." He hits his palm on the counter. "Oh, and last week when I worked with her, she was in a really shitty mood. Thought maybe it was that time of the month, no offense."

Gillian shakes her head. And I don't blame her for being annoyed. I hate when men say that, too. As if we can't be in a bad mood for any other reason.

"Oh, I gotta go help these customers. I'll let you know if I think of anything else," he says before walking off.

"I wonder who she was talking to on the phone? With the big plans?"

"Well, to be fair, she didn't say she had big plans. She just kind of let Ted think she did."

I look at Gillian. "True."

Jazzy makes her way behind the bar, and I flag her over.

"Hey," she says. "You know this is the second shift your daughter's missed."

"I know," I start.

But Jazzy keeps going. "It's not cool. Luckily, Ted could cover, but if not, I'd be here alone again."

"I get that, but Jazzy, no one has heard from Adrienne. She's not at her place and she's not returning any of my texts or calls."

"Have you checked with her fiancé?"

I almost fall out of my chair. "Fiancé?"

"Yeah, he probably knows where she is."

"Adrienne's not engaged." Is she?

"Yeah, I think she is. A few weeks ago she said her boyfriend was gonna propose. Had a ring for her and everything. And then the other day I asked about her fiancé and she didn't correct me."

I desperately root around in my purse, my body heating up as if I'm standing next to a heating vent. When my fingertips light on the photograph, I tug it out and hold it up. "This him?"

"I never met him," she mutters, then takes the photo from me. "But damn, he's hot. Go, Adrienne. No wonder she never introduced us. I'd keep him all to myself, too."

I take the picture back and mutter a thanks.

How could my daughter have a fiancé and not tell me?

And if this is true, what more is she keeping from me?

Blowing out a breath, I glance around the room, at the patrons laughing and drinking as if they hadn't a care in the world. Does anyone in here know what happened to Adrienne? Know where she is? My gaze sweeps the room, studying people's faces as if I'll find the answers in them.

My heart seizes in my chest. A man wearing a hood stands in the parking lot, staring through the window directly at me. His face is blurred by how dirty the window is, but his dark eyes are clear, narrowed, pointed in my direction.

It's the same man I saw at the church. I'm sure of it.

"Gill." I tug on her arm, glance over at her briefly. "Look."

When I point to the window, no one's there. He's gone.

"What?" she asks.

"Nothing." Shaking my head, I feel silly. It was probably a coincidence. A customer outside having a smoke.

I reach for the drink in front of me, ignoring the tremor that has set into my bones.

11

THE FIANCÉ

Past

She stood at the edge of the cliff, staring down at the water below. My hand was on the small of her back. One little push and she'd fall, splitting her head on the rocks below. I drew my hand back and blinked, erasing the thought.

These kinds of thoughts were nothing new to me. I had them from time to time. They'd been happening since I was a child. My earliest memory of it was when I was five, and we'd gone out on my uncle's boat for the day. I didn't know how to swim, so my mom made me wear a life vest. It was bright orange and bulky, and she'd tightened it so much I could barely breathe.

Whenever she wasn't looking, I'd unhook it and slip it from my shoulders. In the afternoon the adults were at the front of the boat, laughing and drinking. I was at the back, life vest discarded on the bench beside me, reminding me of an orange peel. I'd stood up and peered into the water. I saw myself tumbling into it, then sinking like a stone to the bottom.

The compulsion to act out the thought in my mind was so

strong, I ran to my mom and stayed glued to her side the rest of the day, afraid what I might do if left alone. It played on repeat in my mind: me, jumping into the cold, dark water, my body sinking to the bottom, never to surface again. My skin would cool, my lungs constricting.

It's not real. It's not real, I'd think over and over again in an attempt to bring myself back to reality.

Sometimes the compulsions were idiotic, silly. Throwing my cell phone out the car window or yelling out something embarrassing during class.

After my dad remarried, a lot of them involved my stepsisters. Like when my oldest stepsister, Jenna, would sit in front of the fireplace on cold evenings, I'd imagine picking up that long ponytail of hers and dipping it right into the flames, watching them lick up her hair and onto her scalp. That one got so bad, I rarely came out of my room if I smelled wood burning.

"Come on," I said now, a hand gentle on her arm as I led her away from the cliff. "Let's walk this way."

It had been her idea to go on a hike. I'd taken her on a picnic to a similar area just last week. I was learning that she liked to be outside. She liked nature and sunshine.

I liked her.

"Oh, my God. Look!" she suddenly squealed.

My head snapped up to look at her. A butterfly had landed on her finger. The butterfly's wings were black and orange with specks of red and gold. They shivered in the wind, but remained upright as it perched on her finger.

"I've never in my life had a butterfly land on my finger. And look, it's totally staying." Her tone was excited, and her mouth stretched wide into a broad smile. But she kept her hand and arm steady, unmoving, clearly afraid of scaring the butterfly off. "Get a picture."

I'd never seen someone so excited about a butterfly, but I

scrambled to take my phone out of my back pocket. My fingers were a little slick from the heat and the hiking, so it took a couple of tries to swipe into my camera app.

But the butterfly was still on her finger. "What do ya got glue on there or something?" I joked as I snapped a photo. Just in time, too. The butterfly launched off a second after I'd captured the moment.

"Did you get it?" She came closer.

"Yep." I flashed the screen toward her.

Her grin deepened. "That was so cool." She looked up at the sky. "They're beautiful, huh? And amazing how they can just, you know, fly wherever they want to go. Like, they're just…so free."

It was a common theme with her. This idea of freedom. Being here in this town, with her, felt like freedom to me. But I knew as long as we stayed here, she'd feel trapped. Stuck in the place she'd grown up in.

I didn't want that for her.

I wanted her to be free like that butterfly. I just didn't know how to make that happen yet.

I sat on my bed, scrolling through my laptop. I'd been staring at jewelry for the past hour. My eyes were weary and blurring a bit at the edges. I blinked, silver and gold bleeding together, sparkles swimming as if I was looking at them through water. But it had to be perfect. I knew what I wanted. And that was what made this so fucking difficult.

There were lots of butterfly pendants. Gold ones. Filligree ones. Silver ones. Brass ones. But none that looked like the one that had landed on her finger. The one that had made her so happy. I searched through other designs, briefly considering a gold heart. But no, it had to be the damn butterfly. We hadn't been dating long. We didn't have tons of stories and experiences the way couples who had been together for years had. But we did have this.

I wanted the necklace to have meaning. Not something I'd randomly picked out, but something I'd put a lot of thought into.

It seemed that in order to get what I was looking for, I'd have to have it custom made. The account with several butterfly necklaces was called *BeautifulThings*. I clicked on the contact button and sent a message.

12

THE MOTHER

Present

"Where have you been?" Shane is standing directly in front of the door when I walk through it. Clearly, he's been waiting for me.

His tone is aggressive and my heart clatters in my chest as I hang my purse and keys on their respective hooks. Shane had sent me a dozen texts in the past hour, but I'd ignored them. It was easier to feel brave when I was at the bar, though. With him standing in front of me, radiating intense energy, my courage is waning.

"I was at the Float Down, checking to see if Adrienne was there...which she wasn't."

"Took you over an hour to see if she was there?"

"Then we were talking to her coworkers," I explain. "Trying to get information."

"We?"

I step around him. "Me and Gillian."

"Gillian. Of course."

Making my way into the kitchen, I ignore the implication.

Shane thinks Gillian's a bad influence, as if I'm a teenager and she's the rebellious kid in school. I know he blames her for the fact that I've been pulling away from church lately. And I can see why he thinks that. The optics aren't great. I did start on this path right after meeting her. But mentally, I'd left it all a long time ago. For years religion had been my world. The glue that held me together. I'm not sure when exactly that changed. It wasn't one explosive moment. A large abuse or indiscretion. It was multiple small ones over many years that had chipped away at the beliefs I'd held on to so strongly for much of my life.

Gillian just helped me face what I already knew. I'd been standing at the edge of the diving board for so long, sweat beading my back, tocs curled over the side, cool turquoise water underfoot. Gillian simply gave me the nudge I needed to finally jump off.

The first time I saw Gillian, she was guiding her mom, Beth, up to the doors of the church. Beth Hadley had been a longtime member of Grace Community, attending before we'd even arrived. She had stage four colon cancer, and a few weeks back she'd told me her daughter was coming to take care of her.

"You must be Beth's daughter?" I approached the woman wearing torn jeans and a Rolling Stones T-shirt, her short pixie spiked all over her head.

"Yep, that's me." She jutted out her hand. "Gillian." Her nose ring sparkled in the morning sunlight. The edge of a tattoo peeked out from under the sleeve of her shirt, winding around the pale skin of her upper arm.

"Tatum." I shook her hand and smiled. "Nice to meet you."

"Same," she said before helping her mom inside.

As they passed me, I glanced down at my black dress and cream cardigan, feeling like a frumpy old lady. Turning around, I watched Gillian guide Beth into the back pew. Then she sat down next to her, glancing around, looking slightly uncomfortable. Kristen turned from where she sat a few rows up and eyed Gillian, her lips pursing slightly.

"I heard she's an atheist," Kristen had whispered to me after service.

Her words made me a little nervous, but I wasn't sure why.

A couple of weeks later I stopped by Beth's to check on her. I knew her daughter was with her, but she hadn't been back to the church since the first time she came with Gillian, so I was worried.

I wasn't prepared for how steeply she'd declined in just two weeks. Her face gaunt and pale, her eyes lifeless.

"I'm so sorry," I said to Gillian, who nodded somberly. After setting my purse down and taking off my jacket, I rubbed my palms together, wondering what I should be doing. Beth was asleep, so I turned to Gillian. "Is there anything I can do? Something I can help you with while I'm here?"

Gillian shook her head. "Just sit with me?" It came out like a question.

"Oh," I said a bit surprised, but not unpleasantly so. "Okay. Sure."

"Can I get you somethin' to drink? We have water, and maybe some iced tea in the fridge."

"Sure, but you stay seated," I said. "I'll grab us a drink. Do you prefer water or iced tea?"

"Water's fine," Gillian said politely. Today she wore a different band T-shirt. Guns N' Roses.

I filled two glasses with water and then carried them into the family room. Beth lay in a bed by the front window. Her breath rattled in her chest.

After handing Gillian the glass, I sank down onto the recliner across from her. We sat together in silence listening to Beth's inhalations, exhalations.

"I know what you're going through," I said finally. I hated awkward empty silences. Always felt I had to fill them if no one else would. "I lost my mother a few years back." I took a sip of my water and then set it down on a coaster on the end table. "I wish there was something I could say to make it better, but I honestly don't know what that is. Shane would know what to say. He is so much better at this than I am." I let out a little laugh. "You can probably tell."

"I'm sure that's not true. In fact, I'd much rather have you here than him. When I saw him at the church, he spouted off some scripture to me about how Jesus heals." She said it like it had upset her.

"And that wasn't comforting to you?"

"It's bullshit."

"Excuse me?" My insides knotted.

She lowered her voice and leaned forward. "My mom has stage four cancer. She's in hospice. Her doctor has given her two weeks at best. But it could be days. Jesus isn't healing her."

I gripped my water tighter, having no idea what to say to that. Maybe Jesus wasn't going to heal Beth, but he could heal. It wasn't bullshit.

I'd left that day feeling frustrated. Mad.

I went home and spent the next couple of days researching healings in the bible. A few days later, armed with all of my research, I'd marched right into Beth Hadley's house with the express purpose of changing Gillian's mind. Of proving her wrong.

Of proving the validity of the scriptures.

But Gillian wasn't swayed.

"No offense to you or your beliefs, but you can quote all the scripture you want, and it won't change what I think."

"Why not?"

"Because I don't believe in scripture. I think it's written by men. It's a recounting of historical events at best. Lies at worst."

I opened and closed my mouth, a fish out of water. I had no idea how to respond.

"I think it's okay for us all to think and believe what we want. My mom believes so fervently in Jesus and I'm okay with that. Why can't you be okay with what I believe?"

"Because...because..." My lips quivered and moisture filled my eyes. What was happening to me? I wiped frantically at my tears, feeling like an idiot. She was losing her mom and I was the one crying?

This day had not gone according to plan at all.

"You okay?" She placed a hand over mine.

I sniffed and drew back. "I guess...because I need to believe it. I need the hope that it brings."

Her expression was open, curious.

I continued. "A couple of years ago I got sick, and the doctors couldn't figure out what was going on. For months I went through test after test and was told I might have anything from a brain tumor to MS to something as benign as an inner ear infection." She handed me a tissue and I dabbed at my eyes. "My symptoms went on for months with no relief and I was desperate for God to heal me. Everyone kept telling me He would." I sighed. "When He didn't, I fell into a depression. I felt like it was my fault or something."

"It wasn't," Gillian said. "You're not that powerful. You can't control your own health."

I laughed at the bluntness of her statement. I thought of all the things my friends and Shane had said to me. That I was sick because of my lack of faith, or some unrepentant sin in my life. And they were all said with concern and a prayerful smile. None of them were said in the blunt, unapologetic way Gillian had just spoken to me. And yet, they'd hurt me so deeply, caused me to question everything I'd known.

At Gillian's words my chest expanded, my shoulders re-laxed. She was right. I couldn't control my own health, and it wasn't my fault I was sick.

"I'm still not better. I mean, it's not as bad as it was. Now it kind of comes and goes. I don't say anything, though. I'm tired of talking about it. I'm tired of it, period. But I get angry a lot. Angry because I have believed so strongly that God would heal me, but He hasn't. If He can, then why doesn't He?"

Gillian was quiet a moment. She ran her tongue over her top lip and rested her hands on her knees. "I think illness is a human condition. People get sick and people die every day. There's nothing we can do about it. It's all a crapshoot."

"That's a depressing way of looking at it."

"More depressing than believing in a god who can heal you but chooses not to?"

"I'd like to think there's a balance in there somewhere."

"Then that's what you have to find," Gillian said.

13

THE DAUGHTER

Past

Mara had been right. Dating Dylan was fun. My parents trusted him, so we were able to go out all the time. At first, I preferred doubling with Mara and Wyatt. We usually went to the movies or dinner, out for ice cream. Once we went miniature golfing. I loved having Mara there. It felt comfortable and easy, the conversation flowing in a way it wouldn't if I was alone with Dylan. A couple of times Dylan held my hand under the table at dinner or slung an arm over my shoulder at the movies. Wyatt would do the same. Mara and I would look at each other and smile.

It was all very PG. All very rom-com.

My parents would've been so proud.

But last Saturday everything changed. The four of us had gone on a hike near the river. Probably not a great idea for a ninety-degree day in June. About an hour in we found a secluded beach. By then we were all drenched in sweat, our faces red and damp. The boys immediately peeled off their shirts and jumped in. Mara and I hadn't worn our suits underneath, so we stood in the sand and watched. The water looked like heaven—cool and inviting.

After a few minutes Mara said, "I'm gonna dip my feet in." She took off her shoes and socks and walked slowly into the water. "Oh, man, this feels great." Wyatt, who was swimming around, splashed her and she squealed.

Sweat slid down my back. I couldn't stand it anymore. Why should the boys be the only ones having fun?

Oh, screw it. I tugged my shirt up over my head, then unbuttoned my shorts and wiggled out of them.

Mara gasped. "Adrienne, what are you doing?"

"I'm goin' in." I stepped out of my shorts, leaving my clothes strewn in the sand.

Mara's eyes were wide as I waded into the water in nothing but my bra and panties. But that's technically all that bathing suits were, right? How was this any different? It's not like I was naked. Plus, it's not like my bra and panties were sexy. They were plain. Chaste. Picked out by my mom.

The cool water felt so good on my skin, as good as I'd hoped. As I lowered down into the water, I glanced out to where Dylan and Wyatt were, and they looked as shocked as Mara. But there was something else simmering in Dylan's eyes. Lust, maybe?

It gave me a funny, fluttering feeling in my gut. I welcomed it, pleasantly surprised. I'd started dating Dylan out of convenience, joking to Mara that I was in an "arranged dating" relationship.

Was I attracted to him now? It sure felt like it.

Wyatt swam past me toward Mara and the shore. Dylan came up to me, circling his hands in the water to stay upright.

"That was pretty ballsy," he said, one lip curled upward in an amused look.

"Why is it any different from what you and Wyatt did?"

He laughed. "You know why."

I rolled my eyes. "Man, guys have all the fun. You can go swimming at any time. You can pee outside."

"You wanna pee outside? Think that'd be fun?"

"I want the option." I dipped my head back, water coating the edges of my hair. "I think girls should be allowed to do anything boys can do."

"I have the feeling you don't need permission from anyone to do anything."

As untrue as it was, I liked that he thought that. And I liked that it didn't scare him away. I wanted to be as ballsy as he thought I was.

"You're right. I don't," I said, propelling my body forward in the water. Then I pressed my lips to his. He was stunned at first and his lips were frozen in place. But then he responded.

It was a good first kiss, even though I realized I had nothing to compare it to.

But it wasn't the kiss that changed our relationship. It was what happened after our kiss.

"Can I take you out tomorrow, just the two of us?" he whispered to me in the water, when our lips broke apart.

"Sure."

On Sunday Dylan picked me up like always, shaking my dad's hand and making small talk. Explaining that he was only taking me to dinner, and he'd have me back by ten. It was a school night, after all. Their conversation always made me feel small and insignificant, a child on a play date who had to stick to their nap schedule.

But instead of taking me out to a restaurant, Dylan and I went through the Taco Bell drive-through and then he drove me up to Top of the Town, the famed make-out spot up on one of Rio Villa's tallest hills overlooking the river. It's not an official name, just something the kids in town have dubbed it. My parents had warned me away from Top of the Town for years, making it sound like something terrible would happen to me if I came here.

But it wasn't terrible at all.

It was wonderful.

We kissed until my lips were red and swollen. Until my heart raced, adrenaline buzzing through my veins. When he dropped me off that night, my head was in the clouds, my body all tingly.

He took me out two more times after that and both times we ended up at Top of the Town, steaming up his car windows. Tonight, when he took me there, he slid his hand under my shirt, his fingertips feeling me up through my bra while we made out. It felt good. It felt right. I knew it shouldn't, but it did. I longed for him to tear the bra off, to touch me for real.

I'd been in the bathtub since he brought me back home. I'd been in here so long, the bathwater was lukewarm, and my fingers were pruny. Before getting in, my body had been simmering like a pot on the stove about to boil over.

I had to finish what he started.

Afterward, I scrubbed my body clean.

If your right eye causes you to sin, gouge it out and throw it away. If your hand causes you to sin, cut it off and throw it away.

What do I do if my skin caused me to sin? Skin myself? Peel it away?

And what if I didn't feel ashamed? What if I liked it?

What if I wanted it to happen again and again?

14

THE MOTHER

Present

My text thread with Adrienne is a sea of blue bubbles. All texts from me that have gone unanswered. I scroll up, reading through the last one she responded to. It was a couple of weeks ago when I'd scheduled our mani/pedis. The ones we're supposed to be getting this morning. She'd responded with: *Cool. Can't wait.*

For weeks I'd built up the fantasy in my head. Sitting in plush chairs, our feet submerged in warm, soapy water while we gabbed and flipped through glossy magazines. It was the kind of day I'd always dreamt of having with her as she got into her teenage and young adult years. When Curtis was still living in Rio Villa, he and Shane would meet for coffee or go out to lunch. They even went to a men's conference together once. And every time they hung out, I wished Adrienne and I had that kind of connection.

Finally, it seemed we were headed in that direction, and I'd been so excited. I thought she had been, too. She'd said she couldn't wait.

She wouldn't take off and flake on me, would she?

I take one last gulp of my now cold coffee and set the mug in the sink. Out the kitchen window, I see Ruth puttering around in her front yard, watering her flowers and pulling weeds like she does most mornings. Marissa's car pulls out of her driveway a few houses down, most likely taking her two kids to school. Shane's car is gone. He left early this morning for work. Normally, I would've already gone for a walk, either through the neighborhood or, more preferably, around the river. I know Shane thinks I lost my religion just because I no longer find it in musty Bibles or wooden pews, or songs sung by a choir. But I haven't lost it. I now find it in the rising of the sun, the rush of water in the river, the sky when it's a bright cornflower blue. Maybe I always found it there.

This morning I can't bring myself to take a walk, though. I'm anxious to get to Adrienne's apartment to see if she's returned.

Wiping my hands on a nearby towel, I start to turn around, but the figure of a man stops me cold. A man wearing a dark hoodie. The same man I keep seeing. The sunglasses are back. I can't get a glimpse of his face. I'm certain those dark eyes are hidden behind the lenses, though. He's standing on the sidewalk across the street, staring at my house.

I race to the front door and fling it open. My eyes fly across the street, sweep the sidewalk. I lost him again. Desperate, I clamber down the front porch stairs. Where is he?

What does he want?

An hour later I'm on my way to Terrace Grove Apartments, praying that when I get there, Adrienne will answer her door. She'll be apologetic, and I won't even be mad that she took off without telling me. I'll be so thankful she's home and safe.

At the stoplight I glance in the rearview mirror and heat shoots up my back. The blue sedan a few cars back has been following me this entire drive. I squint into the rearview mirror, trying to get a good look at the driver. But I can't. The windows are tinted.

Who has tinted windows? No one I know.

I turn into Adrienne's apartment complex, palms damp. When I look back up, I can't find the car. It didn't follow me into the lot. Breathing deeply, I pull into a parking space. Then I wipe my hands on the thighs of my jeans. Maybe the car wasn't following me. But I am being followed. By the man in the hood. I keep on high alert as I make my way to the building. I don't see the car or the hooded man anywhere, and I make it inside and up the stairs.

After reaching Adrienne's door, I knock for several minutes, and then let out a low groan. My fantasy didn't come true. She's still not here. I lean my head against the wall and stare up at the ceiling, trying to figure out what to do next. Where could she be?

My cell rings out from my pocket. Hope springs up like a fish leaping out of the murky water. But it's not Adrienne. It's a number I don't recognize.

I press the phone to my ear. "Hello?"

"Tatum, it's Officer Delucchi."

I swallow hard at his formal greeting. Why Officer Delucchi? Why not Tony? Fear blocks my throat, and I can't make any words come out.

"I wanted to let you know that there's no sign of Adrienne in any of the surrounding hospitals or shelters. Also, we were able to pull surveillance video of her pulling a large amount of cash from her bank a couple of days ago, as well as a video of her leaving her apartment complex Wednesday morning."

"Was she with anyone?"

"No, she was alone."

All the hope I'd felt before answering the phone has died down now, a plant without sun or water, limp and shriveled.

"Okay, thanks, Tony."

So that's that, then. She left on her own. I've been reluctant to believe it because I want to think I mean more to her than that. I want to believe she wouldn't flake on me or leave me hanging like this.

But it seems I've been grasping at straws this whole time.

"No problem," Tony says. "It's gotta be a relief, right? And don't feel bad. My wife still worries about Tucker all the time, too. It's the curse of being a parent, I guess. I'm just glad this had a good outcome. Hopefully, she went somewhere fun."

The idea of her going somewhere fun rattles a question loose. "Wait, you said there's a video that showed her leaving her apartment in the morning. Did she have luggage with her?"

A few beats. I hear voices in the background, a car driving past. "The way the cameras are situated at her complex it only caught her driving out. It didn't show her walking to her car."

"Okay, thanks again." I hang up.

If she'd left in the morning, that would've given her plenty of time to call her work—and me. It doesn't add up.

From the apartment to my right, I hear the television playing. The voices are tinny and overly dramatic. Cartoons, probably. I recall my conversation with the woman inside. It hadn't been helpful. Surely, someone around here knows something.

I head toward the door to the left of Adrienne's and rap on it. I hear movement inside, but no one answers. I try again.

A man who looks to be late twenties, maybe early thirties, answers the door, opening it barely a sliver. His hair is disheveled, and a thick beard covers the lower half of his face. His eyes are bloodshot, and he reeks of smoke.

"Yeah?" he says, clearly annoyed.

"Sorry to bother you," I say, using what I like to call my "pastor's wife tone"—soothing and friendly, polite. "I'm Adrienne's mom. She's the woman who lives—"

"I know Adrienne," he cuts me off.

"Right. Well, she's been gone for a couple of days and hasn't been in contact with anyone, including her work. I wondered if you knew where she went."

"Nah, we're not like close or anything. We don't like sync our calendars or some shit." He lets out an amused laugh like I'm an idiot.

It takes me a second to formulate a response. "Yeah, no, I understand that. I just... I didn't know if maybe she'd said something in passing."

"Nah, we don't talk. I mean, other than when I bang on her wall and tell her to shut the fuck up."

My cheeks flush. "What? Why?"

He runs a hand through his hair. "I'm in a band, I'm up all night and I need sleep, you know? But then she and some guy are over there all day shouting, arguing, maybe. I don't know, bro, but I liked it better when she was never home."

"Never home?"

"Yeah, I hadn't heard anything from that chick in ages. I thought she moved. But then all of a sudden...bam...she's back and louder than ever."

I blink. "Her and this guy? Were they fighting a lot?"

"A few times, maybe."

"How long ago was this?"

"A week, maybe two. Don't know, dude, the days all blur together, you know?"

I'm sure for him they did.

"Well, I got stuff to get back to." He points with his thumb over his shoulder.

"Of course. Thanks," I say as he closes the door in my face.

Maybe this guy she was arguing with had something to do with her disappearance. Had she gone to see him, and their fighting escalated? Or maybe he found her. Maybe he made her pull out that money. Was she being blackmailed? Involved in something shady?

That could be why she'd been so secretive.

And it could be why that man in the hoodie is following me.

I head back down the stairs, push through the glass doors and step out into the parking lot—and there he is, as if I'd conjured him. The guy from the church, the bar and my house. He's walking toward me.

Fight or flight kicks in, and my muscles tense. But I hold my ground. "Why are you following me?" He's closer now, and I recognize the dark eyes, the sharp jawline, the dusting of stubble. "It's you."

15

THE FIANCÉ

Past

We were sitting on the couch, beers in hand, chips and dip on the coffee table in front of us. She was next to me, her head resting against my shoulder. She picked her head up, taking a long pull of her beer as she played with the fingers of my right hand. "What's your favorite color?"

She did this a lot. Asked random questions. I didn't mind too much. It meant she wanted to know me. And, at least this time, it was noninvasive. One that didn't cause a cold sweat to break out along my upper lip and forehead like some of her other more prying ones.

"Blue," I said.

"Why?"

"'Cause it's the color of water…and you know how much I love being near the water."

"No, that's too easy."

I know, that's why I'd liked it.

She had no trouble sharing about her family life, her parents, her childhood. And I knew she wanted me to do the same, but it wasn't that simple for me.

"What about you?" I asked before she could pry any further into my life. "What's your favorite color?"

"That depends," she said, still absently fiddling with my fingers. "If we're talking about clothes, then black, 'cause... you know...slimming. And if we're talking about in nature or in coloring crayons: red. Always red. It's bright and bold, and you can't miss it. But yeah, I like the bright blue of the water. But if we're talking sentimental value, then definitely green."

"Why green?"

"It's the color of my eyes, my mom's eyes and my grandpa's eyes."

"Okay." One corner of my lip tugged upward in amusement. "Well, I didn't realize we were supposed to have so many. So if we're talkin' clothes, Imma still say blue. And if we're talkin' nature, Imma still say blue." She giggled. "But for sentimental reasons, I'll also go with green, because it's the color of your eyes."

She turned then, rewarding my answer with a kiss.

"This has gone on long enough. You've made your point. You can come home now," Mom said, using her impatient tone.

I held the phone to my ear and paced the floor in my living room. The blinds were open, and the sun was shining, painting stripes on the carpet.

"And where is home, exactly?" I asked sarcastically. My parents split when I was eight, and after that I lived with each of them half the time. One week with Mom, one week with Dad. It helped that their homes were mere blocks apart. At least, it helped me. It bothered the shit out of my mom. Having to run into her ex and his new wife when she was out for a walk or driving to the grocery store.

When I turned eighteen, Mom sold the house Dad had been helping her pay for for years and bought a smaller one across town. A few weeks later her boyfriend moved in. That was when I moved out for good, opting to live in the granny flat at Dad's.

It seemed like a good decision at the time.

It turned out to be a shitty one.

"Oh, come on. It couldn't have been that bad at your dad's. You had all that room to yourself."

"If you think it was so great, why don't you try living there?" I'd worn a path in the carpet with my footprints from all the pacing. I stopped myself and perched on the edge of the couch. Sitting didn't stop the movement, though. My legs bounced in tandem, up and down, up and down.

She let out a loud "ha," then said, "No thanks. Been there, done that."

"Then you get it."

A sigh floated through the line. "You can always stay here, you know."

"I'm not coming back. I'm happy here. I've got a place. I've got a job. A girlfriend."

"Wait, what?"

"Which part?"

"You know which part. The girlfriend."

"Yeah, we've been going out a couple months now. And she's…well, she's…amazing."

"And you're just now telling me?" she spat out angrily.

"Yeah, 'cause I knew you'd react like this."

"Do you blame me?"

"It'll be different this time," I said firmly.

"How can you be sure?"

"'Cause she's different."

"Oh, God," she groaned. "It's not different at all. You're doin' it again."

"I am not."

She huffed loudly. "Okay, well, promise me you'll be careful."

"I will, Mom," I responded as if I was a small child again.

"Okay, love you," she said the way she always did when ending our conversations.

"Love you, too," I said back, same way *I* always did.

16

THE MOTHER

Present

"You're…you're him. Adrienne's boyfri—" I stop, remembering what Jazzy said last night. "Err…fiancé."

He blinks, taken aback. "She told you about me?"

I want to say yes, but I won't lie. If I do, it might get back to Adrienne, and I've been so careful to be truthful and vulnerable with her recently. "No." My heart is still going full speed ahead and sweat has gathered along my hairline. Now that we're face to face, I find I'm nervous. "A friend of hers told me."

He's quiet a moment, chewing the inside of his lip, then he says, "Yeah, I'm her fiancé…or, at least I think I am."

"What do you mean?" I ask.

He flips his hood off his head, and it falls against his neck. His black hair is tousled and messy but in that way that looks effortlessly styled. Men are lucky that way. My hair's been in a ponytail since Adrienne went missing. I don't want to take the time to fix it. If I leave it down it'll look a lot like his, but on me it will be clear it's not a style. He looks right into my eyes, and I see the conflict raging inside like a storm brewing.

"We were supposed to go away together but she never showed, and…I don't know…I've been worried she got cold feet or something." His tone is dejected, and he stares hard at the ground. I know that look. I've had it so many times when Shane's disappointed me.

The implication of his words hits me and my stomach drops. "So you don't know where she is?"

"No, I was hoping you did," he says.

"That's why you've been following me?"

He gives an almost imperceptible nod while staring down at his calloused hands.

"You should've just come up to me," I say. *Why so mysterious?*

"I wanted to," he says desperately. "But I didn't think you knew about me, and I didn't want to scare you."

"So you followed me around wearing a hoodie?" I cock my brow. It doesn't make sense and I'm not sure I'm buying it. I don't know what to think of him yet.

His cheeks color a little—a soft wash of pink—and, coupled with the lopsided frown and softening of his eyes, it made him appear almost childlike. "I'm sorry about that. I just wanted to find her, and I thought maybe she was with you. I—I was hiding because I thought maybe she needed space and I wanted to give that to her. I just needed to know she was okay." His voice breaks on the last word and I have the compulsion to reach out and touch his shoulder or arm, something to comfort him.

But I don't. I keep my arms pinned to my body. "When was the last time you saw her?"

"I haven't seen her at all this week. We were supposed to meet up on Wednesday at my place. I'd booked us a trip to

Napa. But she never showed. I went by the bar and her apartment, and she wasn't there."

I think about what Tony said, about her leaving that morning.

"I was angry. I thought she'd stood me up, so I went to Napa by myself," he says.

"You went alone?"

"Yeah." He shoves his hand into his pocket and pulls out his phone. After tapping on the screen with his thick index finger, he flashes the phone toward me, exposing a photo of him standing in front of row after row of grapevines as far as the eye can see. His thumb accidentally swipes left and another photo comes up. Adrienne grinning widely, his face pressed to hers.

"Oh, sorry." He's about to click out, but I stop him.

"No, I'd like to see," I say softly. He scrolls through a few more. In all of them, she's smiling. Broadly. Radiantly. "She looks happy."

"We make each other happy," he says with a slight grin. And I believe him. He looked happy in the photos as well. Now he frowns, lowering the phone. "That's why it was so hard to be in Napa without her. I'd had this plan for a romantic getaway. I'd booked us in a couple's suite, and it was too lame without her, so I came back yesterday. When she still wasn't at her apartment, or responding to my dozens of calls and texts, I thought I'd check the bar to see if she was there—I recognized you from some pictures, and, you know, she looks so much like you—I wondered if you knew where she was...or if she was staying with you. So that's why—"

"You went to the church and my house," I finish for him, then shake my head. "But no, there's no way Adrienne would ever come back home." If he knew her as well as he's saying, he'd never think that.

"I know about all the issues she's had with her dad. But I also know that you two have been getting closer. She really looks forward to when you visit her on Wednesdays."

Obviously, he's privy to more than I'd given him credit for. "That's why I'm having a hard time with your story—" I stop, blink. "I'm sorry. I just realized I don't know your name."

He juts out his hand, his grip firm but in a comfortable way. His smile is warm. "Seth."

I shake it. "Tatum."

Now that I got that out of the way, I continue, "If you and Adrienne had plans to go out of town, why didn't she tell me? And why didn't she call out at work? According to Jazzy, she was supposed to work Wednesday and Thursday. Also, she and I had plans to get mani/pedis today. Did she tell you that?"

"She didn't. I'm sorry," he says. "I honestly don't know why she didn't call you or her work. I assumed she had. But it was kind of a last-minute trip." Features sagging, his gaze falls to his feet. "Things have been kinda tough lately. We've both been working long hours and we work opposite shifts, so we hadn't spent a lot of time together. So I surprised her with this trip, hoping it would help us connect again, you know?"

I did know. In the early days of our marriage, before kids, Shane and I both worked. We were like ships passing in the night. Back then I lived for date nights or romantic vacations. Anything to feel that initial spark again. To get away from the monotony of everyday life.

"It was a little bit of a whirlwind, and she was busy in the days leading up to the trip—working and packing and shopping."

"Shopping?"

"Yeah." He smiles, and it's so genuine it disarms me. "She wanted some new clothes for the trip."

I think about the money she pulled out. When Tony had said a large amount, I figured he meant drastically large—but maybe he just meant enough for a shopping spree. But that doesn't add up for me. I know she makes a good amount in tips. Why not use that money? Or her credit card? Why would she need a large amount of cash?

"Were you two fighting at all?" I ask, the neighbor's words floating through my mind.

"No," he says. "I mean, no more than the average couple. Everyone argues sometimes."

I press my lips together. "But anything to suggest why she'd skip town?"

"I don't think she skipped town," he says firmly. "Not anymore. At first, I thought maybe she had, but if that were the case, I'm sure she'd be back by now. Or, at the very least, she'd be in touch. I've called and texted her so many times. Told her how much I love her." His voice catches. He swallows hard, running a hand through his hair. "I know she'd be in touch, if she could."

"That's what the police think," I tell him. "Have you spoken with the police? They'll listen to you. Here." I reach for my phone. "I'll call Tony—Officer Delucchi—he's an old family friend."

Seth puts his hand out. "I've already talked to the police."

I blink, surprised. "You have? When?"

"This morning."

"Tony didn't say anything."

"It wasn't him that I spoke with."

"Was it Officer Plunkett?"

"I don't remember his name," he says, his mournful tone suddenly harsh. "They've already made up their minds."

My shoulders dip, and I blow out a breath. "Yeah, that's how they seemed yesterday in her apartment, too. Didn't matter what I said. They'd already drawn their conclusion."

"You've been in her apartment?"

"Yeah, I saw the flowers you sent—"

"What flowers?" he interrupts.

"There were fresh flowers on the counter in the kitchen, and they had note with them. But they weren't your initials. Unless you go by..." I trail off. I don't want to share something secret of Adrienne's that I shouldn't, especially with a man who is essentially a stranger.

But his reply is reassuringly quick. "Did they start with an N?"

I nod, relieved that we once again seem to have puzzle pieces that click together. "N.S., yeah. How did you know?"

He works his jaw. "There was a guy hanging around the bar, talking her up, making her uncomfortable. Nate, she said." He spits the man's name out like a sour candy he couldn't keep in his mouth any longer. "Did she tell you anything about him?"

"No."

"Well, he seems worth looking into, sending creepy flowers to a woman he barely knows and spent an evening hitting on. Do you think we can get back into Adrienne's apartment?"

"Maybe. We can ask the front desk."

"I'd like to see the flowers and the note, see if we can find out where he bought them from. Maybe they can tell us where to find him."

"There's only one florist shop in town. Well, three if you count the grocery stores," I say, and he blinks. "Yeah, let's see if we can get inside."

I don't know a Nate. There's a Nathan who attends Grace, but he's never gone by Nate. Who is this man who's been bothering Adrienne at work? I try to think back to my Wednesday night trips. Guys paid a lot of attention to Adrienne, sometimes flirted, but nothing that worried me. As we head inside, I turn to Seth. "You really think this Nate person did something to her?"

"I don't know." His face is grim. "But I think it's a possibility."

★ ★ ★

Keys in hand, I make my way up the stairs, Seth right behind me.

"Did you talk to Adrienne about the trip to Napa last Sunday over the phone?" I ask.

"Sure. Why?"

"One of her coworkers—Ted—he said he overheard her talking to a person on the phone about some plans she was looking forward to."

"That was probably me, then." His lips curve upward on one side.

We reach Adrienne's door and I stick the key into the lock. The apartment manager gave it up so readily, it made me wonder if the police were even necessary the other day. I might have been able to get in without them. Then again, I think it was Seth's charm that worked on them, not mine. I can already see why Adrienne fell for him. I just can't understand why she wouldn't want us to meet him. He's the kind of guy Shane and I would like, which can't be said of all her ex-boyfriends.

But I also know her life has been spent in a fishbowl, and she's tried desperately to stay hidden in the little plastic caves.

"The thing I don't get, though, is…" The door opens. We step through it. "If she knew that day, why not tell her work right then?"

"I think Jazzy takes care of the schedule. Maybe she wasn't there that day. Also, she and Jazzy weren't getting along that great lately."

"Really?"

"Yeah, ever since Jazzy got promoted over Adrienne, they butted heads a lot."

The apartment smelled like vanilla and flowers. It was light and airy, the blinds open. Wouldn't she close them up if she'd been leaving for a few days? Or is that not something impulsive, romantic twentysomethings think of?

Seth continues. "She'd been thinking of getting another job."

I look at him. "I didn't know that."

He moves toward the counter, studying the vase of flowers. Some of them were wilting. "Yeah, it was something I'd been wanting her to do for a while. A bar isn't a safe place for a woman like her to work."

The statement rubs me the wrong way. "A woman like her? What does that mean?"

"She's beautiful and friendly, and men take advantage of that." He picks up the card and inspects it. "Bountiful Bouquet Florist."

"Yep, that's the one florist in town. I know Marie, the owner." I take out my phone. "Does it list a number?"

"Yeah." He rattles it off and I dial.

"Thank you for calling Bountiful Bouquet. This is Marie. How can I help you?"

"Marie, it's Tatum Murphy." I walk aimlessly through the living area. I've never been able to stay still while talking on the phone.

"Hi, Tatum. How are you?"

"I'm good. Hey, Adrienne had some flowers delivered the other day. We were hoping to send out a thank-you, but there's only a set of initials on the card. We're pretty sure we know who sent them...but if you could just confirm?" I'm hoping that didn't sound too sketchy. Out of the corner of my eye, I see Seth heading into Adrienne's bedroom. He's not wandering aimlessly the way I am, though. With the hard set of his shoulders and quick gait, it seems he's moving with purpose.

It piques my curiosity. I'm about to follow him when Marie answers, stopping me in my tracks. "Sure. I remember who sent those. Newt Simpson."

I'm stunned. *Newt?* He's not at all who I expected. "Oh... okay. Do you happen to have a phone number for him or...?"

"I'm sorry, Tatum, I can't give that out. If you want us to send him a thank-you from Adrienne, I can."

"No, it's okay. I know his address. He's attended Grace before," I say. "Thanks so much."

I walk in a daze toward Adrienne's room. It's so different from her room growing up. Opposite, really. Not that I'm surprised. Back then, I'd been the one to decorate. I gave her the bedroom I'd wanted as a child. Lots of pink, lace and frills. She's chosen to decorate in black, white and grays.

Seth sits on the edge of her bed, his fingers angrily stabbing at the keyboard of a laptop.

"Shit." He presses the heel of his hand into his forehead. "I'm locked out."

I lean over his shoulder and read the screen. "Well, only for fifteen minutes." I'm confused by his desperation. "What are you hoping to find on it?"

He shrugs. "Don't know. I just thought…" Shaking his head, he stands, abandoning the laptop, and then begins pacing. "I'm just lookin' for clues, you know?"

I *do* know.

"All right." I pick up the laptop and tuck it under my arm. "I'll take a crack at it."

He stops abruptly, lifting his head. "Nah, it's okay. Don't waste your time. There's probably nothing on it. It's not a Mac, so it's not synced to her phone."

"Nothing's a waste of time at this point. Who knows? Maybe she's got her calendar or something on here. It's worth a shot."

He hesitates, crossing his arms over his chest, but then says, "Okay, but let me know right away if you get in. I'd like to look through it with you."

"Okay." I open my phone to my contacts and hand it to him. "Guess we should exchange numbers, then."

After typing for a few seconds, he hands it back. I send him a quick text. "Now you have my number."

"Thanks," he says gruffly; then, "Any information on who sent the flowers? An address or something?"

"It's not the guy you mentioned. It was Newt Simpson."

"Who the hell's that?" he grinds out, and the harshness of his tone alarms me a bit.

"You don't have to worry about Newt. There's no way Adrienne's... Well, he's quite a bit older than her and... I don't know what to say, other than that there has to be a logical explanation for why he sent these." I pause, still puzzled by the whole thing. Why would Newt send Adrienne flowers? "I know where Newt lives. I'll head over and figure this out. Wanna come with?"

"I actually would like to stay here and keep looking around, if that's cool."

I hesitate a moment, but I don't know why. Seth is probably the person who knows this place best. He'll notice if something is out of the ordinary.

"Sure. Just bring the key back to the office when you leave," I say. "Call if you find anything, and I'll call after I talk to Newt."

"Deal."

I smile briefly, before hurrying out of the apartment, laptop in hand.

17

THE DAUGHTER

Past

On a Wednesday night a few months back, I was tending bar and looked up to see my mom walking through the front doors of the Float Down. I'd thought there must've been an emergency. Dad dead or in the hospital. Curtis dead or in the hospital. Someone had to have been dead or in the hospital. What other reason would Mom have for coming here? I'd worked at the bar for almost two years and she'd never stopped by. As far as I knew my mom had never been in a bar before. And she didn't look comfortable. Head ducked, her gaze flew around the room like a bee buzzing from flower to flower.

But then she spotted me, and her eyes brightened. Then she did the most shocking thing of all. She asked me to make her a drink. And not just any drink. A drink I'd just made for another woman in the bar. A Manhattan.

There was no emergency, she kept assuring me. She'd simply wanted to visit me at work. To spend time with me.

For another mother and daughter this might have been normal. For us, it was not. And I was highly suspicious.

It's not like she was a bad mom. I had a lot of happy childhood memories of her and me. She loved me. I had no doubt about that. And she was always trying so damn hard to do the right thing. To do right by me.

The problem was that when push came to shove, she sided with Dad.

She'd never stood up to him for herself or for me.

That Wednesday night our conversation was shallow at best. I'd never shared anything real with my mom. Certainly not anything I didn't want getting back to Dad. And one trip to the bar wasn't going to change that.

I was impressed that she finished her Manhattan but discouraged her from ordering another. I knew she had to drive home.

When she left that evening, I thought that would be the last time I saw her at the Float Down. It was clear she was nervous about Dad finding out. She swiveled her neck so violently it practically snapped off anytime the front door opened, as if she was certain it would be someone she knew. Someone who would tell on her, despite how many times I told her that people in her and Dad's circle didn't frequent the Float Down.

It was why I chose to work here.

In high school I'd briefly worked at Dolly's Ice Cream. One time I gave Mara and one of our other friends an extra scoop in their cone and didn't charge them, and my supervisor Tim mentioned it to my dad the following Sunday at church. Dad made me apologize and pay the shop back for the ice cream I "stole."

The summer I turned seventeen, I desperately wanted to go to lifeguard training at the local pool, but Dad wouldn't let me. Said he didn't want me getting a job where I had to wear a bathing suit. I forged Dad's signature and went to the training, anyway. In the middle of it, he showed up and made a huge scene, forcing me to leave. Apparently, there'd been a women's prayer meeting at church that morning, and one of the ladies had dropped her daughter off at the training and saw me. She'd run into Dad on her way in and mentioned it.

After graduating I worked for a couple of years at Fanciful Boutique. It only sold women's clothing, so Dad never went there. Mom did, though, and so did her friends. Not to mention that Stella, the owner, went to Grace Community. I felt like I was being watched all the time. I probably was.

Things only got worse after what happened to Kim—or, rather, the way everyone else referred to it as what I did to Kim. For a few months before landing this job, I'd been working as a server at Jose's Cantina. The tips were good, and the margaritas were even better. I'd sometimes hang out after I was off, sharing a basket of chips and a margarita with one of the other servers. But most nights someone I knew from Grace Community would come in for dinner with their family. The finger pointing and whispering got to be too much.

When Mom and Dad started coming in on a regular basis, I knew I had to quit. The last thing I wanted was to work somewhere my dad could keep his eye on me. I was twenty-two at the time. A little too old for a parental chaperone.

But that was the thing about my dad. He never saw me as an adult. I knew with certainty that he would try to control me for as long as he could.

As awful as it was when he kicked me out of the house, it was also kind of a relief. To not be living under his roof and his rules any longer.

And it was why I was working my ass off to save enough money to move out of this godforsaken town.

In the meantime, the Float Down was a good place to stay seemingly under his radar.

That was why I felt on edge when the following Wednesday Mom showed up at the bar again. A part of me wondered if Dad had put her up to it. Was Mom a plant? Was she trying to get information out of me to take back to him?

But when she once again sat at the bar and ordered another Manhattan, her gaze once again shooting around like a skittish cat, I knew she was telling the truth. Dad had no idea she was here.

So then, why was she?

"What's really going on, Mom?" I leaned over the bar, looking her in the eyes.

"I told you. I want to spend some time with you. See you in your element."

"Come on. It's me. I know you. You're not really the hang-out-in-a-bar-on-Wednesday-night type."

She bristled. Sipped her drink. "People can change."

"Is that what's happening?" I asked incredulously. She didn't look different. She wore the same jeans and navy sweater she always had, her hair in the same shoulder-length bob, hardly any makeup on her face. But then again, she was in a bar, having a drink. "You're changing?"

"Yes, actually." She sat taller.

This piqued my curiosity. "In what way?"

"I'm just…well, trying to find myself, I guess." She tossed out an off-handed laugh and took another sip of her drink. "Sounds silly at my age, huh? I'm almost fifty, and I'm trying to find myself."

I didn't think it sounded silly at all. I think it sounded like the most honest thing my mom had ever said to me.

"And what are you learning?" I asked her.

This time she took a long pull from her drink. "That I don't know a thing."

18

THE FIANCÉ

Past

Rings, rings and more rings. They swam in front of my face, one after another, until they all looked the same. I rubbed my eyes. Blinked. Then looked at the computer screen again, at the rows upon rows of engagement rings. Which one would she like? I had no clue.

She didn't wear much jewelry. Small earrings. The necklace I gave her.

She wore that necklace every single day. Well, at least, now she did. When I first gave it to her, she wore it sporadically.

"You're not wearing your necklace," I'd said when she'd arrived at my house a few days after I'd gifted it to her, neck bare.

She'd absently reached up to touch the spot where the pendant should've been. "Oh, yeah, I didn't wear it today. Didn't really match my outfit."

It felt like a fucking slap in the face. I frowned. "It has so many colors in it. I think it matches most outfits." I reached out and touched her neck. "I like when you wear it."

She'd flinched beneath my touch—and it pissed me off a

little—but then she nodded. And after that she'd worn it every time we'd been together. So I forgave her.

I loved seeing it wrapped around her neck. A ring would feel a thousand times better. A ring would mean she belonged to me.

I'd never seen her wear a ring, though, so I didn't know what style she'd pick. And I couldn't ask her, then she'd know what I was planning, and I wanted it to be a surprise. We hadn't been dating long. Only a couple months. I wasn't stupid. I knew it was too soon to propose. But I didn't see the point in waiting. Not when I was this sure.

I was ready to make her mine, and so I planned to do it. As soon as possible.

I'd reached the bottom of the webpage, when I saw the words: *Want to sample rings before you buy them?*

Yes, yes, I do, I answered internally.

I clicked on the link and was redirected to a page where I could choose three rings to be sent to my house for a small charge. I could send them all back or just the two I didn't want.

Perfect.

Now I just had to pick the three I wanted to sample. Groaning, I dove back into the sea of rings. As I moved my mouse over each one, I imagined holding it in my hand and getting down on one knee.

And I imagined the broad smile on her face when she gave me an emphatic yes. Even though we hadn't been together long, I was sure she'd accept.

Sure, she hadn't said *I love you* yet, despite the fact that I'd said it multiple times. But I knew how she felt about me.

The first time I'd told her, she stared at me a moment and then she reached for me, drawing me close. She might not have said the words, but she showed me with her mouth, her hands, her lips. That was her way. She valued action over words. She'd been hurt by the people who claimed to love her. It was no surprise that she was hesitant about saying the words.

Not everyone felt the need to verbalize it. My mom was one of those women who said it all the time. So much so that it lost its meaning. It became a way of ending a conversation, used in place of goodbye or talk to you later.

But she'd never been affectionate. She could barely be bothered to give me a goddam hug, even when I was a child. Even when I cried. Even when I came at her, arms outstretched. Probably good since she was shitty at it. The few hugs she did give me were awkward and stiff, worse than not being hugged at all.

It wasn't like that with us, and it never would be.

Smiling, I clicked on one of the rings, adding it to the sample kit.

19

THE MOTHER

Present

I step up to Newt's front door. A couple of houses down two men stand in the front yard, eyeing me while sharing a joint. Across the street a man works on a broken-down car parked in his front lawn. Staring at Newt's barred screen door, I'm not sure where to knock.

Finally, I settle on the screen. I wait a few seconds, but I doubt he can hear the knock from inside. So I press the doorbell to my right. The muffled ring pierces through the front door and it's followed by footsteps. My muscles tighten.

The door wheezes like an old man after a coughing attack as it's pried open. Newt's beady eyes stare at me through the dust-covered screen door.

"I'm not givin' any money to the church, lady. I don't have anything for them starving kids in Africa. We've got our own starvin' kids here."

"I'm…um…not here for money." And when have I ever asked him for money? If anyone had been in this neighborhood asking for donations, it wasn't our church. "I'm Tatum Murphy."

"I know who ya are. Pastor's little wife. If you're not here for money, then you must be here to convert me, and let me say, you're barkin' up the wrong tree. If Mama couldn't do it, you can't, either." He clutches the door, pushing it closed.

"Wait, please, I'm here about Adrienne," I practically shout.

The door wheezes again as he slowly opens it farther. "Adrienne? What about her?"

"You sent her some flowers. I just was wondering if you could—" my nerves are high. I swallow them down "—tell me why."

"She knows. Ask her."

"I would if I could…she's…well, no one's heard from her in a couple of days. And I'm concerned, Newt. Do you know where she is?"

He throws up his hands, palms coated in dirt. "I don't know nothin' about that. I just wanted to thank her for helpin' my dad. He was drunk and she called me to come get 'im. She's always there for him. And she's one of the only people in this town who knows I've been clean and sober for months now. She's always kind about it. I think she gets it. Town's written both of us off." My gut twists at his words. At the truth in them. I feel sick. "I just wanted to show my appreciation."

Tears prick at my eyes, and I blink several times. Sniff. "Thanks, Newt. Sorry I bothered you."

"I hope you find her," he calls as I head back to my car. "She's a good one, that girl of yours."

I sit at the kitchen table, mug of tea steaming in front of me. Outside the window a car drives past; kids play in the yard a few doors down. Everyone going about their lives, while for me, everything has stopped. Ceased to matter. Everything except finding out where Adrienne is.

Resting my chin in my hand, I think hard. What would Adrienne use as a password for her laptop?

My first guess had been her birthday. When that didn't work, it occurred to me that I should've asked Seth what guesses he made. I'd texted him, and he responded almost immediately. I now have his list next to me.

Most of them are words or dates that mean nothing to me, so they must be anniversaries of theirs. Perhaps his birthday's in there, too.

Next, I try the word *Charlie*. He was our family cat when she was little, and she adored him. But no, that's not it, either.

I tap my finger to my chin. What dates or words are significant to Adrienne?

My next few attempts are variations on her name: AdrienneM, Adriennem1, AdrienneM!, then I add in her middle initial: AdrienneGM, and for my last guess I use her full middle name: Adriennegrace.

And now I'm locked out.

Thirty minutes this time.

A text comes through from Seth: Did you get in?

I respond: No. Locked out.

Bubbles appear and then transform into words: I can come get it if you want. Give it another go.

No, don't waste a trip over here for that, I type back. You can send me your ideas if you have more. I'll ask Mara, too.

Ok, comes his reply.

The front door opens. "Tatum!" Shane calls out, his footsteps loud in the entryway.

It's only the afternoon. What's he doing home so early?

"In here." I slam the laptop closed and slide it under the bed. Then I tuck my phone into my pocket and swiftly head into the hallway. "I wasn't expecting you."

He points to a brown stain on the front of his dress shirt. "Lost a fight with a coffee cup, and I have an important meeting later. Came home to change." He looks over my shoulder. "Busy day, huh?" I follow Shane's line of sight to the indentations on our comforter.

"I was just relaxing. Trying to clear my head," I say.

"That's good." His eyes soften and he places his hands on my shoulders. "I'm really sorry about how I've treated you the last couple of days."

"Oh. Um…thanks." I'm so stunned, I can't stop myself from asking, "What changed?"

He steps past me, peeling off his jacket and discarding it on the bed. "I talked with Tony this morning at bible study."

"Does he know something new? Something about Adrienne?" I don't even try to mask the desperation in my voice.

"No." He starts unbuttoning his shirt, and my heart sinks. *Of course not.* Bible study was this morning. I'd heard from Tony since then. "But he told me how scared you were at Adrienne's apartment yesterday…and I realized I'd been too hard on you. You're a woman, so it makes sense you'd be struggling with this."

"What?" I ask through gritted teeth.

"I get it. You're guided by your emotions. It's what makes us different, and that's okay." Leaning over, he kisses my cheek. "Because I'm here to help balance you out."

Balance me out?

A dozen arguments linger on the edge of my tongue. I want to let them loose, but I know it won't matter. It won't change his mind. He's had a lifetime of this way of thinking. One argument with me won't erase that.

When he'd first come in, I'd planned to tell him about Seth. About my day. About our theories. But I won't now. Instead, I press my lips together and stay silent, adding one more secret to the pile.

20

THE DAUGHTER

Past

I think back on the last time I saw Kim often, wishing I'd done things differently. Wishing I'd never gone out that night. Wishing I'd listened to my gut. Wishing she was still here, happy and whole. Despite what the townspeople think, I cared about her a lot. I never wanted anything bad to happen to her.

I knew my actions that night would have consequences. I just had no idea how catastrophic they'd be. I'd been on thin ice with my dad for a while. After graduating high school I'd immediately enrolled in Junior College. Unlike Curtis, I didn't have the grades to get into a four-year. And I had no clue what I wanted to do with my life. The first couple of semesters I passed most of my classes, but then my motivation fizzled, and I started dropping more classes than I finished.

"The agreement was that you can live here as long as you're in school," Dad would say.

"I am in school," I would counter.

"You need to be in full-time school and passing," he'd respond, red in the face.

That hadn't been the initial agreement, but Dad's expectations were known to change as quickly as the channels when a flip-happy TV watcher had the remote. It was too late to make him happy, anyway. I was down to one class this semester and last I checked I was getting a D in it.

Kim and I had gone to Jose's Cantina for dinner. We'd spent the afternoon at the river. Our skin was chilled, our heads fuzzy from the sun, sand and lack of hydration. We probably shouldn't have ordered a margarita, but we were enjoying having a day off from the boutique together. Usually, Stella rotated our days off. And I was desperate to numb my mind, to stop thinking about how shitty things were at home. How unhappy my dad always was with me, and how I could never please him. Besides, we were stuffing our faces with chips and salsa and had both ordered burritos the size of our heads. We figured the food would soak up the alcohol in our bellies.

We weren't counting on *them*.

Parker Sebold and Clayton Winston.

Even though I generally stayed away from guys I'd grown up with, Parker had, in my mind, always been the one who got away. Kim and I had known Parker and Clayton most of our lives. They never ran in the same circle as Kim, though. I hadn't, either. She and I weren't friends when we were younger. Her family always attended Grace, but Mara and I had often seen Kim as a Goody Two-shoes. She was the girl who always knew the weekly scripture and would tell on us if we were talking during Sunday school.

It shocked us all when she got knocked up her senior year of high school. She gave the child up for adoption, but the pregnancy was rough, and her grades suffered. She wasn't able to go away to college, so she stayed behind, got a job at the boutique.

I started working there a little after that. And we became

fast friends. She was way cooler than before. No longer a Goody Two-shoes.

It was like she and Mara had switched places.

Kim was now the fun one and Mara was the lame one. Ever since Mara had started dating Isaac, she'd turned into an old married lady. All prim and proper like the moms we made fun of at church. I figured it was only a matter of time before she was married and having babies.

It was Kim who noticed them first. She spoke through her margarita glass, her eyes skating over my shoulders. "It's Parker and Clayton, and they keep staring at us."

"Really?" I whipped my head around.

"No." She shot her arm out, slapping her hand over my wrist. "Don't look."

I never understood when girls did that. "You can't say that and not expect me to take a peek," I said sullenly.

"Fine but be more discreet."

In this town there was no such thing as discreet.

Our waiter appeared at our table seemingly out of nowhere, like an apparition. He set down two more margaritas. "From the guys over there," he said with a large smile.

"Wanna invite them to join us?" Kim asked over the top of her margarita.

"Sure," I said.

While she went to talk to them, I smoothed down my hair and licked my lips. Then I tugged my top a little lower.

"Hey, Adrienne," Parker said, pulling up his own chair and plunking down next to me.

"Hey." I bit my lower lip in what I hoped was a seductive way.

"How's it been going?"

"Good."

Clayton and Kim made their way to the other end of the table and were immersed in their own conversation.

"Hear you're in the clothing business now."

I laughed. "It's not my dream job, just something I'm doing right now."

"What is your dream job?" He winks. "Gonna go into the family business? Be a pastor like the old man?"

"No." My stomach soured. I reached for my margarita. This was why I didn't mess with local boys. They always had to bring up my dad.

"Don't be like that. I was just asking a question."

"How would you like it if I asked if you were going to be a farmer like your dad?"

"I'd like it just fine, 'cause you'd be right."

"Really?" I licked salt from my glass. "I thought you went away to school."

"I did." He takes a chip out of the basket, takes a bite. "Wasn't for me."

"So now you're gonna stay here and help run your family farm?"

"Somethin' wrong with that?"

Maybe it shouldn't have been, but it was an immediate turn-off. The idea of a local boy tying me down in any way, even for one brief evening…no, thanks. "No, not at all."

I made polite conversation through one more round of margaritas and then bowed out.

"Sorry, guys, but I've got an early shift tomorrow." I bobbed my head toward Kim. "You do, too."

"She's right," Kim said, a slur under her words.

"We can give you ladies a ride home if you want," Parker offered. I knew what it was code for, and I wasn't interested.

Kim didn't seem interested, either. She threw me a subtle shake of her head. *Not vibing with Clayton, I see.*

"Um…no, it's okay. Thank you, though," I said.

"You shouldn't be driving," Parker said.

"Well, neither should you," I pointed out, and it was the

truth. When he stood, he swayed to the side. "Don't worry, we'll call an Uber."

It was the better plan. I could have—should have—gotten out my phone and clicked into the app. We didn't even need to share an Uber with the boys. But a couple of months ago Kim and I had gone out for drinks and gotten an Uber home.

The next morning Dad came tearing into my room.

"Where's your car?"

I clutched my blanket, groaned, pried my eyes open. I felt like I'd slept on the beach, like my eyelids were full of sand. My mouth was so dry I had trouble responding to him. "At the bar," I mumbled.

"What?" he said so loudly it made my head pound harder.

I rolled over to sit up, to face him. "I left it at the bar."

"You were so drunk you couldn't drive home?"

"No, I was so responsible I called an Uber," I corrected him, a flush of anger with his interpretation of my decision yanking me from my stupor. I sure as hell was wide-awake now.

"If you were responsible, you wouldn't be out drinking all night with your friend."

"Oh, yeah?" The words burst out, diamond-sharp from years under pressure, tamped down in my gut. "Where would I be, sitting in the pew, bible in my lap, singing with no inflection like your other cult followers?"

"How *dare* you talk to me like that, Adrienne."

Another snarky remark was on my tongue, but I pressed my lips together, caging it in. I was twenty-one. I should be able to drink if I want to. *Should* being the operative word. With Dad, nothing was that simple, and as long as I lived in his home, I'd have to put up with his overbearing nature and list of irrational rules.

I knew better than to cross him. His bark was not bigger than his bite. I knew he wanted to kick me out. The only reason he hadn't was because of Mom. But if I pushed him too hard, he'd do it. He'd pull that trigger.

And I had nowhere else to go.

If I went home without my car tonight, Dad would give me shit. And I didn't want to deal with it.

Cool air enveloped us as we walked into the parking lot. I breathed it in, allowing it to revive me. I blinked a few times, slapped my cheek.

I'll be okay, I thought. *My house is literally five minutes away.*

Kim leaned over, eyes glazed and cheeks red. Her pupils danced around, never quite landing on me. I felt fuzzy-headed and a little unsteady on my feet, but I hadn't drunk as much as Kim. She could knock those margaritas back. I was a sipper.

"Come on, Kim." I opened the passenger door and helped her inside.

"I thought we were getting an Uber," she said.

"I'm good to drive," I assured her.

It was that statement I regretted for years.

I was in no condition to drive. I knew that. Kim knew that. But ultimately, it was my decision. A decision that landed my car squarely into a pole on the side of the road, when I swerved too far to avoid an oncoming car. A car that wasn't even going into my lane. But the light tricked me, and I thought it was.

And Kim caught the brunt of it square-on in the passenger seat. Traumatic brain injury. It's been two years and it still hasn't fully resolved.

Kim and her family never forgave me. My dad never forgave me. Half this town never forgave me.

But my dad expected me to count myself blessed, because he pulled strings so that I didn't lose my license or spend any time in jail. Just community service. Well, that and I had to pay him back all the money he paid Kim's family to cover her medical expenses. Over a hundred thousand dollars.

Money I'd been paying him monthly for two years and I'd hardly made a dent in it.

Everyone thought I got off scot-free, but trust me, I hadn't. I was in my own form of prison.

21

THE MOTHER

Present

It's busy. Way busier than I've ever seen it. I'd never been to the Float Down on a Friday night. Wednesdays are much different.

Jazzy isn't working. Sienna and Ted are. Gillian and I snag the last two seats at the bar and flag down Sienna.

"I'll be with you two in just a minute," she says, tapping her long fingernails on the register.

"No problem," I call out.

When I called Seth to tell him about my visit with Newt, I told him that I thought I should go to the bar tonight to find out more information about the guy who was bothering Adrienne. Nate.

"Yeah, for sure," he'd said.

"You can join me if you want," I'd offered.

"Nah, I'm gonna follow up on some leads on my end."

My heart rate spiked. "Did you find something at her place? Something useful?"

"I'm not sure. Maybe. I'm looking into a couple of things. I think it's best if we divide and conquer. Don't you think?"

"Yeah," I agreed, grateful to have him on my side. Even if he was a complete stranger. It felt so good to know that there was someone else out there who loved my daughter and was actively searching for her.

If only Adrienne's dad were more like him.

"Welcome in. What can I get you, ladies?" Sienna's long blond hair is pulled up in a high ponytail; her face is bright and dewy; her lips so glossy she could probably slide across the floor with them. "Oh, hey, you're Adrienne's mom… Tammy?" She gives me an apologetic look.

"Tatum," I say, saving her from having to list off every T name she knows. We order our usual drinks, a beer for Gillian and a Manhattan for me.

"Hey, Sienna," I say when she slides our drinks across the bar to us. "I heard that some guy'd been hanging around the bar lately, possibly bothering Adrienne."

Sienna flips her ponytail back and lets out a light laugh. "I mean, guys are always hanging around the bar and lots of them bother us. You'll have to be more specific."

"This guy was maybe named Nate, and he's not from around here."

"Oh, yeah. I think I know who you're talking about. He definitely was interested in Adrienne, but I don't think she was bothered by it."

"You don't?"

"Well, if she was, she probably wouldn't have gone home with him the other night."

Heat races up my spine. "What night was this?"

"Tuesday," she says without hesitation.

The night before she went missing. That can't be a coincidence.

If Adrienne was engaged and happy with Seth, why would she go home with a different guy?

Seth was the one who told me about Nate. If he had known Adrienne went home with the guy, wouldn't he be angry? She's his fiancée, after all. How angry would he be?

Angry enough to hurt her?

22

THE DAUGHTER

Past

I always laughed during rom-coms when the girl hooked up with the guy in the same breath that she tells him, "I never do this sort of thing."

They really expected me to believe that the girl met that guy and instantly knew he was worth throwing away all her standards for?

I never could've authentically said that line because I *did* do that sort of thing…a lot. Not with just anyone, though. I had standards. Rules I'd set out for myself. Not like the unattainable ones my dad had for me growing up.

Nope. Mine were attainable.

The main one was that I wouldn't hook up with anyone I'd known growing up. Ever. Period. Another rule—this one I held a little loosely, rather than 100 percent of the time—was only going home with guys who weren't from around here. There were some cool guys who came into the bar who lived in Rio Villa or the surrounding areas. And, as long as I hadn't grown up with them and they didn't attend Grace Community, I'd consider them.

But the most attractive guys to me were ones new to or passing through town.

That was why when Mr. Tall, Dark and Handsome Stranger walked through the doors of the Float Down one slow Sunday night when I was tending bar alone, I found myself rubbing my lips together and smoothing down my hair.

"What can I get you?" I'd asked, batting my lashes and leaning seductively over the bar. Before he could even answer, I'd said, "Wait. Let me guess." I'd sized him up, enjoying every second. He reminded me of Milo Ventimiglia, with his crooked smile and dark, floppy hair. It was clear he did some sort of manual labor. His fingertips were calloused, his arms muscular. "Double IPA on tap?"

"Sounds perfect." The tone of his voice was crisp and sharp, and cut straight through me—a warm knife through butter. He flashed me a crooked smile, and my whole body warmed. Unusual for me, honestly. Guys didn't usually have a visceral effect on me.

God, now who was sounding like they were in a rom-com?

I poured the beer into the glass and then set it on the bar in front of him. It foamed down the sides, and I quickly wiped it.

"Sorry about that," I said. "I guess I made it a little too full."

"It's fine." He lowered his lips to the edge of the glass and sipped.

Bill, one of my regulars, flagged me over from where he sat on the other side of the bar. "Excuse me," I muttered and made my way over to the man with the red bulbous nose and white tuft of hair. "Another vodka on the rocks?"

He nodded gruffly, but I'd already started pouring.

"Enjoy," I said, sliding it in his direction. Ice cubes clinked in the glass.

"Friendly guy," Mr. T.D.H. commented when I returned to where he sat.

I shrugged. "He's fine. Just old and miserable. Pretty typical for people in these parts. You'd understand if you lived around here." I was fishing, but I couldn't help it. I wanted to know about him.

"I do live around here," he'd said.

"Then how come I've never seen you before?"

"What? You know everyone in this town?"

"Pretty much. Been here my whole life." I frowned. "Unfortunately."

"I take it you don't like it here."

"It's not the area so much as the people," I said.

"Ouch. You don't mince words, do you?"

"Oh, come on, you can't take offense to that. I don't even know you."

"I'm Seth." He smiled again. God, his smile was ice cream-meltingly good.

"Adrienne."

"See, now we know each other." He lifted his glass in a faux-cheers. Then he took a sip. "If you're so unhappy here, why don't you leave?"

"God, I wish it were that easy." Sighing, I leaned over, elbows on the bar. "You ever watch *Wayward Pines*?" I asked him.

He shook his head.

"Oh, you should. It's really good. I mean, if you like scary shows. Anyway, it's about this guy who keeps trying to leave this town but can't. Like every time he drives out, he ends up back there. Sometimes I feel like that's me. Like I can never escape this place. Like no matter how hard I try, I'll never be able to leave."

He stretched his lips back in a wince-like expression. "Yikes, that's pretty dark."

Feeling stupid, I pushed myself back up, straightening my spine. "Sorry."

"No, don't be. It's fine. I'm learning a lot about you...and this town." He sipped his beer. "I'm starting to wonder if maybe I should've picked a different one."

Now I felt even more stupid. My cheeks reddened. "How long have you been here?"

"Not long," he said.

It wasn't very specific, but not everyone spilled their guts to strangers the way I apparently did. "What brought you here?"

His fingers played with the bottom of his glass. "I was craving a change of scenery. I've always wanted to live in a small town, and I loved the idea of being near the water. But—" he bent down a little and whispered conspiratorially "—between you and me, it was prices that drew me to Rio Villa specifically."

I nodded, understanding. It was one of the things that kept me here, too. The affordability. The surrounding areas were much more expensive.

I also understood about needing a change of scenery. I felt like that a lot.

"Must be nice," I said wistfully. "Being able to just take off, start over somewhere new."

He studied me a minute. "If you could leave, where would you go?"

No one had ever asked me that before. I think most people around here assumed I'd live here forever. But then again, people had always underestimated me. "I don't know. For a while, I really wanted to go to San Diego. I don't know why, really. I think because I'd seen a picture of the beach there once and it looked like so much fun. People everywhere, having a good time, surfing or playing in the waves. Lying in the sand or running on the beach. They were smiling...and, I don't know...they looked...free."

"And you don't feel free?" he asked.

I blinked, then laughed nervously. "Are you, like, a therapist or something?"

He shook his head. "Nope. Just a guy who's curious."

Curious. I liked that. Men who hit on me at the bar were normally predictable. They'd tell me how good I looked or ask me what my favorite drink was. If they were assholes, they'd jump quickly to asking what position I liked or if I was into it rough. But not many of them had wanted to know deeper things. Things that mattered.

"No," I answered. "I don't."

"What would make you feel free?"

"You sure you're not a therapist?" I cocked a brow, and with another laugh answered, "I don't know. I always thought I'd feel free once I moved out of my parents' house and got away from my dad. But here I am, on my own, and he's still controlling me." I pause, gnaw on my lower lip. "And now I fantasize about getting out of this town, but…sometimes I wonder if I'll ever really be free. I mean, is it possible to run from the things you've done, the person you've always been, the expectations that have been set for you?"

"I'm not sure it's possible to outrun your own demons," Seth answered my rhetorical question. "But I'm certainly trying."

"Whoa, who's the one being dark now?" We both laughed. His beer was empty. I snatched it from the bar. "Let me go grab you another."

He ended up staying until closing. Then we talked in the parking lot for almost an hour. We had a lot in common, namely issues with our parents. But other things, too. We both loved swimming, hanging at the beach and tasting craft beer. And we both dreamed of a better life than what we had now. I'd assumed he'd invite me back to his place, but he'd been the perfect gentleman, instead asking for my phone number.

It had been years since a boy asked for my phone number.

It felt silly, how giddy I was, but at the same time exciting and oddly adult.

He didn't call for three days. I was starting to think he never would. That maybe he'd only asked for my number because he'd been drinking and now that he'd sobered up, he wasn't interested. But then his number popped up on my phone.

I was so excited, I almost answered on the first ring. But I didn't want to seem too desperate. So I let it ring three times—one for each day he'd made me wait—and then I picked up.

"Hey," I said, hoping I sounded breezy and casual, as if I hadn't been waiting desperately for him to call, like a teenage girl with a major crush.

"Hey," he responded, matching my tone. "It's Seth. We met a few nights ago...at the Float Down."

"Oh, right. Seth, hi," I said, and was proud of myself for how cool I was being. "How's it going?"

"Good. Hey, I was wondering if you wanted to hang out today," he said. "I was kinda hoping to take a walk by the river, maybe have a little picnic...but I don't know the area that well yet. Thought I could use your help in finding a spot."

It wasn't exactly a romantic ask. I wasn't even sure it was a date at this point, but there was still no way I'd say no. Not to Mr. T.D.H. There weren't many guys like him around here. I'd be a fool to turn him down.

I led him to a spot my parents often took us to when we were kids. It was close to the water, but removed enough that we didn't have to sit on the shore. There was a large grassy area with some benches and trees.

"Here we are." I spread out my hands in game-show-like fashion.

"It's perfect," he said, his gaze lingering on my face a beat too long. My cheeks flushed.

On the way here, we'd only made awkward, stilted small talk.

How was your morning?

Weather's so nice today, huh?

Are you liking it so far in Rio Villa?

This is a nice car.

As he took off his backpack and unzipped it, I chewed on the inside of my cheek, racking my brain for more interesting topics of conversation. Our first one had flowed so well. Why did it feel so hard today?

Maybe because I was in my element then. Also, there wasn't any pressure or expectations.

He spread a blanket out over the grass, a *whoosh* of wind hitting the backs of my calves with the motion. Then he pulled out a six-pack of beer, a bag of chips and a jar of salsa.

I rubbed my palms together and threw him a wink. "Now, this is my kind of picnic."

"You weren't expecting something fancier?" He cocked a brow.

"What, like champagne and cheese and crackers?" I lowered myself down onto the blanket and grabbed one of the cans. "No, trust me, I'm not that bougie."

"Then I think we'll get along just fine." He sat across from me.

Eyeing him, I popped the top off the beer. It cracked and fizzled. "Was this like some kind of test?"

"If it was, you passed," he bantered back in his easy way, reminding me of how it had been the night we met.

"Lucky me." I winked as I brought the can up to my lips. I noticed his gaze rested on my mouth and stayed there a moment. *God, I hope he kisses me,* I thought as I took a sip. The beer was a little warm. We'd never serve it this way at the bar. But it wasn't too bad.

Over his shoulder I spotted a rope hanging from a tree on the side of the shore.

It made me smile. "I dared Curtis to swing from that rope once. Well, maybe not that exact rope. Looks like they've upgraded it, but there's always been some rope tied to that tree. I think I was probably like eight or nine, so he was like eleven or twelve. At first, he said no. He was never much of a risk taker. But I called him a sissy pants until he did."

"Sissy pants, huh?"

"Oh, yeah, sissy pants was about as bad as my language got back then. If Mom had heard, I probably would've gotten in trouble." I laughed lightly, and then continued. "It worked, too. He did it, but he was so scared. I remember he was holding on so tight, he swung back and forth like three times before letting go."

"So I'm guessing Curtis is your brother?" Seth asked, wiping salsa juices from his lip.

"Yeah."

"Does he live around here?"

"No, he lives in Arizona with his wife."

"You two close?"

I snort. "Not even a little bit. We're very different. He's like a miniature version of my dad."

"And you're not," he finishes.

"Definitely not," I say. "What about you? Do you have any siblings?" I'd asked the question when he was midbite, and he held up a finger as he chewed dramatically. I laughed. "I'm as bad as a waiter, huh? Must be the bartender in me."

He grinned as he swallowed down his chip. Then he answered with, "Nope. Only child."

"Really? What's that like?" I asked.

"Lonely."

Moved by the vulnerability of his tone, I reached over and covered his hand with mine. Our eyes met and then everything happened in what felt like slow motion. Like I really was in one of those rom-coms I hated. His free hand lifted to cup my face. Our heads bent toward one another, our lips meeting. He tasted like beer and salty chips, and surprisingly, it wasn't a turnoff. The kiss was long and deep, slow.

Adrenaline pumped through me, every nerve ending in my body tingling. I wanted it to continue, to see where it would lead. That was why when he dropped me back off at my place, I'd asked him to come up.

But he declined, instead giving me one last lingering kiss in the parking lot before leaving. He was the perfect gentleman—way more so than any of the church guys I'd dated—and the irony in that was not lost on me.

We went out a few more times before he finally brought me back to his place. He lived near the Float Down in the rural part of Rio Villa. His little rental house was set back from the road, his nearest neighbor almost a half a mile away.

"It's so peaceful here like we're in our own little world, away from everyone else. All by ourselves," I'd mused as we sat on his couch sipping beer. This time I'd brought my favorite IPA and had made sure it was extra cold. My eyes widened as a thought struck. "Ooh, almost like we're on that beach in San Diego. The one I told you about."

"Okay, you're gonna have to show me this picture."

"Well, I can't show you the exact one, but I bet I can find something similar on Google," I mutter while pulling out my phone. After a few minutes of searching, I say, "Aha. I think I've found it." I hold the screen toward him.

"Oh, that's Coronado Island," he said. "So you wouldn't technically be free. You'd be trapped."

I laughed. "Better to be trapped on an island than here." His body stiffened, and I rushed to fix my mistake. "I mean, not *here* here. Like not here in this house here. In fact, here in your home is the only place I've felt free in Rio Villa for years…maybe ever."

"Then think of this as our own private Coronado Island," he'd said.

"I like that."

"Even though this place is nothing like being on an island."

"Sure it is. It's quiet. Remote. Away from everyone and everything," I said dreamily. "Apartment life is nothing like this. It's so loud, I can hear everything my neighbors do. Like, the lady on my right has so many kids. I don't even know how many, but they're always screaming or running or something." I shake my head, push my hair from my eyes. "And then the guy to my left, he's in a band. Not a very good one, either." I have no idea why I shared that, so I shake my head and continue, "So he keeps, like, super weird hours, up until late and sleeping during the day. And his friends or bandmates or whatever are always over."

"Sounds like you know this guy pretty well."

"No, I actually don't."

"But you know his band isn't very good."

"Oh, yeah." I wave away his words. "He's always posting flyers in the lobby, so I went to one of his shows once."

"And did you guys...you know..." He kind of shrugs in a sheepish way. "Ever date?"

"Why? Are you jealous?" I teased.

But his face was serious. "Should I be?"

Oh, he's for real.

Warmth spread through me. I had wondered if I should've been concerned about the whole gentleman thing. Like maybe he wasn't physically attracted to me. Like maybe it was all one-sided. That I was pushing something that wasn't meant to be. I liked knowing that wasn't the case. That he was taking things slowly because he cared, not because he didn't.

"No," I assure him. "I never dated the guy. We barely know each other. Trust me."

"Can I?" He leaned forward, an intensity in his gaze that I hadn't seen before.

"Can you what?"

"Trust you."

"Huh?" Had I misread something? Had I done something wrong? Swallowing hard, I played with the hands in my lap. "I'm sorry. I'm not really sure what you're asking me."

He paused a moment before scooping up my hands and placing them in his. "Okay, I'm sorry. I know that came out of left field. I guess I'm just trying to say that I'm starting to...you know...really like you. And I'm...well, call me old-fashioned, but I'm not the kinda guy who dates more than one girl at a time, so..."

"Oh, yeah, no, I get that." I felt relief at this. "I'm not see-ing anyone else."

It was as if he'd been waiting to know he had me all to him-self. He'd kissed me, then, hard and fast, his hands lowering to my shirt, tearing it from my body in an animalistic way. I think he may have even ripped one of the seams. I didn't care, though. It didn't scare me. It turned me on in a way I'd never been turned on before.

As his hands and mouth explored my body, for the first in my life, I didn't feel like me. I felt like an entirely different person in an entirely different world. Being with him *was* like an escape. From this world. This life that I'd been trapped in.

And I started to wonder if maybe together the two of us could find the freedom we were looking for.

23

THE MOTHER

Present

When I slide into bed beside Shane, he rolls over and reaches for me. As he kisses my face, his palms slipping under my shirt, frustration burns through me. I wriggle away from him, but he's not deterred. He comes closer, his mouth missing mine, but landing on my cheek, my nose, my ear. His hands are insistent as they press into my chest.

"Shane," I say harshly.

"What?" He presses his body to mine, his erection hard against my leg. "It's Friday night."

Our daughter is missing, I want to say. But I don't. He doesn't think Adrienne is missing. He thinks she's skipped town for a few days the way she has before. This isn't like those other times, but I'm tired of arguing that point with him. He refuses to hear me. He's already made up his mind. Talking to him about it only makes me more upset.

I relax my body, allow myself to respond to him. Giving in will be easier than fighting against it. It'll be over in minutes, anyway.

The first time Shane and I had sex was a few months before our wedding. Up to that point, we'd been so careful. So full of self-control. The most we'd done was hold hands and kiss. We were hardly ever alone.

But that weekend my parents were out of town. It was a hot summer day and I'd invited Shane to come over and go swimming. I'd worn my yellow tankini. I knew I was pushing it. Normally, I stuck to one-pieces, but I loved that tankini, tiny red flowers dotting its bright, sunshiny background. Shane loved it, too. I could tell by the way he kept staring at me. He couldn't tear his eyes away. It made me feel powerful. Desirable. Sexy. All the things I wasn't supposed to be, and yet, it felt right. I wasn't ashamed. Not then, anyway.

We spent the afternoon splashing around in the pool, only going inside once we'd gotten hungry. My skin was sundrenched, and I shivered when we stepped inside the cool house, AC blasting overhead.

"Cold?" Shane caught me from behind, wrapping his arms around me, my back flush with his bare chest. I leaned my head back and his lips met the side of my face. Then he whirled me around to face him. "You look so good today," he murmured, coming closer. The husky, low timbre of his voice was new, foreign. I liked it.

He kissed me on the mouth, then. My towel fell to the floor, puddling at my feet. His hand cupped the back of my head as the kiss deepened. It was unlike any kiss we'd had before. Our others were soft and chaste. This felt intoxicating.

My tankini top was a halter, and it wasn't difficult for Shane to get it off. It took seconds for him to untie the straps at the back of my neck. Then the top fell forward. When his hands touched me, it was like my skin was on fire. But in a good way. A very good way.

I'd never felt so alive.

I hurriedly fumbled with the string on his swim trunks. We

were both naked by the time he lowered me down onto the couch. When he took me, it was primal. Desperate. We were uncontrollable. Somehow, my body seemed to know what it was doing. And I wanted to stay like that forever.

But I couldn't.

And when it was over, Shane immediately regretted it.

"We never should have done that." Not looking at me, he tugged back on his swim trunks. "It was wrong… Oh, God." Groaning, he ran a hand over his face. "It's just…you were wearing that bikini, and—"

"It's a tankini." I had no idea why I felt the need to correct him. "And are you seriously blaming me?" Hugging myself, I reached for my towel, covered myself. I no longer felt sexy and desirable. I felt dirty.

Exhaling, he turned to me. "No, we both did this. We were playing with fire. We both knew it. What is that scripture? Avoid the appearance of evil? Well, we weren't doing that, were we?" He stepped toward me, an apologetic look on his face. "I'm sorry about this. It never should've happened. And it won't again. We will be careful from now on. I promise."

Nodding, I hugged myself tighter.

Sex was never like that for us again. It was never primal and desperate, charged.

Even our honeymoon was a letdown. True to his word, Shane had been careful with me in the months leading up to our wedding ceremony. He barely touched me. Often, he shied away from my touch as well, as if I was riddled with some horrible disease.

Evil. That was the word that went through my mind any time he scooted away from me. Refused to look in my direction.

Avoid the appearance of evil.

On our wedding night I donned the silky ivory lingerie I'd been gifted at my bridal shower. I fluffed my hair and rubbed my favorite jasmine lotion onto my skin. Shane took his time taking off the lingerie. He kissed my shoulders before working his way down, his hands gently massaging my skin. It was slow and soft, so unlike our first time.

I wanted to like it. But his fingertips were cold and moist, his movements so tender they tickled in an uncomfortable way. I longed for the animalistic way of our first time.

And in my head I kept hearing that word: *evil.*

It was like my brain couldn't make the switch. How was this okay today when it hadn't been yesterday?

My same friends who had admonished me when I told them about Shane's and my slipup, had been flashing me thumbs-up on my wedding day, whispering about how excited I should be about my wedding night. They'd given me naughty oils and massage lotions at my bridal shower, giggling behind their hands when I opened them.

When Shane flipped me over, entering me from behind, I'd stared at the wall in front of me, noticing every stain and crack in the cream-colored paint. With each thrust, I heard that word again—*evil, evil, evil, evil*—until he was finally, thankfully, done. That was the first—but certainly not the last—time I faked it.

Then I got in the shower and scrubbed myself clean.

After that, sex became a part of my life; my routine, my wifely duty. I didn't love it or hate it. It's just another box to check.

Fridays have become our unofficial sex night. I'm not sure when it became that way, but we have it every Friday like clockwork. I used to hate the predictability of it, deep down still longing for that first compulsive time, but now I like the knowing. The not being surprised. The ability to be prepared.

Tonight, after we're finished, I lie in bed, staring at the ceiling until Shane's breathing turns deep and steady beside me. Then I roll over and stare at him. At his head cocked to the side, his mouth hanging open. I frown, thinking how unattractive he looks when he sleeps. Back when we were dating, I loved him so fiercely, I never thought I'd ever love anyone as much as him. But that was such a long time ago. A lifetime, really. Now sometimes I feel like deep down I might despise him.

At the age of seventeen Adrienne started dating Dylan Brenner. The Brenners had been attending Grace Community for years. We'd known Dylan since he was a small child. I'd been a little surprised when Shane gave Adrienne permission to go on a date with Dylan. For years he'd not-so-subtly joked that Adrienne wouldn't be allowed to date until she was thirty. Then again, Shane had always liked the Brenners. Thought of them as a nice, religious, upstanding family. Dylan was polite, well mannered. Never got into any trouble. In Shane's eyes, he was good boyfriend material.

One day after school—a few months after she and Dylan started dating—I caught the hint of a hickey on Adrienne's neck. It was clear she'd tried to cover it up with copious amounts of concealer, but by afternoon it had smudged off. I noticed the way they eyed each other at church. The way she avoided eye contact with her father and me after coming home from a date. Sometimes her cheeks were flushed, her mascara the tiniest bit smeared.

They were having sex. Or, at least, were close to it.

And I knew she'd never tell me.

I wasn't going to let my daughter get pregnant like Kim had last year all because she was too scared or ashamed to talk to me or any of her youth leaders about it. At church the leaders pushed abstinence until marriage. They offered no alternative.

I had to be the one to offer it to her.

She had an upcoming physical appointment with her doctor, so I went with her. After the exam, Dr. Hendry asked if there was anything else he could help us with.

"Ummm...yeah, actually." I pulled at the collar of my blouse. "She's been having some...woman issues...you know? Difficult periods. Back pain and horrible cramps." Adrienne's head whipped in my direction, and I could feel the heat of her raging stare. I didn't dare look over. "I had read online that the pill might help with that."

Dr. Hendry nodded. "It's definitely worth a try." He scrawled something down on his prescription pad and handed it over.

"Thank you so much, Dr. Hendry."

Adrienne had stared at me openmouthed all the way to the car. Once we were safely inside, she asked, "Why did you do that?"

"I just wanna make sure you're being safe," I said.

"But I'm not... We're not—"

I didn't want her to lie to me, so I cut her off. "We'll stop at Rite Aid on the way home. You can take it if you want, or you don't have to—totally up to you. And there's no reason to tell your dad about this. Let's keep it between us, okay?"

"Okay." She fidgeted with the seat buckle.

We were both quiet the rest of the trip, barely even talking at the pharmacy. But when we got back to the house, Adrienne had placed her hand over mine briefly before getting out of the car. "Thanks," she'd whispered so softly I wondered if I'd imagined it.

But over the next few weeks Adrienne was different with me. A little more forthcoming. Even initiating conversation at times. And, every once in a while, I'd catch her staring at me with this expression I didn't recognize, but it was positive. I was hopeful, thinking that maybe my actions had bridged the gap between us.

I allowed myself to believe we could one day have the kind

of relationship I'd always wished I had with my mom. I fantasized about us sitting together talking about boyfriends and love. All the things I never could share with my mother, who was cold and distant, overly strict.

But then one afternoon Shane went to pick up one of his prescriptions, and of *course* the pharmacist asked if he'd also like to pick up Adrienne's. It was her next month's supply of birth control. And he'd come home livid.

"What were you thinking?" he'd shouted, red splotches on his cheeks. We'd made a pact when Adrienne was a toddler that we wouldn't fight in front of her, so we were in our bedroom with the door closed. We'd also made a pact that we wouldn't yell, but that had clearly gone out the window today.

"She was having issues with her periods. This is just to regulate them." I stuck to the lie I'd begun at Dr. Hendry's.

"There have to be other medications that will help with that," he said, and I fought the urge to roll my eyes. What did he know about any of this? "What you did was give her a free pass to have sex whenever she wants."

"It doesn't work like that." I crossed my arms over my chest. "She doesn't need an endorsement from me. If she's gonna have it, she's gonna have it. Nothing we do is going to make a difference. Wouldn't you rather her be safe?"

He paused, and I thought for one second that maybe I'd gotten through to him. But then he ran a hand down his face. "That's what this is really about. She and Dylan…" He stepped toward the door, flinging it open before I could stop him.

Adrienne stood in the hallway, bare feet, and tear-stricken face. She'd been listening.

"You and Dylan are done, young lady. You understand?"

Desperately, her gaze flew over her dad's shoulder to meet mine.

"Shane," I called.

But he shut me up with a sharp, knifelike motion with his

right arm. "I've made up my mind." He stomped to the front door, scooping up his keys.

"Where are you going?" I asked.

"The Brenners."

Adrienne whirled around and ran to her room, slamming the door loudly behind her. I hurried forward. "Adrienne, Adrienne." I knocked.

"Just go away. You've already done enough."

Our daughter may be physically missing now, but we'd lost her years ago.

24

THE DAUGHTER

Past

"Hey." I smiled when Seth opened the door to his house, wearing a gray T-shirt and loose jeans.

Ushering me inside, he said, "Welcome to Coronado Island."

I giggled, loving that he indulged all my little fantasies and inside jokes. This was only my fourth time coming over, but he'd made this joke every time except for the first one. Tonight, as he ushered me inside, The Beach Boys played softly from his Bluetooth speaker.

The music caused my hips to sway back and forth as if they had a mind of their own. Seth smiled with amusement, then took my hand in his and twirled me around. Well, at least, he tried. The edge of my foot tipped, catching on the carpet and I toppled to the side. I caught myself on the kitchen counter, which was to my left. I clutched the edge of it as a giggle bubbled up from my throat and spilled out, a shaken soda.

On the counter sat a stack of mail. The giggle subsided and

I reached out to pick up the top envelope, reading the name it was addressed to.

"Who's Jared Thornton?"

"Oh, I don't know. The guy who lived here before, I guess." He snatched the envelope out of my hand so swiftly, I was certain I'd get a paper cut. I rubbed my fingertips over the tender skin.

I'd never known anyone by that name, but if the guy lived way out here, maybe he didn't go into town that often. He could've just as easily run his errands in Guernesville.

"You know, you don't need to keep his mail. You can just write return to sender and put it back in your box. I can do it for you if you want."

"No, it's cool. I'll deal with it." He tossed the envelope on the counter and grabbed my hand. "Enough about that. Let's have dinner. I picked up takeout." He led me toward the dining table. "Fish tacos and Corona beers. To really get us in the island mood."

I kissed his cheek. "This is amazing."

While we ate tacos and sipped beer straight from the bottle, he told me about his day. I now knew what he did for a living. He was a plumber.

"So kind of like a therapist," he'd said a few dates ago when he told me. "I do spend a lot of time weeding through people's shit to get to the root of the problem."

"What about you?" he asked now, wiping his fingers across his napkin. "What was your day like?"

Today had been uneventful. I'd had it off. "Nothing really to report."

"You must have done *something*."

"Cleaned up my apartment. Ran some errands. Oh, I saw my best friend, Mara, today at Safeway," I said. "Or former best friend? It was kinda awkward."

"Why?"

"We don't talk much anymore. Not since she got married. Now that she has a kid, we talk even less." I played with the edge of the napkin in my lap. "It's still so weird to see her with a baby, you know? It feels like just yesterday we were little kids."

"Do you want a family?" he asked, and for one second I felt miffed that he hadn't asked me more about Mara. It felt like he was glossing over what had happened to me today.

But then I realized I was being petty.

He wasn't interested in Mara because he didn't know her. He wanted to talk about me. To get to know me. That should make me happy.

And it did.

"Um…yeah, I do," I said. "You?"

He nodded. "More than anything."

It struck me as odd, although I wasn't sure why.

"I have something for you," he said suddenly, rushing from the room.

I took another bite of my fish taco. It was a little soggy, but other than that it was good.

"Here." When he returned, he held out his palm. In it he held a bright silver necklace, a colorful butterfly pendant hanging from it.

"Wow, this is so pretty." I plucked it from his hand. "What's the occasion?" We'd literally been dating a couple of weeks.

"Do I have to have an occasion to give you a gift?" He was smiling, but I detected a hint of an edge to his tone.

Had I offended him?

"No, it's just… I don't know… It's just…" I smiled. "I love it."

"The butterfly made me think of you," he said. "And your quest to find freedom."

I understood then and I felt bad for questioning the gift. I'd started our relationship with divulging way too much. Rambling about my past and my family. If it felt like we were further along than we should be, it was my fault, not his. We'd started this train at full speed.

"Help me put it on?"

"I'd love to." His fingers weren't soft. The skin was tough, filled with jagged edges, and yet, it felt so good when they brushed over my neck.

The necklace was heavier than I'd expected, the silver cold against my flesh.

"Thank you." I peered up at him. "It's perfect."

Later in the week I was back at his house, and he was once again cooking for me. I watched him as he stirred noodles on the stove, thinking about how I'd never seen my dad in the kitchen. I wasn't sure he knew how to cook anything. It made me like Seth even more. He was making pasta and he wouldn't let me help. Like usual, he insisted I relax.

"You serve people all day long. Let me serve you." After years in the church the word *serve* often triggered me. But not when he said it. Somehow, it sounded different coming from his mouth.

Steam circled his head and fogged up the window in front of him, causing his reflection to morph and muddy like something out of a horror movie. The far wall of the family room was lined with bookshelves. I wandered past them slowly, trailing my fingertips over the spines of the books propped inside. He had some of the classics. *The Shining.* "The Tell-Tale Heart." *Frankenstein. Bram Stoker's Dracula. Misery.*

"You like horror?" I lifted my head toward the kitchen.

He peered over his shoulder and bobbed his head toward the shelf to my right. "And mysteries. I like any story that explores the human condition."

I understood what he was saying. I wasn't much of a reader,

but I did like studying people. In public. At the bar. And I liked scary movies.

I shuffled to the right, where he had a shelf of mysteries. Agatha Christie. Arthur Conan Doyle. Robert Bloch. I picked up his copy of *Psycho* and studied it. "I wasn't allowed to read stuff like this growing up."

"Have you read it now?" he asked as he rinsed the noodles in the colander.

"No," I confessed. "But I have seen the movie."

"The book is better," he said. "Take it and let me know what you think."

I didn't have the heart to tell him I'd never read it. Instead, I said, "Okay. Thanks." As I picked it up, a photo came into view, lying face up on the shelf of a little boy with dark hair and eyes, a serious expression on his face.

Seth?

I turned it over in my palm and read what was written on the back.

Cole, age 8.

A hand at my spine startled me. I gasped. Seth laughed. "Didn't mean to startle you. Dinner's ready."

"Who's Cole?" I flashed the photo toward him.

His face paled, his lips lowering into a frown. "My brother."

Alarm bells went off in my head. "But…you said you didn't have any siblings."

"I don't. Anymore."

My free hand flew to my mouth. "I'm so sorry. What happened?"

He took the photo from me. "I don't wanna talk about it."

"Of course." I touched his shoulder. I felt bad for prying. "I'm sorry."

Leaning forward, he kissed my forehead. "No worries. Let's just eat, okay?"

"Yeah, okay." I followed him to the table where he had a

bowl of steaming hot pasta in the center, our plates and forks set across from one another. "You're amazing, you know that?" I said, leaning into him. He put his arm around me, drawing me close.

"I know I like when you say it." He kissed me again and this time it wasn't on the forehead. It was quicker than I wanted, though. I could tell he was hungry.

We sat and dished up. He piled the pasta high on his plate. It was sweet how he always doted on me, having me over and cooking for me. But it was also kind of strange. How all of our dates were at his house. I sometimes wondered if he didn't make much money and so that was why he didn't take me out. I wasn't one of those girls who thought a guy should pay for everything, but he'd admitted to me that he was old-fashioned, so maybe he thought that. Either way, it was a sensitive subject, and I didn't know quite how to broach it.

"Everything okay over there?" he asked around a mouthful of spaghetti. Red sauce clung to his lips. Noticing, he swiftly wiped at it with a napkin.

"Oh, yes, great." I twirled noodles around my fork. "Sorry, I was just thinking."

"About what?"

I decided to come at it from a different angle. "About how you haven't come back into the bar since the night we met."

"Do you want me to?" He raised his brows, holding his fork over his plate.

"Yeah, I think it would be fun to…you know, introduce you around…and…" A thought struck. "Ooh, you should come in on a Wednesday night. My mom's just recently started coming in on Wednesdays. I'm sure she'd love to meet you."

"You've told her about me?" The question came out like an offbeat clap, loud and jarring.

I shifted in my seat. Licked my lips. "Um…no, not yet. But I'd like to."

"Really? That surprises me." He sat up taller, his chair creaking with motion. "After everything you've told me, I assumed you wouldn't wanna tell people about us."

"Well, I mean, yeah, I like keeping things private, but not necessarily secret." I rolled the fork between my fingers.

"It's up to you." He gave a slight shrug of his shoulders before scooping up a forkful of pasta. "You were the one who said you hated everyone knowing your business and being involved in your relationships."

"Yeah, you're right," I said quietly. I had said those things, that was true, but I never meant that I wanted to keep him a secret. It seemed like he wanted to keep it a secret, though.

He finished chewing, and I watched the swell of his throat as he swallowed it down. "I mean, if you're not worried it will change things, then let's do it. I guess I just thought you liked things the way they are. Just the two of us."

"I do," I said, trying to save face. Then I speared a chunk of ground sausage. Before popping it into my mouth, I said, "I don't know what I was thinking. I just like you so much, I guess, that I wanted to show you off." Feeling foolish, I instantly regretted my words. Needy girls were a turnoff. I'd learned that the hard way. And he clearly wasn't feeling the same way. I really regretted starting this conversation.

He reached across the table and snatched up my hand. "I like you a lot, too, and that's why I don't wanna screw things up, you know?"

"Yeah. Same." I forced a smile. He released my hand and then took another bite. "So I won't tell my coworkers or my mom yet. I guess I'll just settle for Mara."

"Mara? Isn't she your ex-best friend?"

"I mean, yeah, kinda. Mara and I have been friends forever, though. We just sorta go through phases, and right now she's in the young mom phase. But that doesn't mean we're not still friends."

"Isn't she part of the 'churchy' people, though?" He made little air quotes around the word *churchy*, and I nodded. "I think if you don't want your parents to know, you probably shouldn't tell her, then."

"It's just that I've always told Mara everything."

His eyes met mine and he grinned. "But now you have me. I can be the person you tell everything to."

I smiled back. "I'd like that."

25

THE MOTHER

Present

It's barely light outside, the morning sun rising up over the river. There is a chill in the quiet air. I'd slipped out of bed early this morning while it was still dark outside, and Shane breathed deeply in his sleep. In an attempt not to wake him, I'd changed in the bathroom and put my shoes on by the front door. If he'd woken up, he'd probably have wanted to come with me.

We used to frequently take walks by the river together. But lately, I've preferred going alone. While Shane finds solace in church, I find it in nature. In the brightness of the sun, the blueness of the sky, the chirping of birds, the scuttle of a squirrel, the rush of the river as it flows over the rocks. I find it in the strength of the wind, the mighty roar of thunder and the delicate *pitter-patter* of rain. I find it in the glow of the moon and the sprinkle of glittering stars.

It all makes me believe in something greater out there. Something bigger than church pews, steeples, stained-glass windows and men holding Bibles. Something bigger than me.

And I need to believe in that this morning.

As my feet clomp along the trail, I savor the feel of the breeze on my face. The way the air makes me feel acutely alive.

I think that's how I felt when I first started visiting Adrienne at the Float Down. It started as curiosity. As wanting to be near to my daughter. To get a glimpse into her life. But it ended being more about me. About the way I felt sitting on that bar stool, drink in hand, getting to know the beautiful woman before me. The one I'd known since birth, had raised into an adult, yet barely knew. Getting to know her was like meeting a long-lost friend. I see so much of myself in her. The me I stuff down, anyway. Around Adrienne, parts of me were beginning to creep up, expose themselves. I know that's what's been scaring Shane. It scared me at first, too. But the more I've been getting to know these parts of myself, the more I can't ignore them. I can't pretend they're not there.

I think back to the last time I saw Adrienne at the bar. It was the week before she went missing. Racking my brain, I try to recall if I saw the man Sienna was referring to. She said he had dark hair, was attractive, average height. That description fit most men in Rio Villa. If only she could have remembered something more telling. But the truth is, even if she did, I probably wouldn't have remembered seeing him. No one made an impression on me that night. No one acted oddly toward Adrienne. No one seemed to rattle her and scare her in any way.

She tended to Bill, like usual, and a few other regulars. But mostly, she hung by the bar near me, and we caught up. I'd told her that since I hadn't been helping much at the church, I'd been thinking of getting a job in event planning or hospitality. After all the events I'd planned at the church, I had ample experience. She'd told me the Rio Villa Lodge was hiring, but then her eyes got really big, and she'd leaned forward, rag in hand and said, "Or you could start your own company."

"No," I'd said into my drink. "I wouldn't even know how."

Her face had crumpled as if I'd disappointed her. She'd stood, dragging the rag limply over the counter. "You always sell yourself short."

Before I could answer her, she'd gone to refill Bill's glass of vodka.

I'm not surprised by what Newt told me. I'd seen my daughter with Bill many times. She clearly cared for him. I'd thought on more than one occasion how she wasn't entirely unlike her dad. He's spent his entire adult life serving others. Adrienne is doing the same, just in a different way. But I know if I said that to Shane, he'd laugh in my face. And maybe it is a flimsy comparison.

But it's not untrue.

Adrienne has always sold herself short, too.

The ringing in my pocket startles me. I let out a small gasp. I hate that the manufactured sound has broken through the calming tunes of nature.

It's Shane.

"Hey," I answer, picking up the pace.

A bicyclist comes around the corner and I move to the side. The sky is brightening. More people will be coming out.

"Where are you?" he asks, his voice thick with sleep.

"On a walk."

"Alone?"

"Mmm-hmm," I say absently. I went on walks alone all the time. It's never bothered him before. "Why?"

"I just got a phone call from Kristen," he says, and without even knowing the rest my insides begin to squirm with discomfort. "This morning there had been some talk about you at the women's breakfast and she was a tad concerned."

"I'm sure she was," I mutter under my breath, agitation causing my feet to quicken their pace.

"She means well," he says.

"If she meant well, she would've called me, not you. But

go on. Tell me what she's concerned about." I emphasize the word *concerned* in a sarcastic way.

If he notices, he chooses to ignore it. "I guess one of the ladies in the group saw you with a strange man yesterday, and another lady saw you at Newt's place." According to his voice inflections it would seem that the latter bothers him more. *Interesting.*

I want to ask him who the ladies were who felt the need to gossip about me, seemingly keep tabs on my every movement, but I don't bother. Kristen probably didn't say, and anyway, it doesn't matter at this point.

I decided to address the Newt question first. "Newt had sent Adrienne flowers. I'd seen them in her apartment, so I went to find out why. And apparently it was to say thank you for looking out for his dad."

"His dad? Is Adrienne Bill's caregiver?" His question serves as a reminder that he knows next to nothing about his daughter's life.

"No, he comes into the bar. She makes sure he doesn't drink and drive." Two bicyclists are coming in my direction and I wave as they pass. "And the man I was with yesterday is…" I take a breath before ripping off the Band-Aid. "Adrienne's fiancé. I ran into him at her apartment. He's looking for her, too."

"Adrienne's engaged?"

"Yes."

"Well, this changes things. Why didn't you tell me?"

"Because you haven't taken anything I've said seriously." I pause, finally processing what he'd said. "Wait, what do you mean by *this changes things*?"

"Tony thinks Adrienne took off with her boyfriend, but you're telling me her boyfriend is here. So he must be the reason."

My feet falter. "You think he did something to her?"

"I think they might have gotten into a fight, or she simply got cold feet," he says. "Like you did before our wedding."

I *had* gotten cold feet. It was a few weeks before our wedding, Shane and I had gotten in a huge argument and I'd threatened to call off the wedding.

How different would my life have been if I had?

I shook my head, not allowing myself to think that way. I couldn't undo what I'd done. Also, I would never dream away my children. This life hadn't been all bad. There'd been beauty as well. Beauty I wouldn't trade for anything.

"But I'd told you I needed a break, and I went to my grandma's for a weekend. This is hardly the same thing," I point out.

"But that was you. This is Adrienne we're talking about."

I hate that his words make sense. "Maybe," I acquiesce quietly. "But I don't even think they have a date for their wedding or anything. If so, Seth didn't mention it." I make a mental note to ask him. "So why take off now?"

"I don't know," he says. "What's the guy like? Her fiancé?"

"Nice, well-mannered. Good-looking. I think you'd like him," I say and then my eyes widen, as a thought dawns on me. "I should have him over…dinner, tonight, maybe."

"I don't know. If Adrienne wants us to meet him, she should be the one to introduce us."

"I agree, but those aren't the circumstances we're in. He and I have already met and he's anxious to meet you," I lie. I don't think Seth has a very high opinion of Shane. Not after everything Adrienne has undoubtedly told him. Then again, who knows what he thinks of me, either? Shane is right about one thing. Seth hadn't *wanted* to meet me. Adrienne hadn't *wanted* to introduce him. They clearly had been keeping their relationship from us on purpose. But that's why I want to have him over. There's still so much I don't know. And I feel like the more I can find out, the closer I'll get to finding my daughter. "Come on, I think it'll be nice."

He hesitates. Bushes to my left rattle as if a bird or animal is shaking inside. "Okay, fine." He sighs heavily. "Are you on your way home?"

I'm almost to the end of the trail, then I'll be back in our neighborhood. "Yeah, I'll probably be there in ten."

"Okay. See you then."

After hanging up, I shoot Seth a text inviting him for dinner. It's difficult for me to type on my phone as I walk, so I pull to the side of the trail and stand in the dirt. I'm a little unsteady on my feet today. I started to feel slightly dizzy last night. That's part of the reason I'd wanted to go on a walk this morning. Stress triggers my symptoms. Fresh air and deep breathing can ward them off.

Less than a minute later Seth responds, accepting my dinner invitation.

I follow up with: Hey, have you and Adrienne set a date for your wedding?

No.

So that shoots down Shane's idea about cold feet.

Then he says: were you able to get into the laptop?

Not yet, I type back.

Maybe we can try together tonight, comes his response.

He's so anxious to get into that laptop. What does he think is on there?

Is Shane right? Does this whole thing have to do with a fight between them? If so, is there something about it on her laptop?

I've gotten locked out of the laptop twice since I've had it. Mara's ideas for passwords weren't any more successful than mine. At this point I've exhausted all my options. I'd tried the name of her childhood pet, all variations on her name, her birthdate. Seth had tried all their important dates and what seemed to be variations on his name. What other words or dates are important to her?

And then it hits me.

How had I not thought of this before?

Adrienne's birthday is December twenty-seventh.

"Curtis's birthday is in the summer, and he gets all the good presents," she used to complain every year. "And I get ripped off."

So the year she turned ten we started celebrating her half birthday. June twenty-seventh. The one important date I haven't tried yet.

I walk faster, anxious to get home and try it.

Footfalls emerge behind me, coming fast. I whirl around while simultaneously moving to the side of the path, thinking it must be a runner. But then I stop, heart slamming into my chest. No one's there.

I spin in a circle. I know I heard footsteps. It was undeniable.

Where did the person go?

To my right, leaves rustle. I clutch my chest, my heart dancing underneath my palm. The river rushes nearby. My mind jumps to the image of Jane's body being carried downstream. My palms moisten.

Who would do that to her? Dump her in the river like she was nothing more than trash?

No one knew the guy at the bar watching Adrienne. In a town this size, everyone knows everyone. But he was a stranger. Seth says he thinks his name was Nate, but that's all he knows. Seems like a huge coincidence that a strange man would be watching Adrienne at the bar two weeks after another girl around her age went missing. What if Nate is the same guy who went after Jane? And what if he now has Adrienne?

What if there is a murderer dwelling among us?

Preying on the women of this town?

I click on Tony's name in my contacts and press the phone

to my ear with a quivering hand. I audibly groan when his voice mail comes on. After the beep the words tumbled out. "Tony, there was a strange guy at the bar. Nate—I think his name is—and he was watching Adrienne…and…well, you might already know all this. I don't know if Seth—Adrienne's fiancé—filled you guys in. He talked to one of the officers. Plunkett, I think." Stamping my lips together, I think of the one thing Seth wouldn't have told them. But should I share it? Then I shake my head and spill it all. It's the only way. I have to be truthful in order to find her. "She went home with him—Nate—the night before she went missing. I don't think that's a coincidence. What if…well, maybe he's the same guy who…" I can't bring myself to say the words *hurt Jane*. "I think it's at least worth looking into. Anyway, um…call me back, okay? Or, you know, just look into it."

I hang up, my shoulders sagging. I sounded like a rambling idiot. Was any of that even intelligible?

I imagine Tony sharing everything with Shane, all about how worried I've been. How I'm overdramatizing things. But I'm not. I know I'm not.

Bad things do happen, even in small towns like ours. Jane is proof of that.

I hurry forward, suddenly afraid to be out here alone, my feet moving as quickly as I can make them. When I finally reach the end of the trail, I spill out onto the street. A car drives past. I see a man in his front yard watering his grass. My chest swells. I breathe deeply, some of the tension in my shoulders dissipating.

The road slopes upward. Normally, I take it slowly, but this time my feet clatter up it rapidly. When I reach the top, I pause to catch my breath. Turning, I stare down toward the trail. Two bicyclists materialize out of the cropping of trees. But no one else.

Had I imagined the footsteps?

Shivering, I hug myself and spin around, racing toward home.

26

THE DAUGHTER

Past

"Right this way, miss." The hostess, a young woman probably the same age as me, guided us to our table. It was our two-month anniversary and Seth insisted on celebrating it. I'd never had a boyfriend who celebrated monthly milestones, and it was kind of nice. He'd driven me out to Jenner, and we were trying what was touted as the best steakhouse in the area. In the past few weeks we'd hit up a lot of restaurants in the neighboring towns, both of us bored of dating at our respective homes, but still trying to maintain our privacy. I was losing my grip a little on why, though. Sure, I liked having Seth all to myself, and it was fun being in our little bubble. At least, at first. But it was beginning to lose its luster. Mostly, it felt like a lot of work.

"Ooh, pretty necklace," the hostess said once we were seated.

I reached up, fingered the butterfly. "Thank you."

"You didn't tell her it was from me," Seth snapped sharply

from across the table once she was out of earshot. Candlelight flickered eerily over his face.

"Sorry." I dropped my hand. "Habit, I guess."

"You never tell people it's from me?" Even in the dimly lit restaurant I could see his skin was reddening.

"Are you for real right now? I thought we agreed to keep this on the DL?"

"So even with customers, you don't tell them you have a boyfriend?"

"How would that work, exactly?" My hands shook with irritation. I held them down in my lap, nervously fidgeting with them. "If I told my customers, my coworkers would hear. Is that what you want?" Was he tired of keeping this secret, too?

"I don't—"

"Hello, folks. My name is Jonathon and I'll be your server today." A young man in a crisp white collared shirt and black pants appeared at our table. "Can I get you started with some drinks?"

"Um…" I glanced down at the craft beer list in front of me. "Hmm… Moonraker, that's a great one. Oh, wow, your hazy on tap is good as well."

"Sounds like you know a lot about craft beer."

I smile and shake my shoulders. "Well, I am in the biz."

"Really? You work at a brewery or…"

A clatter rang out, a sudden jolt startling me. When I glanced up, Seth was storming out of the restaurant, the front door slamming behind him. Heat rushed to my cheeks.

"I'm… I'm s-s-so sorry. I don't know…" I pressed my lips together, drawing in a quick breath. Then I pushed my wobbly lips up into a smile. "I'll be right back." I unhooked my purse from the back of the chair, and with it dangling from my fingers, I hurried after Seth.

The spring air was cool tonight, and it shivered over my bare arms.

Seth stood by the car, lips downturned, eyes narrowed.

"What was that?" I hugged myself. The wind kicked up, tossing my hair from my shoulders.

"You were flirting with him," he spat.

"What?" I recoiled. "No, I wasn't. I was just making small talk."

"Is that how you always make small talk? With the guys at the bar, too? No wonder you don't want anyone to know about me."

"Whoa, wait up. You're the one who decided that."

"The fuck I did," he said, slamming his hand down on the hood of the car. I jumped back, my heart thudding in my chest. I'd never seen him like this before. I glanced over my shoulder, searching for signs we weren't alone. I wasn't sure if I wanted us to be or not. On the one hand, I wanted backup. On the other hand, this was fucking embarrassing. "The island fantasy was all yours."

I bit back an argument and slowly tugged in a breath. "I'm sorry." It burned my tongue to say these words. He didn't deserve them. But all I wanted in that moment was for him to calm down. "Let's just go back inside."

"No, I'm done. I'm outta here."

Hot tears stung my eyes. I blinked them back as he opened the driver's-side door and hopped inside. When he turned on the engine, I burst forward, yanking open the passenger door. I didn't want to chance him leaving me here in Jenner. As much as I wasn't looking forward to the car ride back to Rio Villa, an Uber would cost way more than I was willing to spend tonight.

I watched the world blur past as Seth drove, the colors blending together like crayons melting on the sidewalk under the scorching-hot sun. My eyes and cheeks were hot with the sting of embarrassment and frustration. Fisting my hands, my fingernails scraped the insides of my palms. I focused on the feeling, the motion, in order to steady my emotions, to keep myself calm.

We didn't say a word the entire drive.

Once we arrived back at Seth's house, I immediately made a beeline for my overnight bag, snatched it up and flung it over my shoulder.

"Where are you going?" Seth walked toward me, forehead pinched in a look of confusion that in my opinion didn't make any sense. Surely, he didn't think I was staying the night after what he did.

"Home." I whirled away from him, heading toward the front door.

He zipped in front of me, blocking it. "Come on, don't leave."

I stood taller, lifting my chin. "I'm tired, Seth. Just let me go."

"No, please stay. I'm sorry."

I backed up, shaking my head. "You can't just fix this with an apology, Seth. The way you acted... It was... Well... It wasn't okay."

"I know. I really am sorry." His shoulders sagged, his head lowering. "I don't know what got into me." I huffed at his lame words, and he caught it. He looked at me and held up his hands, exposing his palms. "Okay, okay, I do. I know why I acted that way." He paused, swallowing hard. I stood still, waiting. "I got jealous, but it's only because I'm so into you, you know? And..." His tongue tucked into the side of his cheek. "And that scares that shit outta me."

"Why?"

He ran his hand down his face, released a loud breath. "My last girlfriend...she cheated on me."

"I'm sorry that happened, Seth, but I'm not her."

"I know," he said. "I know you're not. You're so much better. So much cooler...and so much hotter...and, God, I'm so much more into you." No matter how hard I tried to keep the glare on my face, the corners of my lips inched upward. Clearly taking it as an invitation, Seth moved closer to me, his hands sliding around my waist. I allowed my body to fall against his. His hands found my hair, his fingers burying into the strands. "I got scared, okay? But I'm sorry." He covered my lips with his, and I didn't want to fight anymore.

We became a tangle of limbs and lips, a symphony of panting and kissing. We made our way to the bedroom where we tumbled down onto the bed. We undressed each other quickly with jerky, lust-filled movements. Then Seth reached into the nightstand drawer to his right, dipping his hand inside. It was where he kept his condoms. I stared up at the ceiling, my chest heaving, my breathing labored as I waited. Normally, it only took a few seconds, a quick grab. So when he was still rooting through the drawer at least ten seconds later, I rolled over.

"Where are they?" he muttered under his breath, reaching in farther. The sound of objects clanging around reverberated in the drawer.

I leaned over to look inside. My gaze skated over a couple of ballpoint pens, caps off, a few blank index cards, a travel pack of Kleenex.

"Ahh, found one." His arm was elbow deep in the drawer. As he pulled out the shiny foil packet, something in the drawer caught my eye. The sparkle. The shine. The gold. Was that a ring?

He slammed the drawer shut and then he was on top of me. It only took a few seconds for us to rev back up, to get back to where we were before we hit Pause.

It was rougher than usual, his hands at times holding me too tightly, his thrusts hard and a little painful. Even his expression seemed to mirror anger rather than passion.

It's like he's punishing me, I thought at one point.

Afterward I lay in bed, sore and achy, while he made us

sandwiches. When he brought them back to the bed, I searched his face for signs of the anger he'd displayed during sex, but there weren't any. He was content. His fingers played with mine, and every once in a while he'd pick my hand up and press it to his lips.

I started to wonder if maybe I'd imagined it. He appeared fine. Sweet. Happy.

Shortly after we ate, he fell into a deep sleep. But I couldn't. My mind kept replaying the events of the night, trying to process them. It felt like I'd been on a roller coaster, with sudden twists and turns and terrifying loops. It had been hard to keep up in real time.

In the dark I listened to Seth's even breathing and weeded through it, turning it all over in my mind. And that was when I remembered the ring.

Checking to make sure he was still sound asleep, I scooted to the edge of the bed. Then I slowly tiptoed to his side of the bed and tugged the nightstand drawer open. It emitted a high-pitched squeak and I winced. Stopped. Peered over my shoulder. Still asleep, thankfully. The drawer was only open a sliver, but that was enough. There it was. The ring. I carefully plucked it out, holding it between my fingers.

It was an engagement ring, all right. But not brand-new. The yellow gold had some scuffing on it, and the diamond was set up high in an old-fashioned way. Rings now were platinum, square cut.

And why wasn't it in a box?

I studied it a little longer. In the dark I couldn't see if there was an inscription, but when I ran my fingertips along the inside, I didn't feel any.

Again, I looked over at Seth. His face was turned toward the opposite wall, but his broad shoulders and defined back were still, and I could detect his even breathing. He was facing my side, though, so I knew I needed to get back in bed quickly.

I wondered if maybe the ring was his mom's. Or grandma's, although it didn't seem *that* old.

He didn't talk much about his mom. About his parents at all, really. Mostly, he mentioned them in generalizations. I rolled the ring around in my palm. It was odd, actually. I've told him so many things. Specific things. Before now I'd never stopped to think about how he hadn't exactly reciprocated that.

He remained somewhat of a mystery.

It would be just like Seth to buy an old-fashioned ring, though.

He stirred, stretching out his legs and letting out a soft groan. Pulse spiking, I lowered the ring back into the drawer and shoved it closed. Then I hurried back to my side of the bed and slowly got into it. Just in time, too, because he threw an arm over my chest.

As he nestled into me, he murmured, "I love you." I froze. It was the first time he'd said that, and he was asleep. "So much," he added, tagging on a contented sigh as he wiggled his body closer to mine.

Did he mean this or was he simply dreaming?

I couldn't be sure. Honestly, I couldn't even be sure he was directing it to me. He could've been dreaming of someone else. Still, it begged the question.

Did I love him?

It was that question that chased me into my slumber. I dreamt that Seth and I were at a restaurant. A fancy one, not unlike the one we'd tried and failed to eat at earlier tonight. As Seth sliced his steak, blood oozed out, coating his plate. My stomach turned.

"Try it," he said, holding out his fork, a dripping piece speared through one of the tines.

Wincing, I shook my head.

"Eat it!" he demanded, thrusting into toward me.

"No." I drew back, but he grabbed my hand. Held me in

place. Force-fed me the steak. It was mealy and soft. Long after I swallowed it, the putrid metal taste lingered on my tongue.

When I awoke in the morning I was drenched in a cold sweat. I slipped into the shower while Seth was still sleeping. Then I got dressed and gathered my things.

"Taking off?" He sat up in bed, propped on his elbows.

"Yeah, I have work later." I hoisted my bag over my shoulder.

He slid out of bed and swaggered up to me. "Hey, I'm sorry again about last night. I wanted everything to be perfect, and then I fucked it up."

"It's fine," I said, and then wished I hadn't. It wasn't fine, and I didn't know why I was excusing it. What was it about him? I looked at his muscular chest and piercing eyes and almost laughed out loud. Oh, God, I was turning into one of those girls. The ones I made fun of. The ones who got charmed by some hot guy and let him make a fool of her.

"I'll make it up to you." He rested his hands on my hips. "I promise."

I smiled. He wasn't one of those guys, though, was he? He wasn't going to make a fool of me. *Oh, God, I hope not.*

"Why don't I take you out tonight? A do-over."

"I don't think tonight's gonna work. I'm working late and…" I shook my head.

"Tomorrow night, then."

"I'll let you know." I wriggled away.

"I love you," he said suddenly, tugging me back. So he had meant what he said in the middle of the night.

I stared at him, willing my mouth to do something. Anything. But what? In that moment I knew I couldn't say it back. I liked him. A lot. But love? That wasn't something I said— or did, for that matter—very easily. I also wasn't the kind of person who said it when she wasn't certain that she meant it.

He raised his brows. I'd been mute too long.

No words were forthcoming, so instead, I kissed him. When I drew back, I avoided looking at the sad expression on his face. I looked at the floor, my shoes, my hands.

"I really should get going," I mumbled, moving around him.

"Text me about dinner," he called after me. "There's something I wanna talk to you about."

I thought about the ring in his nightstand drawer, and I walked swiftly away from his house, the chill of the morning at my back.

"What's going on with you?" Jazzy asked that night at work. "You're... I don't know...more ditzy than usual."

"Gee, thanks," I muttered, shaking my head. "I didn't realize I was such an airhead."

"I said *more* ditzy," she repeated, punctuating the word *more*.

"Which implies I'm always ditzy," I explained.

"Sorry." She threw up her hands. "I'm no English major, so sue me."

I couldn't help it. I laughed. This was typical Jazzy. I never should've taken offense to it. She wasn't mean. She just wasn't articulate.

"Anyway, whatever you wanna call it," she continued. "You're acting off."

We were in that lull in the late afternoon where there were only a handful of customers, all of whom were nursing their one drink before heading home for dinner. I leaned my back against the bar and fingered my necklace.

"I don't know...it's just..." *Oh, the hell with it. I can tell Jazzy. It's not like she even knows the guy, and I'm so tired of keeping this secret.* "I've kinda been dating this guy."

"Oooh." Jazzy waggled her eyebrows. "I didn't know this."

"Yeah, we've kinda been keeping it on the DL," I explained.

"Well, tell me about him. Is he cute?"

"Cute is an understatement. He's seriously hot."

"Oh, my God, girl, why have you been keeping him a secret? I wanna meet him."

"It may not matter now," I said.

"Why not?" Her eyes widened. "Oh, my God, he didn't cheat on you, did he?"

"No." I wrapped the silver chain around my finger. "He would never do that. He's totally into me."

"Then what's the problem?"

"He's just… I don't know…moving too fast." I released the necklace and it fell against my chest. "I think he might be about to propose."

Jazzy clutched her chest. "Nuh-uh. Oh, my God. Are you gonna say yes?"

"I mean, we've, like, just started going out."

"Yeah, but you said he's hot and totally into you. What more do you want?"

I swallowed hard. That may be enough for Jazzy, but not for me. It was way too soon to get engaged.

I wasn't sure I even wanted to keep dating the guy, let alone marry him. As much as I wanted to forgive him for last night, deep down I was still upset about how he acted. Maybe if it had been the first time he'd behaved off, but it wasn't. It was so early in our relationship for him to be showing me these kinds of red flags.

I thought about Jazzy's question again: What more did I want?

A stark realization hit. It wasn't about what I wanted. It was about what I didn't want.

I *didn't* want to be controlled.

I *didn't* want to be afraid.

27

THE MOTHER

Present

Shane has breakfast and coffee ready when I get home. It takes all the willpower I can muster to sit patiently at the table with him and partake. I'm anxious to get onto Adrienne's laptop. I shovel in the eggs and toast so rapidly I almost choke a couple of times. But I wash it down with a swig of hot coffee.

"You were hungry," Shane observes from across the table where he eats methodically.

"Yeah," I mumble around a mouthful of eggs. By the time I finish, Shane still has half his food left. I swallow my last bite down and then carry my plate to the sink. After rinsing it and sticking it in the dishwasher, I say, "I'm gonna hit the shower real fast." I turn around in the doorway of the kitchen. "Oh, and Seth is coming over tonight at five."

"Okay." Shane picks up his half-eaten piece of buttered toast, lifting it to his mouth.

I hurry into our bedroom and close the door. Then I slide my arm underneath the bed and tug the laptop out. Keeping my ears perked and eyes peeled toward the door, I race into the bathroom. It's no secret to Shane that I'm looking into Adrienne's disappearance. That's painfully clear at this point. But I know he's not happy about it, and if he finds out I'm trying to snoop on her computer, he'll think I'm stooping to a new low. It's a conversation I don't feel like having.

I lock the bathroom door and turn on the shower.

Then I lower down onto the closed toilet seat and open the laptop. I have the rush of adrenaline like someone engaging in illicit behavior. It's similar to the rush I feel when I go to the Float Down on Wednesdays. I imagine it's how Adrienne felt when she snuck in cigarettes or alcohol, or a boy.

I type in 0622, but it's not enough characters, so I add the year. And I'm in!

It worked!

Her half-birthday. That was the password all along.

As her screen loads, I think back to those June 22 celebrations. She and Mara in the backyard, faces planted in fuchsia frosted cupcakes, pink balloons tied to the fence.

Once everything is populated, I start searching. If I thought the adrenaline rush I'd felt earlier was significant, it's nothing compared to now. It's warm in here, steam smothering the mirror. I should change the temperature of the water, but I'm too focused.

Seth's right. She doesn't have her computer synced to her phone. She probably can't, since it's a Dell, not a Mac. At least, that's how Seth made it sound. I don't really know how all this works. But I do find her calendar and it looks like an updated one. She has things written on some of the dates.

I locate this week.

I smile when I see she'd put our mani/pedis in. She also has her work schedule inputted. I sit up straighter, skin heating up and not just from the shower water that pounds behind the curtain.

There's nothing in here about a trip to Napa. Seth's name doesn't appear on here at all.

I search her home screen again. There's no texting or messaging app. There's a camera roll, though, and I go into that.

Here she has photos of her and Seth. On a hike. On a picnic. Out at the river. My heart swells. She *had* been happy with him. He's telling the truth.

My gaze lingers on the most recent one. It had been taken a couple of weeks ago. Her arms are wrapped around him. At first glance it's a sweet photo, but as I stare at it a little longer, it becomes clear that her smile is a little forced. I know my daughter. I can tell when she's not happy. And in this photo, she's not. Another odd thing is that I don't see a ring on her finger. I zoom in to be sure. If she and Seth were engaged, why wouldn't she be wearing a ring?

I think back on my conversations with Seth. I'd never asked him how long ago he proposed. Had Jazzy said? If she had, I couldn't remember. According to him, they hadn't set a date yet, so maybe that's because he'd just proposed.

Exiting the camera roll, I find myself back on Google.

I shove my tongue into my cheek and think. A couple of years ago Kristen had come to bible study distraught because she'd found out her husband had been chatting with other women in online forums. She'd caught him late at night on his computer a couple of times and had an inkling something wasn't right. But ultimately, his browser history was the nail in the coffin.

I move the mouse up, deciding to check Adrienne's. I don't know what I'm hoping to find. She's not a cheating spouse, after all. But I figure it can at least give me a picture into her thoughts lately.

Her last search stops me cold.

She'd read dozens of articles about Jane's murder.

Why was she reading about that so much?

Had she been afraid?

I click on the articles and scan them. But they're all the same, and all information I'd known.

It's the next search that causes my insides to knot: *Carolyn Spencer, murder Aptos.*

Heat works its way up my spine as I read the articles. Another young woman, murdered. Strangled. Her body thrown into the ocean. Only parts of her had been recovered. Sharks got to the rest.

The air left my lungs. Why had Adrienne been searching these murders?

Her other searches are just as confusing. Names I don't know. Max Lincoln. Jared Thornton.

But the last one I do: Seth Lafferty.

I hadn't known that was his last name, but it must be. How many Seths could she know?

But why had she been searching her boyfriend's name?

I click on the search, but it yields no results. At least, no successful ones. A bunch of LinkedIn and Facebook accounts, none of which are him.

So I move to Jared Thornton. Click on the sites she'd searched. I find a bunch of images and social media accounts that mean nothing to me. I wonder if any of them did to her. And why? What had she been looking for?

Last, I try Max Lincoln. Again, a mishmash of images comes up. None of the photos look familiar.

"Tatum? You okay?" Shane hollers through the door. "You've been in there awhile."

"Yeah, fine. Washing my hair." I slam the laptop shut, hide it under a towel and peel off my clothes. Then step into the shower.

28

THE DAUGHTER

Past

My phone buzzed in my pocket, but I didn't bother looking. I knew who it was.

Ever since I'd seen the ring in Seth's nightstand, I'd been avoiding him. After my conversation with Jazzy about it, I'd been more confused than ever. I needed time to think. I didn't want to make an impulsive decision either way.

It was Wednesday night, and we had a steady stream of customers. I kept looking for Mom, certain she'd walk through the doors any minute. Funny how much her visits disconcerted me at first. Now it was something I'd come to rely on.

On my break I checked my phone.

It hadn't been Seth, after all. It had been Mom.

Dad had stayed home tonight, not feeling well, so she wasn't coming by.

I texted back that I understood, and hopefully, I'd see her next week. Then I blew out a frustrated breath and shoved my phone back down into my pocket. Of course Dad would keep her from coming by.

She'd been visiting me for more than two months now. Did he seriously not know?

I couldn't imagine keeping that secret from my husband this entire time. And how lame that Mom would even have to. I'm her daughter for fuck's sakes. What kind of father keeps a mother from her daughter?

Break over, I got Bill his vodka on the rocks. As soon as I got a chance, I'd need to ask Jazzy how many she'd served him while I was away from the bar. If he'd had too many, I'd have to call his son Newt to come get him. I usually called Bill an Uber at the end of the night, but a few months back he'd had a fall walking from the Uber to his front door, and ever since then Newt preferred to drive him home and make sure he was safely inside when he was particularly hammered.

After serving Bill his drink, I grabbed a rag to clean up the counter. As it swirled over the mahogany, my frustration rose. It was always like this with Dad. One small flame could turn into a fire that would obliterate everything in sight in a matter of seconds. That was all it took. One thing. Because, let's face it, it could never stay one thing. It was all the things. All the ways he'd hurt me. All the things he'd taken.

It would never be an isolated event.

It couldn't be. My brain wouldn't allow it.

I probably should've talked to a therapist about all this. Mara had been encouraging me to do so for years. But she had no idea what it was like having a dad like mine. She had a great relationship with her parents. She was the good kid. The golden child.

I bet my parents wish she was theirs.

It wasn't like Mara hadn't tried to help me over the years. Growing up, she was the person I ran to more than anyone else. And she loved me as best as she could. It wasn't her fault that her family was better than mine.

I'd only ever been candid about all this with one person.

"You know you can shut me up at any time," I'd said to Seth a few weeks after we'd started dating. We were on a walk by the river, the smell of fish and sand wafting under my nose.

"I'd never do that," he said.

"I'm not scaring you?" I asked.

"Not at all," he said. "Am I scaring you?"

"No," I answered, thinking it was an odd question. He hadn't been the one word-vomiting about his dad all night.

My shift tonight went by so slowly. I hadn't even realized how much I looked forward to seeing my mom until I didn't. My heart ached somewhat as I closed up the bar.

By the time I stepped outside, I felt dangerously close to crying. How silly was that? I was twenty-four years old, and I was going to cry about not seeing my mom?

It angered me. And I wasn't only angry with my dad. I was angry with Mom, too. Why couldn't she grow a pair, stand up to him? Do what she could never do when I was growing up. Stand up for me for once, goddammit.

Wasn't I worth that?

I stormed up to my car and hopped inside. After turning it on, I peeled out of the parking lot. But I didn't go home.

I ended up back at the one place I'd felt free lately.

Seth's house.

My fake Coronado Island.

It was dark inside, but still I ran up to the door and knocked. Waited. Seconds ticked by. Then minutes.

Where was Seth?

My stomach knotted. What if he was with another girl?

If he was, I didn't have the right to be mad. I'd been avoiding him. What did I expect?

Desperate, I knocked a few more times and then jiggled my leg up and down with impatience.

When I gave up a few minutes later and started trudging

back to my car, shoulders sagging, lights swept over me. I froze. Was that him?

When the car turned down his driveway, my heart lifted. Hugging myself, I waited. It was spring, but it was late, and the air was cool.

"What are you doing here?" Seth asked gruffly when he stepped out of the car.

Instinctually, I stepped back. It's not the greeting I'd expected. I cupped the back of my neck with my right hand. "Um… I… Well, I… I missed you."

He sighed loudly. "I'm sorry. It's just been a long night." When he stepped into the porch light, I saw that his pants were wet and caked in mud. His hands were dirty and stained as well. And there were bits of dirt and some other substance on his face, maybe a few scratches. It was hard to see in this lighting.

"Oh, my God, what happened?"

"Mainline sewer break. Got the call when I was already off for the day. Too urgent to leave for morning," he said like I'd know what all of this means.

I didn't.

After we stepped inside, he looked at me apologetically. "I'm gonna need to take a shower."

"Of course."

Without another word, he hurried into the bathroom. From inside, he hollered, "There's beer in the fridge. Help yourself."

"Okay, thanks." I slowly moved into the kitchen. It was a mess; dishes piled high in the sink. I shivered. It wasn't much warmer in here than outside. I opened the fridge, locating the beer he'd promised. After grabbing one, I rooted around in the kitchen drawers for an opener. Once the cap was popped, I lifted the bottle to my lips and took a long sip.

I could hear the shower going, the rush of water through the piping. A funny feeling descended into my stomach, and

I wished I hadn't showed up unannounced like this. Condensation from the beer bottle dampened my palm. I carried it into the family room and set it down on the end table, relieving my hand. Then I sank down onto the couch, tucking my legs up under my body.

"Sorry about that," he said when he emerged, hair wet and tousled, flannel pajama pants riding low on his hips, chest bare.

I swallowed hard. "No, I—I'm the one who's sorry. I shouldn't have shown up out of the blue like this."

He shook his head. The scent of soap lingered in the air. "Don't worry about it. I'm glad you're here. It was just a rough day. That's all."

"For me, too. That's… Well, that's why I came here."

Brows knitting together, he sauntered toward me, taking a seat next to me on the couch. "Why? What happened?"

"I was at work and…" I drew in a breath, wondering if I was truly about to tell him I was upset about not seeing my mom. Admittedly, I shared a lot with him, but this? How would that make me sound? I exhaled, closing my eyes for a moment, then opening them again. "Never mind. It's… It was nothing. Stupid. I feel better now…seeing you."

He cursed, running a hand through his hair. "I knew it. I knew something bad would happen to you working at that place. We need to find you a new job."

"What? No, I love my job."

"It's not a safe place for you, Adrienne." He swept my hands up into his. "Trust me."

I jerked my hands back. "Not a safe place for me? What does that mean?"

"I know what guys think about when they see a woman as beautiful as you."

"So do I, and I can handle that," I said.

He leaned back. "I thought that's why you came here.

'Cause you wanted my help. So that's what I was trying to do. Help."

"I was upset that my mom didn't show up tonight to see me." I ran my tongue along my lower lip. "Okay? I know it sounds stupid, but that's why I was upset. I guess I like seeing her more than I thought I did. It had nothing to do with a guy."

"Oh, God." He ran a hand down his face. "I overstepped."

"Yeah, you did."

"I just worry about you there. That's all."

"Right, because I'm a poor little weak woman making men feel all sorts of things just by looking the way I do. I've heard it all before, okay? My whole life, growing up. It wasn't okay for my dad to say and it's not okay for you to say. You don't get to control me. It's my life. Why can't anyone see that?"

"Hey, hey." He placed his hands on my thighs. "That's not what I'm saying. I'm not trying to control you. I care about you. That's all. Okay? I think you're gorgeous and I thought you were going to tell me that some asshole harassed you or worse…and…and I let my emotions get the better of me." I noticed he used that phrase a lot. "But only because I like you so much. Love you, actually." He used that one a lot, too. "Please don't be mad at me." He flashed me his lopsided smile.

God, he was cute. I kind of hated him for it. But my stupid lips weren't getting that memo and they began lifting at the corners.

"I missed you. Let's just… Let's not talk anymore. Let's just have a good night together." He opened his arms. "C'mere?"

I wanted to say no. I wanted to make him pay for what he'd said to me. To drive the point home that it wasn't okay. But he was shirtless and smiling, and my stomach was doing that fluttering thing, and then I was in his arms. And then in his room…and then in his bed.

29

THE FIANCÉ

Past

Something's different about her.

"New lipstick?" I asked, studying her crimson lips.

"Yeah, you like it? I got it for you."

I wanted to believe her. That she'd been in a store, perusing the aisles and picking out something she thought would be sexy for me. But that image wouldn't stick. It kept being replaced by her flirting with that rando at the bar. She'd been wearing this lipstick then, too. And she'd been smiling and giggling and touching his arm. My skin was hot as if I had a fever and it itched like that time I touched poison ivy on a hike with my dad.

Are you stupid? Look what you did to yourself, he'd said in frustration a couple of days later while I scratched the shit out of my arm, wishing the itching and burning would go away.

She swaggered up to me, her face close to mine. I touched her cheek, pictured myself smearing that red lipstick all over her face with a forceful swipe of my hand. Worried I might actually do it, I dropped my arm, tucked it behind my back.

Earlier tonight I'd gone to the bar to surprise her. Have a drink. Chat. I thought she'd be happy to see me. But as I walked up to the front door, I'd stolen a glance in the window to the right of it. And there she was. And there *he* was. A strange man sitting in front of her. That wasn't the part that pissed me off. It was the way she behaved around him. Laughing demonstratively. Fluttering her lashes. Smiling a little too big, teeth and all, like she was having the time of her life.

With *him*.

Without me.

I only watched for a few minutes. But that was long enough. Long enough for me to envision myself storming inside to slam my fist into the dude's face. Instead, I clenched them and raced back to my car. Then I peeled out and sped back home. Once I'd cooled down, I texted her, asked how things were going.

It took her a full hour to respond. But when she did, she said she was on her way over.

"I know it's not blue or green," she teased now, sliding her hands up my chest. "But I figure, what guy doesn't like red lipstick. It's a classic."

Red. Her favorite color. Or at least, one of many. The thought made me smile, despite my earlier frustration. She had that effect on me. The ability to make me smile through all the shit. Even make me forget the shit altogether.

Her mouth was on mine, then, the red lipstick being smeared, all right, but not by my hand. By my lips. When we drew back, she laughed. I must've had the red lipstick all over me now. "Very sexy." She didn't attempt to wipe it off, just kissed me again.

I wrapped my arms around her middle and carried her to the bed. She giggled and kissed my neck repeatedly. She wanted me. Badly. She got like this sometimes.

I'd always thought it was her love for me that brought it

out. That, although she couldn't say the words, she could show me. Like this. Like now when she lay in my bed, tugging me on top of her.

But that damn image of her with that other man wouldn't leave my mind.

Was it him she was thinking of right now or me?

She moaned, closing her eyes.

"Open them," I demanded, and maybe a little too harshly by the startled expression she bore when she looked at me. So I softened my tone. "I wanna see those beautiful green eyes."

She smiled then and I grabbed her wrists, stretching her arms over her head. I took her then. Harder and more forcefully than usual. She liked it, though. I could tell.

I did feel a little bad, however, when I saw the bruises forming on her skin. I kissed them lightly as I lay next to her in bed, wrapped in blankets and slick with sweat afterward.

30

THE DAUGHTER

Past

I carried a tray of drinks to a group of loud women who'd come in an hour ago and had already, in my opinion, exceeded their drink limit. I knew from experience that they still had a few more in them. They lived in Guernesville and came in from time to time, a night out away from their men. They generally had a good, if not boisterous, time, and always took an Uber. So I let them have their fun.

After depositing the drinks, my phone buzzed in my pocket. I waited until I was back behind the bar, before turning away from the customers to momentarily check my phone.

Come over after work?

Seth and I had fallen back into our rhythm these past few days, me heading to his house every night after work. But it had been a long, busy night already and I knew I wouldn't feel like driving over there. I hadn't had the forethought to leave a packed bag in my car, either, so unless I headed back home first I wouldn't have any of my stuff. It all seemed too exhausting.

I'm tired. I think I want to sleep in my own bed tonight.

My own bed. All alone. Stretched out. It sounded glorious. I was already looking forward to it.

"Excuse me?" A male voice interrupted my thoughts. I shoved the phone back into my pocket and whirled around.

A man I'd never seen before sat on the bar stool directly in front of me. He flashed a friendly smile that instantly put me at ease.

"What can I get you?" I asked.

"I'll take the hazy on tap." He had a nice voice, and it reminded me of someone. A little quiet, but that only made him feel more approachable, less threatening.

Some guys came in here demanding drinks with their loud, booming voices and I was immediately on alert.

Jazzy's laugh floated above the crowd. As I poured the hazy into a beer mug, I caught sight of her talking to the group of women. I was grateful she was handling them for the time being. They could be high-maintenance, all of them ordering something different, wanting to try drinks they'd heard about but couldn't remember the names of, only some of the ingredients. It could be a lot.

"Here you are." I slid the hazy toward the strange man with the nice voice.

"Thank you." He tossed a wad of cash on the counter. "Keep the change."

Ah, that was it. He sounded old-fashioned, like his voice was coming from a black-and-white movie. And I should know. I'd seen a lot of them. We hadn't been allowed to watch very much modern TV growing up. Who was it that he reminded me of, though?

"How is it?" I asked him after he took a sip.

"Great. Thanks." He flashed a thumbs-up, and I had it. *Marlon Brando.*

Bill waved me over in his usual gruff and mute way, merely an impatient flick of his wrist once he had my attention, and I refilled his vodka.

"Busy tonight?" Marlon Brando asked when I got close to his side of the bar again.

"Yeah, but that's typical for a Saturday."

"You seem to handle it well." His gaze flickered toward Bill. "Even with that guy."

"Bill? Yeah, he's harmless." I leaned over and whispered, "I feel sorry for him. Lost his wife a few years back and now he spends every night here getting drunk off of vodka."

Marlon frowned, his head slowly bobbing up and down. "That's really sad."

"I figure keeping his glass full is the least I can do." I slid my arms off the bar, standing up. "People don't give bartenders enough credit. It's really an important, compassionate service we're providing here," I joked, and he let out a small chuckle.

"Hey, I buy it. I know I've never been unhappy around a bartender," he said, wearing his easy smile. "Is that why you got into this line of work? To make people happy?"

"No, I didn't really choose this line of work. It chose me," I answered, honestly.

"Ahh, very philosophical," he teased, stroking his chin.

"Just call me Aristotle." Out of the corner of my eye, I saw Pamela, one of our regulars, approaching the bar. I ambled over to her. "Hey, Pamela. Glass of red?"

"You know it."

"I have a blend open. That good?"

She nodded, and I went to retrieve the open bottle. As I poured her glass, I noticed Marlon watching me, and my body felt all tingly. I was anxious to get back to our bantering. After handing Pamela her glass, and adding it to her tab, I hurried back over to him.

Only foam was left, stuck on the sides of the glass, a thick layer coating the bottom.

"Another?"

"Sure, why not?" He shrugged.

When I handed him his fresh glass, he looked at my neck and said, "That's a really nice necklace."

"Oh." I reached up to touch it. "Thanks."

"It looks custom made. Is it from someone special?"

I sighed. The spell was broken. "Um…yeah, my boyfriend gave it to me."

There was an awkward pause. "He's a lucky guy," the stranger said.

"Yeah, he is." My mouth tasted sour. Here I was flirting with this guy, secretly hoping it might lead to something, and I had a boyfriend.

One that wanted me to come over tonight. What was I thinking?

And…oh, shoot.

"Excuse me." I held up a finger to Marlon and turned my back to him. Then I pulled out my phone.

The last text that came through was from Seth and it read:

I can come to your place.

About ten minutes later he'd texted:

????

"That your fiancé?" Jazzy asked a little too loud as she nudged me with her hip while she passed me. I glanced around. Marlon was watching me. My face reddened. I spun around to tell Jazzy she was wrong. That I wasn't engaged, but she'd already made it to the other side of the bar and was making a drink.

I bit my lip and texted back:

Sure. Sounds good.

His text came back immediately, like he'd been waiting. It was simply a thumbs-up, followed by the kissie-face emoji.

"Hey, do you mind taking out the trash bins real quick? They're starting to overflow," Jazzy spoke over the chatter of the room.

I nodded, glancing at the trash nearest me. *Oh, God.* It *was* overflowing. I'd been so focused on Marlon I'd been neglecting my duties. By the look on Jazzy's face, I could tell she'd noticed as well. I felt bad for allowing her to shoulder the bulk of the work on such a busy night, especially since Ted had called out. Usually, there were three of us on Saturday night.

After tying and gathering up the trash bags, I lugged them outside. As I dragged them across the parking lot, the screeching of tires startled me. I craned my neck to look, and heat shot up my spine.

Was that—?

The car sped down the street, a bolt of lightning.

For a second I thought it had been him—Seth—but no, it couldn't have been. He was just texting me. He'd tell me if he was here. If it was him, why would he speed off like that? No, there were lots of blue sedans in this town. I was being paranoid.

I tossed the bags into the Dumpster and scurried back inside.

The next morning Seth and I got up early and drove to a little diner in Guernesville. We sat outside at a circular table, had coffee and pastries.

"Isn't this nice?" Seth lifted the white mug to his lips. Foam painted his mouth when he drew the mug back.

I giggled, reaching out to wipe it off. He kissed my fingers as I did, and I giggled again.

He checked his phone, and my stomach clenched. He had work later, and the drive alone had eaten up a lot of our morning.

"It is nice, but…" I ran my fingertips over the rim of the mug. "You know, I don't think we need to keep driving a half an hour away for coffee or food. We have diners and cafés in Rio Villa."

"But look how relaxed and happy you are here. Not worried at all about being watched."

"True."

He leaned back in his chair, coffee in hand. "Don't feel bad. I don't mind it at all."

Was I feeling bad? I didn't think so. I didn't even think I was the reason we kept driving out of town to go on dates.

But was I?

It was muddied in my mind now. Who had started this idea of keeping our relationship secret?

He seemed to think it was me. I'd thought it was him.

But maybe I was wrong.

"Have you started reading *Psycho* yet?" he asked.

"I mean, I've been trying." I set my mug down on the circular table between us. "It's kind of slow. It was much quicker to just watch the movie."

He let out an amused laugh, hands wrapped around his mug. "It'll pick up. Just wait 'til you get to the twist."

I clutch my chest. "I already know what's going to happen."

"Still. Just keep reading," he said with more firmness than I thought was warranted.

"Okay, I will," I answered, feeling a little like a student who'd been schooled by her teacher.

He glanced down at his phone. "Oh, we should head back soon." His coffee cup was mostly drained.

I had quite a bit left in mine, so I slurped up as much as I could. Took a few more bites of my chocolate croissant. I didn't want to go to the trouble of getting a to-go cup.

"What time is your first job?" I asked, wiping chocolate from my fingers.

"I don't know. I'll have to check my work orders. I left my laptop back at your place."

Nodding, I gathered up our trash. Then I carried it to the bin. A cool breeze circled me, bringing with it the scent of jasmine.

We didn't talk much on the drive home. But we did sing along to nineties music, and that made the drive go by fast.

When we got to my apartment, I stuck my key into the lock, but the knob moved before I even turned it. "That's weird," I said aloud. "Did I leave my door unlocked?"

"I don't know. I didn't notice," he said.

"I could've sworn I locked it." I pushed the door open and stepped inside. At first glance everything looked the same. Nothing out of place. TV: check. Bluetooth speakers: check. Laptop plugged into the wall: check. I must've been so distracted I forgot to lock the door.

"What the fuck?"

The sharpness of his words caused my head to swing in his direction.

"My overnight bag's gone," he said.

"What?" I walked over to him. The spot where he'd dropped it was empty. "But that doesn't make any sense. Why would anyone take your overnight bag?"

"I don't know." He scratched the back of his head in agitation. "But it's gone. Look."

"Are you sure you didn't move it before we left?"

"I'm sure," he snapped.

Why his bag and nothing else? I lifted my head, my gaze scouring the room. Maybe because it was easy to grab. And I didn't have anything of value. Maybe the robber walked in and was instantly disappointed in my cheap flat screen and years-old Bluetooth speaker. The only thing I have of value are some old rings of my grandmother's and a bracelet my mom gave me for my sixteenth birthday.

I raced into my room and looked in my jewelry box. All there.

Returning to the family room, I said, "I don't get it. Did you have some expensive clothes in there or something?" I was trying to make light of things, to add a little humor, but it didn't work.

"No, but I had my work laptop," he said, seething.

"Why would they take your laptop and not mine?"

"I don't know." He paced back and forth, wearing a line in my carpet. Then he stopped abruptly, stared right at me. "You were the one who insisted on going out for coffee. I wanted to stay in."

I almost laughed at the absurdity of his accusation. It was only because I was almost out of my specialty coffee beans, and despite what the commercials said, I didn't think the best part of my morning was having Folgers in my cup. "You think I had something to do with this? What the hell did you have on that laptop?"

"Nothing… Work stuff." His jaw tensed, his hands fisting at his sides.

"What kind of work stuff?" I always thought it was odd he had a work laptop. He's a plumber. Didn't he just need tools? What was he doing on a computer?

"Work orders, invoices, emails, stuff like that." His eyes flashed. "What does it matter?"

"Did you have anything else in your bag? Money or something?"

"No." He groaned. "I wasn't even gonna bring up the lap-top, but I didn't want it to get stolen from my car. Fucking irony, fuck!"

Feeling bad for not taking him seriously, I pulled out my phone and looked up the number for the police department. He was clearly worried about the work implications. I had to remind myself often that he wasn't a contractor. He worked for a company, used their trucks and equipment. It made sense that he'd worry about something of theirs being stolen.

"What are you doing?"

"Calling the cops."

"No!" He said the word so forcefully I froze. "It's a fuck-ing laptop. They're never gonna find it. They won't even take it seriously. It'll be a waste of time." With a dramatic exhale, he said, "Sorry. I'm just gonna head out. I gotta call my boss. Let him know. Find out what he wants me to do."

31

THE MOTHER

Present

"Your home is lovely," Seth says, glancing around.

It feels strange having him here. Wrong. Adrienne should've been the one to introduce us. The one to invite him over. We should all be having dinner together. Adrienne should be home and safe. My eyes are wet again. This keeps happening.

"Did you want to try to get into the lap—"

"Um…actually, I'm locked out again," I say, cutting him off, grateful that Shane's head is deep in the fridge, trying to locate a few bottled waters. It's a bold-faced lie. I'm getting better at them. "Twenty-four hours this time."

"Really?" I can't tell by his expression if he believes me or not.

Shane emerges with three waters, slamming the fridge door closed with his elbow.

I smile at him as he hands us each one. "Why don't you give Seth a tour while I finish dinner?"

He nods back, sweeping his arm in front of him as a way of invitation. As Seth follows him down the hallway, I blow out a breath, my mind whirring with what I'd found on Adrienne's laptop—the photo of her without an engagement ring, wearing a forced smile. And the Google searches about murdered women, along with a search of Seth. I'm still not sure what any of it means. Or if it means anything at all. But I have to find out, and I have to be careful about how I do it.

Stirring the noodles on the stove, heat cascades over my face. As I stare down at the boiling water, I catch snippets of the men's conversation as they move about the back of the house.

"Is this Adrienne?"

"Yeah, first grade."

"Cute," Seth says. "God, she's really changed, hasn't she?"

It's an odd statement. Of course she's changed since first grade. Who hasn't?

I envision the photo they're talking about. Adrienne, two pigtails on either side of her head, bright pink barrettes, crooked grin. Then I think about what Adrienne looked like the last time I saw her. Hair long and spilling down her back, no barrettes, but same crooked grin. She hated the asymmetry of her mouth, but I loved it. I thought it gave personality to her almost perfect features. I often teased her that her beauty is so intimidating that God had to give her something to make her approachable. I don't think she's changed that much, just gotten older.

A door opens and I stiffen. *Adrienne's room.* Or, at least what used to be her room. It's now turned into my sewing and project room, but I left up Adrienne's corkboard full of photos and notes from growing up. And there are boxes of her school papers and photo albums in the corner. Shane rarely goes in there. I normally have it to myself.

An itch forms on the back of my neck. Reaching up, I scratch it.

Feet shuffle on the carpet, muffled voices traveling from

down the hall. The itch spreads. I wriggle as I check the noodles. Soft and pliable. I dump them into the colander in the sink, steam kissing the window above it.

After throwing them into a bowl, I mix in the meat and sauce. The salad is already prepped and on the table.

They haven't returned, so I follow their voices. They're still in Adrienne's former room.

I step inside. Seth has one hand in his pocket and he's staring at the photos tacked to Adrienne's corkboard.

"...mission meets old-fashioned fun approach has been very effective. I think we started it over thirty years ago now," Shane is saying, pride in his tone.

It comes as no surprise that he's talking about Grace Camp and not his missing daughter. While their backs are to me, I take a minute, my eyes scanning over the dozens of photos of Adrienne when she was younger. Smiling. Laughing. Jumping. In some, she's with Mara, their arms slung over each other's shoulders, all gangly limbs, and metal mouths. In all of them, the woods are prominent behind her, tall, dark green trees peeking over her shoulder.

She never liked going to church, but she did like summer camp.

"Did Adrienne go every summer?" Seth asks.

Shane nods. "Since she was in kindergarten."

There is a beat of silence before Seth says, "I wish I'd known her then. She looks so sweet and innocent."

I shiver, a prickle of apprehension dotting my spine. It's not so much his words as his tone that alarms me. It's the second time since he's arrived that I've caught that tone. Almost like he's angry with her. Angry with who she's become.

"Dinner's ready," I say.

Seth peers over his shoulder, his gaze lighting on me briefly before turning back to the photos.

I understand the compulsion, though. Adrienne has that

kind of beauty. The kind you never want to stop staring at. I know all mothers think their kids are beautiful, but in Adrienne's case I wasn't the only one. When she was a baby, I'd get stopped every time we left the house, neighbors in awe of her large eyes, porcelain skin and heart-shaped lips. And it only got worse when she was older, every boy in the youth group following behind her like lovesick puppies. Shane used to joke that he'd have to lock her up and throw away the key. I laughed then. I'd thought it was a joke.

Shane heads out of the room. Seth's hand makes a fist at his side as he continues to stare at the photos. My stomach twists.

"Ready?" I say, and his muscles relax a bit, his hand opening.

"Yes." With a kind smile, he turns away from the wall and follows me out of the room. Once in the hall, I turn off the light and firmly close the door behind us.

I dish the pasta onto our plates, the red sauce bleeding all over the white ceramic. It turns my stomach, the way it takes everything over, encroaching on the salad and staining the edges. I push the tines of my fork around the plate.

"So, Seth, that's an interesting name," I say. "Were your parents religious...or?"

"No. Just liked the name, I guess."

"Well, it's a nice name. A biblical one," Shane says, and I take a bite of pasta.

That was a dead end.

I try something else. "Do you and Adrienne go to Napa often?"

Seth looks up, the fork in his hand covered in sauce as he holds it suspended over the table. His jaw works as he chews the pasta he'd stuffed into his mouth as if he hadn't a care in the world, despite his fiancée being missing. "Huh?"

"Napa. That's where you two planned to go last weekend, right?"

"Right." He wipes his mouth with his napkin, bright red immediately appearing against the stark white. "Um...no, we'd never been. This was going to be our first time."

"But you'd been before?"

He nods.

"And you're still sure she never told you about us getting mani/pedis?" I ask, picking at the skin around my bare nails. The ones I'd been hoping would be shiny and lacquered by now.

He shook his head as he took another bite.

"It's so strange to me that she would've made plans with me if she already had plans with you," I continue.

He shrugs. "Maybe she forgot. It was a last-minute trip. I only booked it last week."

Not a bad answer. Believable, even. We'd made our plans several weeks ago. I'd wanted to lock her in the minute she agreed. Maybe that was why she hadn't changed it on her calendar.

Shane subtly nods as if he buys Seth's explanation.

"What's the name of the hotel you booked?" I asked, unable to let it go.

"Oh, not a hotel. An Airbnb."

"Like through a homeowner or a rental company?"

Shane shoots me a look like I'm overstepping.

"Um... I don't know, just an Airbnb?" He's sitting comfortably, slowly chewing his food, but I detect a slight tremor in his hand. The one holding the fork. Light glints off the metal.

"Do you remember the name of it?"

He swallows. Shakes his head.

"But I thought you ended up going. Staying there."

He wipes the corner of his mouth. "I did. But I was so upset about Adrienne not...being there. I... I didn't pay much attention. I could look it up for you." He reaches down, feeling his pockets. "Oh, shoot. I think I left my phone in the car. I can...go get it."

Shane holds out his hand. "Nonsense. Stay put. Finish your dinner." He throws me an exasperated look before turning back to Seth. "Tatum tells me you're a plumber?"

Seth nods, his shoulders visibly relaxing as if relieved to be out of the hot seat.

"How is that going?"

"Okay."

Shane spears a piece of lettuce. "Must be a tough job."

"The job itself isn't bad. It's the customers that make it hard." Seth shakes his head. "Had this guy the other day. Called about a leak in his bathroom sink. The job before his took a little longer than expected. The guy was already mad when I got there, kept griping about how late I was. And I wasn't. I was still within the window of time given, but barely. Anyway, it was my last call of the day and I'd used some parts on my truck I hadn't planned to. Long story short, I didn't have the parts I needed for his sink. Guy lost his mind." Seth shakes his head. "Entitled prick. He's lucky I didn't slash his tires on my way out." He lifts his head, eyes meeting Shane's, and he flashes an easy smile. "Not that I'd ever do that."

"Right." Shane nods, laughs lightly as if that wasn't an odd anecdote to share, especially to the father of his supposed fiancée.

When I met Shane's parents for the first time, I'd been on my best behavior, showing them only the best parts of myself. I laughed at their antiquated jokes and smiled uncomfortably under his father's thinly veiled misogynistic remarks. Even now when his parents make their twice-monthly phone calls, I'm careful not to share much. If they have any idea about my crisis of faith this year, it has to be from Shane. I've never mentioned it. Sometimes, I'll test the waters a bit, throw out a doubt or two, but when it's not well received, I'll quickly rein it in, backtracking.

Is that what Seth is doing? Testing the waters? Seeing if we would find it appalling for him to puncture a customer's tires?

Had he actually done it?

The fact that he even thought it reveals an angry streak. We deal with disgruntled congregants all the time. I can honestly say I've never thought of slashing one of their tires. If Shane has, he's never verbalized it.

I think about what Jazzy said about Adrienne going home with that stranger at the bar a few nights before she went missing. What if Seth had found out about it? If an upset customer could anger him enough he'd want to slash his tires, I can only imagine what he'd want to do to his fiancée if he found out she was cheating on him.

I shudder.

Shane puts a hand on my arm. My muscles tighten. "You okay?"

"Yeah." I breathe out.

Their plates are empty, nothing but smears of red sauce and oily salad dressing. My plate is mostly full, but there's no way I can force a bite.

"Can I get anyone anything else?" I stand, reaching for my plate. "Coffee? Dessert?"

Seth tosses his napkin on the table. "I actually need to head out."

"Oh?" I pause, fingers closed around the edge of the plate.

"Early day tomorrow." He scoots backward, the legs of the chair scraping the floor.

"You're still working?" I ask.

"Still gotta pay the bills."

Agitated, I run a hand through my hair. "God, I'd really been hoping by now we'd have found her."

"She'll be back soon, trust me." Shane leans back in his

chair, not a care in the world. I want to punch him in his face. I'm not a violent person by any means, but when it comes to my kids, a fierce protectiveness comes over me. "I know Adrienne. She's taken off for a bit, but she'll be back."

"You really think so?" Seth sits forward, chin resting on the bridge he'd constructed by threading his fingers together.

"I know so," he says.

"What makes you so sure? You haven't spoken to her, have you?" Seth's eyes are wide, his brows gathered together in a look that's so hopeful, it makes me wonder if my distrust of him is misplaced.

Shane frowns, shaking his head. "She'd never reach out to me." His head bobs up to where I'm standing. "To either of us, actually." The statement stings. He's probably right, though. Adrienne and I have been becoming closer, but we're not close. "There was a time when I'd say she would for sure contact Mara…"

"We've checked with her," I say softly.

"Right, yeah, I don't think they're as close as they used to be. I really don't know who she's closest to now." He reaches for his glass, one ice cube and a few drops of water at the bottom. When he lifts it to his lips the ice cube slides to meet his mouth.

"I thought it was me," Seth says darkly.

Shane looks at him, eyes apologetic. "I'm sorry. I didn't mean—"

"It's fine." Seth stands, waving away his apology. "I really have to get going. Thank you for the meal and the hospitality." He looks at me. "I'll let you know if I hear anything or think of anything…"

"I'll do the same," I say.

Shane walks him to the door while I clear the table. My phone lights up from where it sits face up on the far counter. I check it. I have a voice mail from Tony.

I listen. "Hey, Tatum, I got your message. I understand your concern, but I can't go looking into people based on a whim or feeling. I have to have some kind of evidence or suspicious behavior, at the very least, and being new to town isn't suspicious. Also, I would need more than a first name." My cheeks warm with every word he says. It's just like I figured. He thinks I'm being ridiculous. "And as far as Adrienne's fiancé, we don't have any record of him coming into the station at all. I don't know what he told you, but no one here's talked to him. If he has information to share, have him call us."

Numb, I lower the phone. I hear Shane's footsteps retreat into the family room. From the window above the sink, I watch Seth walk toward his car parked along the curb. He lingers beside it for a minute, looking at something on his phone. Then his gaze sweeps up and down the street. My stomach knots.

When he looks back up at our house, I instinctually duck. After a few seconds I dare to peek back out. He's getting into his car. Light from his phone flashes as he affixes it to his dashboard the same way Shane does when he uses his GPS. But surely, that's not what Seth is doing. He knows his way home.

Early day tomorrow.

Heat shoots up my spine. When I'd talked to him two days ago, he'd said that he was off this week; that was why he and Adrienne were going out of town. He shouldn't have work tomorrow. I think about how he'd eaten so fast, left so abruptly.

About Tony's message.

He's hiding something.

I slam down the handle of the faucet and hurry toward the front door where I'd last discarded my slip-on tennis shoes. I shove my feet into them and reach for my purse and keys.

"Hey, Shane," I call out. His back is to me, the television on. "We're low on coffee. I'm gonna head to the store."

He cranes his neck. "Now?"

I force a natural smile. "You know we won't survive the morning without it."

"Okay. Drive safe." He returns to his program.

Heart thumping, I step outside. Seth has just pulled away from the curb. I have to hurry. I run to my car. My hands are shaking so it takes a few clicks on the remote before it unlocks. I hop inside. After turning on the engine I back out of the driveway and go right. I frantically scan the road for Seth's car. When I reach the stop sign, I catch him to my left. Relieved, I breathe out, then wait a few beats before following him. It takes all my willpower not to gun it. My heart races, my veins buzzing with adrenaline. I force myself to slow down.

I have a feeling I'm close to finding out answers.

He's going to lead me straight to Adrienne. I know he will.

But only if he doesn't know I'm following.

32

THE DAUGHTER

Past

Bruises bloomed on my wrists and biceps. I traced them in the dark as I lay in bed, Seth sleeping beside me. The sex had been rough again tonight. I could no longer chalk it up to passion or his not knowing his own strength, as he'd once said. It had become a pattern. One that was impossible to ignore.

I'd shown up at his place after work tonight. It had been slow, so Jazzy and Ted let me leave a little early. I'd slumped down on the couch as Seth retrieved a beer from the fridge. He was handing it to me when my phone rang. We both jumped. I'd had the volume all the way up.

I scrambled to answer, the loud ringing already giving me a headache.

It was Ted.

"Hey, dork," I said after answering. Ted's a know-it-all, and the girls and I tease him about it endlessly. He takes it well.

"Hey, klepto," he said.

"What? That's a new one." I smiled, balancing the phone between my shoulder and cheek as I took a swig of beer.

"No, it's not. I think you took the storage key again."

"Oh, man. I hope not." I feel around in my pocket, then look down. Nope. No lanyard. Nothing in my pocket. "I've been pretty good about putting it in my apron pocket. Oh, have you checked there? I left it hanging in the back." Twice I'd taken home the key to the storage closet. I'd accidentally left it in my pocket after retrieving supplies from it.

"Oh, yep. That's where they were. Thanks," he said. "Sorry to bother you."

"No worries." I hung up and tossed my phone down on the couch. As I lifted the beer bottle to my lips, I caught Seth staring at me from across the room. His expression was hard. Angry.

What the hell?

"You okay?" I asked.

"Who was that?"

"Ted." I took another sip. "He couldn't find the storage key."

"You were flirting with him."

A surprised laugh leaped from my throat. "No, I wasn't."

"You were," he insisted, his face reddening, his eyes black. "I'm not an idiot, Adrienne. Don't make me out to be one." His tone was starting to frighten me a little.

I instinctively scooted back on the couch. "Seth, I'm not. I honestly wasn't flirting with Ted. I don't like him at all. You'd know that if you ever came to the bar."

"You're the one who didn't want me going to the bar. Is that why? Because of him?"

I put my hands up. "No, no. I—"

"Is he the reason you can't tell me you love me?"

And there it was. The real issue. The reason he'd been acting so strangely. So jealous. So angry.

I felt sorry for him, then.

His last girlfriend had cheated, and now I couldn't tell him

I loved him. I went to him. Kissed him. Held him. And like always, we ended up here, in his bed.

I was wondering now if that had been a mistake.

Shifting position, I rolled over onto the opposite side, facing away from him. His bedroom was never pitch-dark. A few of his blinds were kinked in a way that allowed natural light to filter in. The moon must've been bright that night because webs of light circled the walls almost like we were under water.

My gaze landed on the nightstand. I hadn't peeked in the drawer since the night I found the engagement ring. A proposal had never happened. With my inability to say I love you and his being so moody, I wasn't surprised.

Besides, it probably was never meant for me. My initial thought that it could be his mom's or grandma's was probably right. Still, I was curious.

I didn't need to peer over my shoulder—if his even breathing was an indicator, he was fast asleep—but to be safe I did steal a glance. Then I inched the drawer open. I instantly found the ring. At least, I thought I had at first glance. But once I picked it up, it was clear that it was a different ring. One small princess-cut diamond set in the center of a smooth gold band. A prickle dotted my spine. I swept my hand inside the drawer until my fingertips grazed something hard and sharp, a diamond. I pulled it out. And all the air was sucked from my lungs. This wasn't the ring I'd seen last time, either. This one was much newer than the others. Pristine. Square-cut diamond, platinum band. Heart pounding, I rooted around in the drawer until I found the one I'd initially been looking for. I held all three in my palm, staring down at them in confusion.

Why three rings?

I'd heard of websites where you could have multiple rings sent to you to sample them, see them in person before ordering. Was that what he was doing? But wouldn't they be in boxes?

Oh, God, this was too strange.

A loud snort erupted from Seth's throat, and I flinched, almost dropping the rings. Alarmed, I tossed them into the drawer and shoved it closed. Then, heart hammering in my ears, I threw myself back down on the bed.

I had no idea what the rings meant. But one thing was clear: I couldn't stay in this relationship. Sure, he was hot, and the sex was good, and he could be really sweet when he wanted to be, but there were way too many red flags. A whole damn field of them.

I couldn't marry him. Not now. Not ever.

And it wasn't fair to keep leading him on.

The year after I graduated high school, half of our youth group at Grace Community got married. High school sweethearts finally old enough to get hitched. I joked with Mara that what they wanted was to get laid, not married. They'd all end up divorced by the time they were thirty.

I hadn't been entirely wrong.

We were only twenty-four and I knew of two couples who had already split up from that group. And I was certain there'd be more. Not all, because some of them probably didn't believe in divorce. They'd stay in their unhappy marriages the same way my mom had.

I'd made a vow to myself back then that I'd never do that. Jump into a marriage that had no chance of working. If I got married, I wanted to be damn sure I was 100 percent in love, and that was definitely not the case.

Regardless of if those rings were for me or not, it's clear his feelings were stronger than mine. The humane thing was to break it off before I got in any deeper.

"Are you for real or is this one of your jokes?" he asked the next morning when I'd finally got up the courage to tell him we were over. He sat up in bed, comforter bunched around his waist.

I stood off to the side, fully dressed and holding my overnight bag. I kept averting my gaze from his body, wishing the entire time that he was fully dressed as well. But I couldn't wait any longer.

I raised my chin. "No joke. I just think… Well, I think it's time."

He shook his head, running a hand through his hair. "You've gotta be fuckin' kidding me. Where is this even coming from? Things were going great."

"Were they, though?"

He recoiled. "I thought so."

I took a breath, slowed down. "I just… Look, it's been fun. And I do really like you. I just…feel like what we have has… you know, run its course."

"Run its course? What does that even mean?"

Shaking my head, I sighed. "Sorry." I was out of words. Out of ways to explain this. I simply wanted to take my stuff and go.

"Wait." He scrambled out of bed, following me. His hands reached out, grappling to grab on to me. I knew I couldn't let him.

I walked faster.

"But I love you."

"I know. I just… I don't feel the same way. I'm so sorry."

"But you could, if you gave it time," he pleaded.

"I'm sorry," I said again, fighting with the doorknob.

"Adrienne, come on. Don't leave like this. Let's at least talk about it."

The door gave way, fresh air spilling into the room. I tumbled out, my chest expanding. Then I ran toward my car as he tried in vain to call me back.

33

THE FIANCÉ

Past

Her blinds were open, lights on, giving me a clear view inside her apartment. I sat in my car, aiming my binoculars up toward the second floor. That was when I caught a glimpse of her, walking past the window. It appeared she was headed toward the kitchen. I shifted position. She returned, this time with a glass of water in her hand.

I was right. She had gone to the kitchen.

I'd been here long enough to know she was alone, and that gave me some satisfaction. It had been two days since she broke up with me. Two days of doing nothing more than thinking about her. Replaying our relationship. The good and the bad. Reexamining. Wishing I'd done things differently. Better.

I should've listened to my mom. I shouldn't have come on so strong.

It was stupid.

She was on the couch. I could only see a flash of her hair, a portion of her shoulder, but it was enough. I could fill in the blanks. I knew every part of her.

I imagined going inside, planting myself on the couch beside her, forcing her to take me back. But that would also be stupid. I'd tried it before. It had never been effective.

I'd have to find another way.

I picked up the engagement ring. The one I'd chosen from the three samples. The one I'd been so anxious to put on her finger.

I still was.

She'd love it.

I knew she would.

I just had to get it on her finger.

A car pulled into the lot. I ducked down, hiding the binoculars under the seat, and then waited. Light doused my car and then retreated, a lit match that had been snuffed out. I heard the engine cut, then a car door open and close, followed by footsteps.

I inched my way up. A man walked up to the apartment door. Once inside, he went to the right. Just like I did when I visited her.

I snatched up my binoculars, sat up taller and placed them over my eyes.

She got up from the couch. My shoulders tensed. Was that man here for her?

She disappeared from view. I gripped the binoculars tighter. Ground my teeth. When she appeared again, I got so excited I bumped the binoculars into the window and it jarred me. I scooted back. She'd refilled her water. I didn't see a man. A light flickered on a couple of windows over from hers.

Of course. The man must've been a neighbor. Why would I even assume any differently?

She was good. Honest. It's why I'd fallen for her.

And I knew she'd fallen for me, too.

I just had to figure out a way to remind her of that. And I would. I'd do whatever it took to get her back. To make her mine for good.

PART TWO

PART TWO

34

THE FIANCÉ

Past

At first, I didn't see Adrienne. I frantically scanned the bar. She told me she'd be working tonight. My heart started to sink, but then she stepped out of the back room, her hair pulled tightly up into a ponytail, an apron around her waist. In her arms, she carried a box. Heart lifting, I made my way toward the counter.

"Hey," she said after I hopped up onto a bar stool.

"Hey." My gaze instinctually moved to the deep scarlet color on the butterfly pendant, the flecks of gold sparkling under the overhead lights.

"Whiskey, right?" she asked, and her tone was off. There were rings around her eyes, bits of mascara flecked on her skin.

"Right," I said.

Her movements were faster than normal. Jerky. She splashed golden liquid onto her skin as she pushed it in my direction. I noticed a purple bruise peeking out from the edge of her long sleeve.

"Hey, you okay?" I knew it was bold, but I had to ask.

"Yeah, fine," she said, not looking at me as she wiped her skin with a rag.

It was clear she didn't want to talk about it. With anyone else, I would've let it go. But I couldn't. I'd been sitting on this bar stool for far too many nights. It was time to take action.

"You sure?" I leaned forward, pinning her with a knowing stare. "'Cause you don't seem fine."

"You don't even know me," she said, no contempt in her voice, just fact.

"That's how obvious it is."

Her eyebrows rose swiftly in surprise. She paused a moment, studying me. Then she shook her head. "Let's just say I've had kind of a shitty week." A man sauntered up to the bar, holding up his hand to get her attention. "Excuse me." I blew out a frustrated breath when she headed in his direction.

While she made the random man's drink, I hurriedly finished mine. The other bartender, a short girl with long blond hair, wiped down a few of the tables out on the floor. I wanted to be sure that Adrienne was the one to help me. I set my glass down loudly on the bar, ice cube slamming against the side. It caught Adrienne's attention. She returned right after handing the man his beer.

"Another?" she asked.

I nodded. "So what happened that made this week so shitty?"

As she made my drink, she kept her gaze trained on the glass. "I guess you could say that my eyes were finally opened."

I sat up taller. "To what?"

"Men who masquerade control as love." She slid the drink to me. "And I'm done with them."

"Them?"

She nodded. "I've owed my dad some money for a long time, and he like, totally lords it over me. I'm so sick of it, you know? So I pulled all my savings. I'm gonna pay him back in one lump sum. Get him off my back. Maybe if I can get out from under his thumb, I'll stop choosing guys like him. Guys who want to control me."

"Your boyfriend?"

"Not my boyfriend anymore." She laughs bitterly. "I thought it would feel good—getting rid of my dad and my boyfriend at the same time. But now I'm just broke and broken up."

I glanced at her neck. "But you're still wearing the necklace from him."

She reached up to touch it and shook her head. "I put it on out of habit, I guess. But I don't need this thing." She turned it until the clasp was under her chin, then she unfastened it and slipped it off. A couple walked inside. Before leaving to greet them, she tossed the necklace into the trash at the edge of the counter.

I watched her walk to the other side of the bar and start talking to the couple. Keeping my gaze fixed on her back, I carefully made my way around the counter to the trash can. The necklace was hidden. I fished around until my fingertip caught on the clasp, then on the shiny metal of the butterfly. I snatched it out and pocketed it. Then returned to my stool.

A few seconds later she returned, sliding a full beer toward me. "On the house." She flashed an apologetic smile. "Sorry I unloaded all that on you."

"I asked."

"Yeah, but still, I shouldn't have spilled my guts like that. I don't even know your name."

"Nate," I said.

"Adrienne," she replied, although I'd already known because of the name tag she wore.

"See?" I smiled. "Now we're old friends."

She laughed, her head bobbing toward the beer. "This is

different from the one you've been drinking, but I think you'll like it."

I lifted the foamy beer to my mouth, took a sip. It was smooth, no hint of bitterness at all. "You're right. I do like it."

"I knew you would." Her lips curved upward slightly. Her eyes were still sad, but at least her face was beginning to brighten.

"Am I that predictable?"

"No, it's not that. It's just something I'm good at." She glanced up as two men walked into the bar. "Like take these two guys for instance. I can tell just by looking at them that the guy on the right will order a double IPA and the guy on the left will order…bourbon…on the rocks. Watch." She ambled in their direction.

I eyed her as I sipped my beer. The guys at the table behind me were talking loudly, making it difficult to hear her conversation. I did catch her name coming out of the mouth of the guy on the right. And I heard the guy on the left ask her about someone named Mara.

When she handed the guy on the right a foamy beer and the one on the left a beveled glass with golden liquid in it, she flashed me a triumphant smile. I laughed, raising my glass as if in a toast.

"See," she said when she returned. "What did I tell you? It's a gift."

"A gift of good memory?" I teased.

"What?"

"Who's Mara?" I asked, and her face fell.

"Oh, you heard that?"

I nodded.

"She's my best friend… Well, she was my best friend… when we were growing up," she said. "We still talk a lot, but she's married with a kid and…it's not the same." She picked at a piece of skin around the nail on her index finger. "Anyway, so yeah, I was messing with you. I knew what they were gonna order. They come in all the time."

"True—"

"Bye, Adrienne," a woman interrupted as she headed out the door.

"Bye." Adrienne offered a short wave.

"You seem to know everyone around here," I mused.

"The hazards of growing up in a small town." She frowned, and it buoyed me. I had the advantage here. I was the new guy. The unknown. And that clearly intrigued her.

"So your boyfriend? Was he someone you grew up with?" I was careful to keep my tone neutral and even, just subtle curiosity. Nothing more.

"No, he was new to town when we met."

"Oh, really? How long ago was that?"

She shoved back from the counter, shaking her head. "I really don't want to talk about him."

Shit. "Yeah, no, of course not. I'm sorry. We can talk about something else."

"Actually, you seem good right now." She eyed my drink. "And I need to check on the other customers." Backing up, she whirled around and walked away.

I was getting somewhere with her. *Why did I have to push it?*

Patting my pocket, I felt the outline of the necklace inside.

"Look, Nate. It landed on my finger!" Carolyn had squealed, *wearing a broad smile, her eyes wide and bright.*

I bit the inside of my cheek and scratched my leg through my jeans. Hard enough to bring me back to the present. Too many months I spent lost in my memories. Bathing in them. Swimming in them. They cocooned me in safety and warmth. Until they didn't, and then I started drowning in them. Sniffing, I reached for my beer, taking a long swallow, focusing on the bitterness of the hops, the coolness of the liquid, the foam at the back of my throat.

"Wow, you downed that fast." Adrienne appeared in front of me, wiping down the counter with a damp rag.

I glanced at my now-empty glass. "Yeah." The word came out quieter than I'd meant it to. I cleared my throat. My insides felt shaky, so I pulled in a breath and sat taller. "I'll have another one, please."

"Same?"

"This one, yeah."

"So you did like my pick." She winked, plucking my glass off the counter. A few minutes later she returned with a fresh one, beer foaming down one side. "Here you go." She wiped the spot where it had dripped onto the slick mahogany.

"Thanks." I palmed the cold glass. "Look, about earlier, I shouldn't have…"

"I'm the one who should be apologizing," she cut me off with the flick of her wrist and shake of her head. "I started the conversation and then I got weird. I just wanna move on, you know?"

I nodded. I understood, but it was disappointing. But I couldn't give up. I'd have to pivot, switch to a new strategy.

I'd get my answers one way or another.

I guess my new plan worked, I thought as I ushered Adrienne into my hotel room.

Getting drunk didn't usually work out so well for me, and, despite being drunk loads of times, I could safely say this was the first time I'd done it as part of a strategy.

Back at the Float Down, I'd continued to order beers until last call.

"Do you have a ride home?" Adrienne had asked after I finished off my last glass.

"Are you offering?"

She stared at me a moment, cocking one eyebrow. "We have Uber around here, you know?"

"You'd let a stranger pick me up in this state?" I slurred, pointing to my chest.

"You're a stranger," she reminded me.

"No, I'm not. I'm Nate. And you're Adrienne. We've known each other for hours now," I said. "Days if you count the other times I've come in here."

She laughed. "Okay, okay. Fine, *Nate*. I'll give you a ride home. Just wait for me to close up and then I'll take you."

I waited, drumming my fingers on the counter and sobering up by the minute. Truth is, I wasn't nearly as drunk as I was pretending to be. I knew how to hold my liquor.

When we finally got back to the hotel, I turned to Adrienne with a smile. "Come in for a drink?"

"You've had enough." Her tone wasn't accusatory, merely amused.

"But you haven't had any," I pointed out, and felt her resolve slipping. "Come on, as a thank-you for the ride home."

"All right." She held up her index finger. "One drink."

Now we were inside, and I was pouring a little whiskey into a white paper cup. Housekeeping must have come by because the bed was made, my clothes were neatly placed on top of my suitcase and there were fresh towels in the bathroom.

I was glad the room wasn't as messy as I'd left it.

"Here you are." I handed Adrienne the cup. She sat on the edge of the bed with her legs crossed, shoulders back and spine straight. *Perfect posture.*

I slouched. Most people did.

She was nervous.

Trying to put her at ease, I unscrewed the top off a bottle of water and sat on the one chair in the room, a few feet from the bed putting distance between us.

"Switchin' to the good stuff," I joked, holding up the bottle.

She smiled, her free hand dropping to her lap.

"Sorry I don't have any beer. Is the whiskey okay?"

"It's good," she said. "But I'm not picky with my alcohol."

"I figured." Her eyes widened. Shit, that came out wrong. "I mean, only because you're a bartender. Not because I think you drink anything…or, I mean…you know…"

"It's cool." Laughing, she waved away my apology. "I know what you meant, and it's true. As a bartender, I have tried a lot of drinks. Anywhere I go, I can find a drink I like."

"How long have you been bartending?"

Smiling, she leaned forward. "Why do I always feel like I'm on a job interview with you?"

I squirmed as she pinned me with a curious stare.

After taking a long pull from her cup, she stood and set it down on the table against the wall. Grin deepening, she sauntered toward me. "Did you really bring me back here to ask me about my job?"

I shook my head. I hadn't.

I'd brought her back here to get more information about her mysterious boyfriend. The one who gave her the butterfly necklace. The one she didn't want to talk about. I'd kind of figured after a few pours of whiskey her lips would loosen a little.

"I didn't think so." She lowered herself down onto my lap, legs straddling me.

I swallowed hard. This wasn't part of the plan.

Framing my face with her soft hands, she leaned forward and kissed me. And not a chaste kiss, either. Her tongue coaxed my lips open, darted inside. My head was screaming no, my brain realizing this was a mistake. But then her hands moved down to my upper thighs, her fingertips brushing over my crotch, and my dick instantly hardened, clearly not in agreement with my brain.

Oh, fuck it.

I tossed my water bottle aside and reached for her, all my carefully laid out strategies flying out the window.

35

THE DAUGHTER

Past

My throat was parched. I needed water.

It was so quiet that for one second upon waking I thought I was at home. But the smell was wrong. Mustier, maybe. And when my eyes dragged down the wall, none of my photos were hung. I looked over at Nate beside me and felt relieved.

Much better.

There was no danger that he'd become too attached or keep a drawer full of engagement rings handy. He was simply passing through town.

I slipped out of the bed, remembering the bottled waters the hotel had left him near the door and the Keurig coffeepot. Leaning against the wall, blue light illuminating the room, I unscrewed the top and took a long draw. The water was lukewarm at best, but it quenched my thirst. I finished off half the bottle before sauntering back toward the bed. My toe hit something, and I swallowed down a yelp.

Bending down, I rubbed my foot.

His suitcase had been the offending object. When I started

to stand back up, I saw the edge of a chrome laptop sticking out from inside it. Everyone had a laptop, so that wasn't what caught my attention. It was the familiar navy blue straps of an overnight bag. I reached inside the suitcase and pulled at the straps, then gasped.

Oh, my God.

It was Nate.

He was the one who broke into my place. Who stole Seth's overnight bag and laptop.

But why?

It didn't matter. I had to get the hell out of here.

My clothes were tangled in with Nate's, causing another wave of shame to wash over me. I unhooked his jeans from mine, and a silver chain fell out of it, a shiny, colorful butterfly winking at me.

My breath escaped me.

Had he fished this out of the trash?

Oh, my God.

What the fuck was this guy up to?

With trembling fingers, I grabbed my clothes and hurriedly threw them on. Then I gathered up all my stuff and turned to leave.

"What are you doing?" Nate stood in front of me, blocking my path.

I sucked in a startled breath, my heartbeat revving up. "Get outta my way," I said in a firm voice, hoping he didn't detect the terror underneath.

"It isn't what you think," he said, hands out in front of him, palms exposed.

"I think you broke into my apartment and stole this laptop." I hold it up. My hands are trembling so bad it looks like I'm swinging it back and forth.

"Okay, well, yeah, you're right about that part, but let me explain why."

"What explanation could you possibly give that would make this okay?"

"Your ex… I—I know him."

"Seth?"

"Well, yeah, I mean, I knew him as Jared."

"Jared?" My mouth dried out. "Jared what?"

"Thornton."

Oh, God. The name on his mail.

The last time I'd been over, I'd seen an envelope addressed to Jared on the counter again. I couldn't figure out why he was still getting mail from the last tenant. Was it not for the last tenant? Was it for him?

Why would he lie to me about his name?

"But I don't even know if that's his real name," he continued. My head swam as if I was being held under water. "Prior to moving to Aptos—that's where I met him—he lived in Oregon. I think he went by Max Lincoln there."

I was finding it hard to draw in a full breath. I thought about the photograph. The word *Cole* on the back.

"Does Seth…um…Jared or whatever…does he have a brother?"

"Not that I know of, but maybe."

"Why change his name so many times? Was he running from something…or someone?" It was all clicking into place now. His erratic behavior. How on edge he seemed.

I swallowed hard.

Oh, God, was Nate the person he was running from?

I clutched the laptop tighter. I could use it as a weapon if need be. A clock to the head with this would be brutal. And I wouldn't hold back.

"Himself, I guess," Nate finally said, and it made no sense. Then he added, "His crimes."

"Crimes?" Swallowing was doing me no good now. I had

no saliva left in my mouth. It was like my glands had stopped working.

He took a step toward me, arms out as if he was an animal trainer at the zoo and I was the unruly lion he was attempting to wrangle. "I know this is going to be difficult to hear, but…" My stomach clenched, as if preparing for the impact of his next words. So far it had all been hard to hear. How could this get any worse? "He killed my fiancée."

No amount of clenching could have prepared me for that. "What?" I blinked repeatedly and my body shook as if I was malfunctioning. It was one thing to tell me my ex-boyfriend had gone by multiple names. There could have been a logical explanation for that. But murder? That was too much. "No," I said, then repeated it louder. "No."

"We'd both worked for the same heating and air company for a short time, and in that time, I'd introduced him to my fiancé, Carolyn," Nate said, ignoring my emphatic protests and pressing on with his story. "One night she and I had gotten into a fight. She headed to the bar with some girlfriends. After a few hours I felt bad, and I went to the bar to make up with her. When I pulled up, I saw her leaving with a guy. Jared—er, Seth. I never saw her again."

"Well, maybe she just moved or something. Maybe she's hiding from you… No offense."

"She didn't, and she's not."

"How can you be so sure? I mean, she did go home with a different guy." And I couldn't blame the girl. Nate was cute, but he was no Seth.

"The police found her body a week later washed up against the rocks on the beach."

The air left my lungs, deflating like a popped balloon. "I'm so sorry," I said. "But how do you know Seth did it? I mean, you could be wrong about who she went home with—"

"I'm not," he snapped. "I'm sure it was him."

"Okay, but sleeping with someone and killing them are much different."

"I'm positive it was him."

I wasn't buying his story. There were too many holes. Plus, I think I would know if I'd been dating someone capable of murder. "Then how come he wasn't arrested? Surely, you brought this theory to the police."

He worked his jaw. "I did. Many times. But there was no way to prove it. And all they had was my word. The boyfriend. Honestly, they'd looked more into me than they had him." He paused. Breathed deep. "That's why I'm here. To prove it was him. To finally get answers."

"How did you even find him?"

"I read about Jane's death. It was exactly like Carolyn's. And then I saw you...and the necklace...and I knew I was in the right place."

I recalled our first conversation. "The necklace?"

"It was Carolyn's. I gave it to her."

"No offense, but a butterfly necklace is hardly original. There are probably thousands just like it in the world. How can you be sure this is hers?"

"Because there aren't thousands. There's only one. I had it custom made. I'll show you." He scrambled to the nightstand, snatched up his phone. With fast movements, he scrolled through his photo roll. He pulled up a picture of an attractive woman—brown hair, dark eyes, easy smile—and he zoomed in on her necklace. "See?"

"Oh." There was no doubt it was the same one. And it gave me the chills, knowing I'd been wearing a dead woman's necklace for months.

"She wore it every day. She rarely took it off. And she had to have been wearing it when she went missing, because it wasn't in her apartment. But it wasn't found on her body, either."

"But you found Seth, so why not go after him? Why me? Why break into my home? Why bring me back here?"

"I didn't… What happened between us… It was…"

"Oh, cut the bullshit, Nate. I'm not stupid. Just answer the question."

"Fine, fine." He scratched his chin. "Like I said, I need proof. Something substantial to show the police."

"Did you find it?"

"I can't get into the laptop. Hey, you wouldn't happen to know his password, would you?"

"Are you seriously asking me to help you break into Seth's computer? You're unbelievable."

"He killed Carolyn. Shouldn't he have to pay for that?"

My head spun. "Look, I'm sorry about what happened to your fiancée. I really am. But you have the wrong guy. Seth's nice. He's not a murderer."

"You yourself said he was controlling."

"Yeah, but like in a needy way. He was kinda smothering. But not killerish."

"Killerish?" He cocked his head to the side.

"I know him, okay? We dated for months. You're a stranger. And a pretty creepy one at that." I yanked my purse off the table and flung it angrily over my shoulder. Tucking the laptop under my arm, I stalked forward.

Nate leaped into action, trailing after me. "Where are you going?"

"Home," I said.

"Wait, come on. Please, just hear me out."

Anger flared. "You used me. I'm done listening to you."

Without another word, I stormed out.

36

THE MOTHER

Present

An uneasiness settles over my shoulders as I continue following Seth. We are getting farther away from Villa Rio. Farther away from home.

Not only that, but we are heading toward the woods.

Where is he going?

I slide into the same lane as him, careful to make sure there's a car between us to shield him from seeing me. Shrugging off the uneasiness, I grip the wheel tighter. I'll follow him to the ends of the earth if he leads me to my daughter.

The sky is darkening, a soft salmon pink fraying along the edges. We've been driving for over a half an hour. Seth's headlights turn on. So does the car in front. I flick mine on as well. How much longer?

A ringing blasts through the small space, and I jerk. It comes from my purse in the passenger seat. I reach inside and pull out my phone.

Shane.

He probably wonders where I am.

If I don't answer, he'll be worried.

But if I do answer, I'll have to lie. There's no way I can tell him where I am. It rings again. My heart clatters.

Reaching out, I turn the volume up on my car radio. It is set to a Christian station. Shane must have been in here last. Sometimes he takes my car for short runs to coffee or the store. I change the station. When the sultry harmonies of En Vogue rush through the speakers, I stop it. Adrienne always teases me about my love of "oldies" as she calls them. But I never mind. I can't get into the current music. I always find myself gravitating to the hits of the 80s and 90s. Maybe it's the nostalgia.

It's getting darker, the pink morphing into a deep blue and then a charcoal gray. But we are still driving.

I check my gas gauge. Luckily, I filled my tank a few days ago. I have a little over half left. We are entering the forest. There aren't any gas stations around here.

I think about the searches on the laptop. The two murders. The men's names. What does it mean?

And why is Seth's name one of them?

Who is this strange man whom my daughter is dating? The one she's never introduced us to? What is she involved in?

I almost don't want to know.

We're the only cars on this road now, so I stay a safe distance back.

It's pitch-dark, trees flanking us. I glance at my phone. No service. My chest tightens. I'm truly alone now.

Has he figured out I'm following him? Is this a trap?

I ease my foot farther off the gas. Put more distance between us. I glance around. It's too late to back out now. I only hope it isn't a huge mistake.

37

THE DAUGHTER

Past

When I got back home from Nate's hotel room, my adrenaline was sprinting like a runner at the summer Olympics. No way would I have been able to fall asleep. After unplugging my laptop from the wall, I carried it into my bedroom, sat in bed and opened it in my lap.

I clicked into Google and typed the words: *Jane Dekker, murder.*

Dozens of stories populated. I went into the first one and read the details. Most of it I knew. She was out with friends, said she was going home, but never arrived. They found her body washed up downriver a few days later. Her friends recalled that a few guys had hit on her while they were out, but she hadn't given in to their advances. And, as far as they knew, she hadn't planned to go home with any of them. I wondered as I read it, if that was a lie. After the accident, so many lies were told. Parker and Clayton lied, said that they'd thought I'd gotten into an Uber.

They hadn't. They'd seen me get into my car and didn't

try to stop me. Only later did they lie to make themselves sound more noble.

Photos were sprinkled throughout the article. Jane looked like I remembered her from around town. Big teeth, big hair, big smile.

I read a few more articles, and finally, in one of them, they'd quoted the fiancé as saying that he knew she wouldn't willingly go home with another guy. They were about to be married. I felt kind of bad for him. None of the friends had mentioned him in any of the other articles, and by the way they'd recounted the night, I wasn't so sure Jane was as pure as he wanted to believe.

Zooming in on the photo with the ring, I tried to get a good look at it. But it got blurrier the more I zoomed in, nothing but a pixelated mess.

Pinching the bridge of my nose, my eyes caught the date of her disappearance. Wait. What day of the week was that?

I went into my calendar. That was the night I showed up unexpectedly at Seth's. The night he showed up late, covered in mud and water, had some explanation about a mainline water break. In the three months we'd dated, he'd never worked at night. Why that night?

I thought of the rings in his drawer. Three of them.

Oh, my God. Could Nate have been right?

I googled Carolyn next. I didn't know her last name, so I went with *Carolyn, murder Aptos*. That was where Nate said he was from. And bingo, she came up. Carolyn Spencer.

There was a photo of her and Nate, and she was wearing the butterfly necklace. I zoomed in, heat snaking up my spine. Nate was right. That had to be the same necklace. And her ring. I zoomed in on it, too. Was it one of the rings I saw in the drawer? It looked a lot like the first one I'd seen, but I couldn't be sure. It was dark and I hadn't gotten a good look at it.

I searched the name Jared Thornton. Dozens of images

and social media accounts populated. After painfully search-ing through many of them, I couldn't find anything tying the name to Seth.

Taking a break, I stretched my legs, grabbed a water out of the fridge. As I did, my gaze fell to the bruise on my wrist. It was an ugly purple now, jagged around the edges. Seth—or whoever the hell he was—had apologized afterward. Said he was so into me he hadn't been able to control himself.

But even at the time, I hadn't bought it. I'd seen the anger on his face.

He could be so gentle, but also, he could be so scary.

But scary enough to kill someone? It was hard to fathom that someone I'd been in a relationship with could have done something that horrible. My brain didn't want to believe it.

It wasn't the time to stick my head in the sand, though. I had to be sure. Either way—whatever I uncovered—I had to find out the truth.

As I headed back into my room, I heard a noise and froze. A footfall. A creak. I held my breath and listened. My heart was thumping so loudly I could barely hear anything else. And then finally, I detected movement in the hall outside, and I breathed out.

This time when I got into bed, I pulled the covers up over my legs. Since I was a child, I'd always felt safer cocooned in my comforter. In the search bar, I typed in the name: Max Lincoln. Like before, I was assaulted with an array of images and social media accounts, not matching up with Seth or any-thing I knew about him.

But then, something caught my eye. A photo of a couple. I clicked on it. And there he was, the man I knew as Seth, standing next to a beautiful woman. I read the accompanying article with growing horror. The woman was named Anna Jeffries. She lived in Oregon. She'd been murdered. Strangled. Her body dumped in a river.

The caption under the photo read: Anna Jeffries with fi-ancé, Max Lincoln. I zoomed in on her ring, but it only got blurrier. I zoomed out. Stared again at the man in the photo. The man I'd been dating for the past three months.

38

THE FIANCÉ

Past

"Fuck." The knock on the door startled me, and I spilled a little of my coffee. A few minutes ago I'd made my second cup in the Keurig the hotel offered, and it was only 7 a.m. It had been a long night. I'd hardly slept. I paused, hesitant. I hadn't been expecting anyone.

My mind briefly lit on last night. Adrienne taking the laptop and leaving upset. Had she gone to the police? Told them it was me who broke in to her home?

The knocking intensified.

Sweat broke out along my shoulder blades as I walked to the door. When I flung it open, I found Adrienne standing in front of me, wearing a sweatshirt and jeans, tennis shoes on her feet. Her hair was pulled back in a ponytail and there wasn't a stitch of makeup on her face. It made her look so much younger than she had last night. At the bar I'd assumed she was in her late twenties, but today she barely looked a day over twenty-one.

"What are you doing here?" I asked, glancing around. She was alone.

"I've thought a lot about what you said last night…and I think there might be some truth to it." Clasping her hands in front of her, her gaze flickered around. "Can I come in?"

I nodded, moving out of her way as she brushed past me. She smelled like vanilla. It made me hungry and my stomach growled. I prayed she didn't hear it. If she did, she didn't react.

"You said that when Carolyn's body was found, she wasn't wearing her necklace. But what about her engagement ring?"

I shook my head. "The police never found it."

"I think I might know where it is."

"What? Where?"

"About a month ago I was at Seth's and I was looking for something, so I opened his nightstand drawer and saw an engagement ring. I thought he was gonna propose and I kinda freaked out. I mean, we weren't quite there, you know?" She played with the collar of her shirt. "Then a few weeks later, a couple of days after Jane went missing, actually, I opened the same drawer and there were several rings inside. Probably sounds stupid now, but I thought maybe he was like shopping around, like sampling rings to see which one he wanted to give me."

It wasn't stupid. "People do that. I did when I proposed to Carolyn. Got three rings to sample in the mail."

I didn't mention that she turned me down the first time. That she'd broken up with me and I'd muscled my way back into her life and proposed too soon. And I'd never admit to anyone what I had to do to get her to say yes.

"You did?" She blinked, then ran her top teeth over her lower lip. She's pretty, and I wonder how Seth got all these women? What was it about him? "Okay, well, anyway, last night I was reading up on Jane's and Carolyn's cases online and in the pictures…well, I kinda think two of those engagement rings were theirs. And the third…well, it might have been Anna's. His fiancé in Oregon. I read the article online. She was also strangled…same as the other two."

I swallowed hard against the lump in my throat. I knew all of this, but it was never easy to take in. "Do you know which one of these names is his real one?"

"I think it might be Cole," she said and then explained about finding a picture on his bookshelf. One that he said was of his brother. "I don't have a last name, though." Exhaling, she lowered down onto the edge of my unmade bed. "How did you find out all this stuff about him? Like all his past names and stuff?"

"After Carolyn died, the police were clearly not taking what I said about him seriously. They looked into me for a while, then an ex of hers and then every time I checked in with them, they said there were no new leads. I knew they'd given up, but I couldn't. So I started investigating on my own. For him to skip town without leaving a trace or any evidence at the scene, I figured this wasn't his first murder. For weeks I scoured all the cold cases I could find and then *bam*, I found Anna's. And there he was. In one of the photos of her. He looked much different, but I could tell it was him. I couldn't find anything that tied him to her murder. But then I remembered a conversation I'd had with him once when we worked together. We'd only had a couple of jobs together, and on one of them I was trying to make conversation, so I asked him why he moved to the Aptos area. He said something about wanting to get away from his cheating ex. If that was her, then that gives him motive."

"Yeah, for Anna, but not for Carolyn and Jane. They were engaged to other people."

"And they cheated," I said. It was a theory I'd put together a while back. One I empathized with more than I would ever admit. I was so angry with Carolyn for cheating on me. I'd loved her so goddam much. I didn't get it. Why she'd want to hurt me. It was what my mom had been so afraid of when I told her about Carolyn. I had a habit of falling in love too quickly. Of getting screwed over.

Still, Carolyn didn't deserve what happened to her. I'd give my fucking right arm to have her back.

"You think that's why he…" Eyes widening, her hand clapped over her mouth. "Oh, my God."

"I don't know if that's why, but it seems to be the pattern."

"In one of our first conversations, he'd asked me about how long I'd lived here in Rio Villa and I told him my whole life. He made a comment about loyalty being a rarity. It was a sentiment he brought up in some of our other conversations, too. Like when I'd talk about my previous relationships and, like, reconnecting with my mom and stuff."

"But he didn't tell you about his previous relationships?"

"I mean, kind of. He did tell me that he'd been cheated on. It affected him. I know that. But he didn't tell me her name or any specifics."

"Yeah, I bet not," I muttered. "Why'd you break up?"

"He was smothering. Jealous. From the beginning. It kinda scared me."

"Did he ever hurt you?"

"No, nothing like that," she said, but I noted that she pulled down her sleeves. I'd seen the bruises. I knew she was lying. I just didn't know why. "It was more just a feeling I had around him sometimes. There was an intensity about him that made me a little uncomfortable. And my job definitely bothered him. He'd always ask about other guys at the bar and stuff. It was too much." She cupped her chin with her hand. "But I never thought something like this could happen. I mean, my God, if he really killed his fiancée, then…"

"I know," I said. She was coming to the realization that she was probably next. "But that's why we've gotta stop him. So he doesn't hurt anyone else."

"I'm still having a hard time believing he did all this. I mean, I've dated other needy guys before, and he wasn't that different from them. I honestly didn't get serial killer vibes from him."

"If he gave off serial killer vibes, he'd never get away with it." I knew better than anyone about the masks we wear and how effective they can be.

She nodded, her features ravaged. I knew all of this was hard for her. "If you saw Carolyn's ring, you'd recognize it, right?"

"Of course."

Her tongue swiped over her teeth. "Okay, I have a plan."

In theory, the plan was simple.

Adrienne and I would go together to Seth's. According to Adrienne the rings were in the nightstand on the far right side of Seth's bed. His bedroom had a faulty window that wouldn't lock properly. While Adrienne went in the front door and distracted Seth, I would sneak in through the bedroom window and find the rings. If Carolyn's was among them, I'd quietly text Adrienne. She'd seduce a confession all while I recorded from the bedroom. Then I'd sneak back out and together we'd take the rings, the recording and Seth's laptop to the police.

I'd finally have the justice I'd been seeking.

But I knew it wouldn't be that simple. There were a million things that could go wrong with this plan. But I didn't say that to Adrienne. She was scared shitless. And rightly so. I didn't want her backing out. This was the closest I'd ever come to getting hard evidence. I had to see it through.

"He sent me a text early this morning," Adrienne had said as they devised the plan, "saying how much he missed me. If I make him think I want to get back together, this should work." It was impossible to miss the violent tremble in her hands. I imagined scooping them up and kissing her. It felt good last night. I wouldn't mind doing it again.

But I knew this was crap timing. I didn't feel like being rejected this morning.

Adrienne had texted him back, saying she missed him, too, and wanted to see him. Bouncing her leg up and down, she'd waited for a response. She only had to wait a few minutes.

"He's on a job, but he said he'd text when he's finished," she'd said. "I work tonight, so hopefully it's not too late."

"Want me to order us some food while we wait?" I'd asked, stomach still growling.

"Sure."

We'd scarfed down an entire pizza by the time Seth texted back in the late afternoon.

Now Adrienne was driving us to Seth's house. She started work in two hours, so we had to move fast. Adrienne had hinted at waiting until tomorrow, but I was too anxious. We had to nail this motherfucker today.

"I'll lose my nerve by then, anyway," she'd said when she agreed.

I was a ball of adrenaline by the time we pulled up to Seth's rental house seemingly in the middle of nowhere. The farther Adrienne had driven from the noise and bustle of the town the more my body moved involuntarily. The more I couldn't keep my legs still. The more my veins buzzed.

"I thought you said he lived in Rio Villa?" I asked.

"Technically, I think he does. He's just in a more rural, remote area," she said as she drove down a long gravel driveway before parking under a large leafy tree. I was crouched down on the floorboards of the backseat. We idled for a few seconds. I lifted my head. She undid her ponytail, fluffed her hair and then swiped gloss over her lips. After rubbing them together, she blew out a long breath.

"Okay, it's go-time," she muttered under her breath before opening her door and stepping out. I stayed still, listening to the crunch of her soles on the gravel. The rap of her knuckles on the front door. Then a familiar male voice. My muscles tensed.

Lying still, I counted in my head, same way I did as a child trying to fall asleep. One, two, three…all the way up to sixty before daring to raise my head. Seth's house was small, painted a tan color with dark brown trim. Bushes lined the side, and two large leafy trees were staggered on the front lawn. To my left I spotted a house a little way down the road, but on my right a vast expanse of tall yellow grass stretched out before me like a body of water. I didn't like the feeling of isolation that pressed around me on all sides.

I carefully opened the back door on the passenger side, since the driver's side was visible to the house. Then I crawled out onto my hands and knees. Gravel poked at the inside of my palm and scuffed my knees as I army-crawled across the driveway.

Adrienne had said that Seth's bedroom was around the right side of the house. Her plan was to keep him occupied in the family room. Once I was certain the house was shielding me, I stood, wiping my palms on my pants, then brushing dirt and debris from my knees.

Adrienne was right. The window didn't latch. It opened easily with nothing more than a slow, soft push. I'd almost gotten it open all the way when it let out a tiny squeak. I stopped. Froze. Listened. From inside the house, I made out the sound of Adrienne's voice, then the repeated clinking of ice coming out of an ice maker. Was he getting her a drink?

Gripping the edge, I hoisted myself up and then assessed the situation under the window. A dresser, but next to that, nothing but carpet. I had to aim for that. I climbed in, lowering down gently, feet falling to the carpet. I paused.

Seth was talking in the other room. The sound of his voice made my skin crawl. I hadn't heard that voice in over a year. Anger tightened around my neck like hands strangling me. Like the hands that had strangled Carolyn to death. God, I wanted to march out there and beat the living shit out of him. I'd fantasized about killing him for the past year. Now, here he was, mere feet away.

But I stopped myself, took a deep breath. I had to stay calm. Stick to the plan. In the moment it would feel good to hurt him, but in the long run it would be stupid. Pointless. Getting evidence against him was the only way to take him down for good. I'd come too far, given up too much, to throw it all away now.

"...should've seen this shoddy workmanship. The toilet literally fell over. It wasn't even affixed to the floor."

"Oh, my God. That's so wild," Adrienne piped up, and I had to hand it to her. She sounded almost normal.

I tiptoed forward, keeping my eyes and ears perked toward the hallway. Unfortunately, the bedroom door was wide open. But the family room wasn't visible from here, so I was good. I headed straight for the nightstand to the right of the bed. The drawer squeaked like a cat squealing, and I stopped abruptly.

"The guy acted like it was my fault, but come on, leaks happen all the time..." Seth was still talking. Dude was always a big talker. I guess that hasn't changed.

Fingers tingling, I was more careful when I pulled this time. Bingo. There were the rings. Three of them. And there in the center was Carolyn's. The one I'd carefully chosen and had lovingly slid onto her finger. I blinked back tears. After shoving all three rings into my pocket, I very slowly closed the drawer and texted Adrienne. Time to enact the next part of our plan. I crawled forward, the rings digging into my side.

In order to get a clear recording, I'd have to position myself as close to the doorway as possible. It would've been best to get into the hallway, but I wasn't sure that would work.

"Everything okay?" Seth asked, and I stopped, mid-crawl, one hand suspended over the beige carpet.

"Yeah, it was just um... Mara...checking in," Adrienne said. "It's been so long since we talked."

"Do you need to respond to her?"

"No, no, I'll call her later. I um…right now, I want to talk to you."

"Talk, huh?" Oh, great. He was going to try to get freaky with her. He sounded pathetic. Was this really what chicks were into?

"Yeah, um… I… I… Well, the main reason I came by today was…um…" *Oh, man, she sounded nervous. Good, he was such an idiot.* "Well, I wanted to apologize for…for breaking things off the way I did…and I also felt like I owed you an explanation."

"I knew there was something goin' on with you." There was rustling as if he was scooting or moving around on the couch. "Go on. I'm listening."

"Uh…yeah, okay," she said. "Well, it's just…"

I got into position right at the edge of the doorway, my body hidden by the wall.

"You're such a good guy, and…"

Ugh. Where's the barf bag?

"Well, I'm not a good person, Seth," she said.

"Yes, you are," he insisted. "Why would you say that?"

"There's something you don't know about me. Something I've never told you."

I pressed my back to the wall, my legs tucked up underneath me. Then I reached down into my pocket, the rough material rubbing against my knuckles as I got out my phone.

"It's my fault Kim is brain damaged," she said.

I'd pulled up the recording app and pressed record.

"Yeah, you've told me about the accident," he said.

"That's the thing, though. It wasn't an accident."

"What do you mean?"

"Kim had betrayed me. I found out that she'd hooked up with my boyfriend. And…well, the truth is I wanted to hurt her when we got in the car that night." Her tone faltered a little, and I felt bad that she had to say this. She'd come up with it on the way here.

"Is that true?" I'd asked her.

"Of course not. Kim didn't cheat with my boyfriend and the accident really was just an accident," she'd said, her voice cracking. "An awful accident that I wish never happened. I'd literally do anything to go back in time and never get behind the wheel that night." She'd swallowed hard, blinked a few times before speaking again. "But it's the only way he'll confess. If he thinks I'm just as evil as he is, then he'll think he has nothing to lose."

It was a solid plan, but I knew it couldn't be easy to say. It was obvious she deeply regretted the accident.

"I get that," Seth said. "My ex cheated on me, too, and I wanted to hurt her," he said. "To make her pay for what she'd done to me. That doesn't make you a bad person."

"Yeah, but wanting to hurt someone and actually doing it are two different things. You didn't actually hurt her. I did hurt Kim. I almost killed her," she continued, her voice wavering. Was she for real? "And the worst part is that I don't even feel bad about it. Does that make me a monster?"

"No, it makes you honest. More honest than most people."

"You don't think that. You probably think I'm a terrible person now."

"No, I don't," Seth said earnestly.

"There's no way you can understand what I'm saying. You're a good person. You'd never hurt anyone. And, as much as I like you, I can't be with someone who doesn't get it, you know? It just makes me feel too bad."

Damn, she's good.

I sat forward, holding the phone out into the hallway as far as I dared. I couldn't risk not getting this.

"But I do get it," he said, desperation in his tone. "We're perfect for each other, Adrienne."

"How can you say that after what I just told you?"

"It's *because* of what you just told me," he said. "You know, everyone gets mad enough to want to hurt someone. It's only the most honest among us who actually go through with it. You and I, we're the same."

"We are?"

"Yeah," he said. "Remember how I told you about my ex and how she cheated on me? We were engaged. And I was so angry. I'd thought she was different from other girls, you know? I thought she was like you. Loyal. Honest. But no, she was like all the others. Like my high school girlfriend who kissed Billy Fisher at a football game. Girls are so weak, you know?"

My arm trembled from being stretched out so far. And I wasn't even sure I was picking up much. They were still so far away. *Fuck it.* I scooted forward and crept into the hallway.

"Anyway, I confronted her—Anna, my ex—but she just denied it. She stuck to the fuckin' lie even after I knew the goddamned truth. Like, did she think I was an idiot? Did she think that low of me?" His voice was amping up. I could feel the energy radiating into the hall. "I was so pissed I couldn't see straight. She'd betrayed me and she couldn't even own up to it. I don't even think she felt bad. That's the thing about these kinds of women. They know the power they have over men, and they love it. They fuckin' eat it up. It's disgusting. And I'd had enough. I wanted her to hurt like she'd hurt me. And I just snapped. I fuckin' snapped, Adrienne."

"What did you do?" she practically whispered.

Here we go. He was going to confess; I could feel it. I moved forward a little farther.

"I strangled her."

I momentarily lost my balance and the toe of my shoe hit the bedroom door. It creaked, the knob thudding against the wall. My muscles tensed. I squeezed my eyes shut, although I have no idea why.

"What was that?" Seth asked.

39

THE DAUGHTER

Past

"I didn't hear anything," I lied.

Reaching out, I grabbed Seth's hands in mine, desperate to salvage this. We were so close to getting the answers we needed. We couldn't afford for it to go wrong now. For so many reasons.

"Anyway, you were saying?" I cocked my head to the side, smiling sweetly.

He wasn't buying it, and I didn't know why I expected him to. The noise had been loud. Obvious. What the hell had Nate been doing? Seth shifted from one foot to the other, his eyes flickering toward the back of the house.

My stomach knotted. I gripped his hands tighter. "It was just the wind."

"I thought you said you didn't hear anything?" He pulled his hands back.

I swallowed hard. "I didn't. It's just... Well, you did, so..."

Shaking his head, he said, "Nah, something's goin' on here." He stood abruptly and walked swiftly down the hallway.

I shot up, too, racing after him.

"You," Seth sneered the minute he entered the room.

Shit. My insides plummeted. I almost ran right into Seth's back. From over his shoulder, I caught sight of Nate near the open window. He must have been trying to climb back out.

"What are you doing here?" Seth asked sharply, then turned to me, his features sagging. "You set me up."

"No, I—"

"I don't know her at all," Nate cut me off. "I came on my own."

"How stupid do you think I am?" Seth's tone was rising, his hands fisting at his sides.

We had to get out of here. I peered over my shoulder, gauging the distance from here to the door. Then I looked up. Seth stood between Nate and me. Even if I made it out, Nate wouldn't. Not without having to go through Seth. I could go get help, but would I get back in time?

Seth had the physical advantage, for sure. Taut muscles lined his arms. I know he spent at least an hour a day lifting the weights in his garage. Nate's arms were scrawny, thin. He looked like he hadn't seen a gym in years.

My palms were sweating. I had no idea what to do.

"What did he tell you about me?" Seth asked me.

I shook my head. "Nothing, he didn't—"

"Shut up." He pressed his fingers into his temples. "Stop fuckin' lyin' to me. What was your plan, huh?"

Out of the corner of my eye, I saw Nate backing toward the window. I kept my eyes glued to Seth. If I could keep him distracted, Nate could escape. Find us help. He seemed mostly focused on me. And I was the one with the advantage. Seth and I had dated. He wouldn't hurt me.

Would he?

"Um… I just… I just wanted to know the truth," I finally

said. He'd figured it out, anyway. Being honest would get me further at this point. Seth valued honesty. That I knew.

"The truth is you're a lying—" His head snapped to the side as if he'd just remembered Nate. "Where do you think you're going?"

Seth moved fast, tugging open the nightstand drawer closest to his—the one on the left side of his bed. His side. I'd never seen what was in that one before. It wasn't filled with photos and rings. This one held something much more dangerous. It filled me with dread. Seth snatched up the gun and waved it first at Nate, who immediately threw up his arms in surrender, palms exposed, fingers spread.

"Whoa," Nate said. "Come on, man."

Seth swung the gun over to me. "Get over there. Stand next to him."

My heart clattered in my chest. If I did what I was told, we'd both be trapped. I should've run when I had the chance. My gaze slid to Nate, and he nodded as if reading my mind. Then he sprang into action, lunging toward Seth.

"Run!" he hollered.

And I did. I sprinted toward the front door, as grunting and scuffling ensued behind me. When I reached the door, I grabbed at the knob. It didn't budge. My sweaty fingers fumbled with the lock.

"Oof." There was a thud.

One of them was down. Was it Seth or Nate?

I didn't look. I'd gotten the lock. I started to turn the knob.

"Adrienne, stop." *Seth.* There was a click, the safety of a gun being released. "If you open that door, I swear to God I'll pull the trigger." I weighed my options. It would only take one swift motion to open the door. But after hearing his story about Anna, I knew he'd make good on his threat. I'd betrayed him. He wouldn't forgive that. My chin dropped to my chest, a breath escaping through my lips. My only hope of getting out of this alive was to do what he said.

I dropped my arm and turned around.

The gun was pointed at me, Seth's face red with anger, his lips pressed into a narrow line. Nate lay at his feet, slumped over in an unnatural way. There was blood on the carpet. The back of my throat burned. *Was he dead?*

"C'mere," Seth said gruffly.

My mouth dried out. What did he want?

I walked stiffly over to him. When I'd almost reached him, he bobbed his head toward the same drawer he got his gun out of. "Open that drawer."

I did as I was told. Ballpoint pens rolled around inside. There were thumbtacks, plastic bags, duct tape. My stomach soured.

"Get the duct tape out," he commanded. Gone was any trace of care or kindness in his tone. It was pure ice now. Bitter and cold, unforgiving.

My fingers were so sweaty it was like I had a condition. It took a couple of tries to successfully pick up the duct tape. My heart hammered so loudly in my ears it was disorienting.

"Tie him up."

"What?"

"Now!"

I flinched. With quivering fingers, I picked at the edge of the tape, lifting one corner enough to peel it. Sticky residue tinged my fingertips. Nate lay on his side, arms bent oddly around his head. He wasn't moving, but as I stared down at him, I saw an ever-so-slight lift and fall of his chest.

Oh, thank God.

I exhaled in relief.

He was breathing, even if it was shallow.

I knelt down beside him, acutely aware of the gun Seth

still pointed at my temple. Sweat beaded along my upper lip. I wiped at it with the back of my hand.

"Come on, get movin'," Seth said.

I'd never tied anyone up before. I wasn't even sure how to. "I'm not really sure..." I looked up at Seth. "I mean, h-how do you—"

"You're stalling. Just do it."

"I'm not. I don't know how..."

"Oh, my God. Really?" He groaned in frustration the same way my dad used to when I couldn't figure something out that he deemed easy. Something everyone should know. "Just grab his wrists, put them together and wrap the tape around them."

Nodding, bile rose in my throat. It was thick and hot, rancid.

Nate's arms were limp in my hands as I picked them up. A part of me wanted him to wake up. I felt so alone and scared. But the bigger part of me wanted him to stay asleep. It was safer for him that way.

"Don't do it loosely, either. I'm gonna check it."

Last year a Facebook friend of mine had reposted this YouTube video on how to escape if you've been abducted. I watched it, so I knew a few tricks in case I was ever tied up. I never thought I'd need to use that knowledge. I wished I didn't have to now.

I put his hands together, thumb to thumb, rather than wrist to wrist, like the video had instructed. I prayed Seth wouldn't notice. Wouldn't realize what I was doing. I wound the tape tightly so Seth wouldn't feel the need to redo anything. And I prayed that Nate would wake up at some point and have the wherewithal to get himself out of the restraints. It was all I could do.

"Now his mouth."

Color drained from my face. "But he's not even awake."

"He will be, and I don't want him screaming."

I'm claustrophobic. Extremely so. I couldn't imagine waking up to tape over my mouth. My belly churned as I ripped off a square of tape. By the time I placed it over Nate's lips, I thought I might throw up all over him.

"Okay." Seth nudged me with the cold barrel of the gun, and I suppressed a squeal. "His phone. Take it out of his pocket."

When I reached in to grab it, my fingertips brushed over the rings. My heart seized, and I sucked in a breath.

"What is it?" Seth asked.

"Nothing." I couldn't let him find out about the rings. He had no reason to suspect Nate had them. My fingers itched to grab them, stuff them in my own pockets. But he'd see. I couldn't risk it. I pulled out the phone, the screen facing us. It was recording.

"Goddammit." He grabbed it from me. "This was your plan, huh? To record a confession." He shook his head. "Hand over yours."

My heart sank even further as I put it into his palm. My one lifeline. Gone.

"Your turn. Get down on your knees," he said. His tone was like venom. Poisonous and slimy. His eyes were black like a snake's.

Shaking, I lowered down to the floor. He snatched the duct tape from me.

"Hands behind your back." Swallowing hard, I did as I was told. His hand was gruff as he grabbed my wrists, pinning them together. I couldn't use the same strategy on myself as I had on Nate. I heard the rip of the duct tape. Had he put down the gun? Moving my head as little as possible, I glanced behind me. He was crouching down, the gun in his lap.

I envisioned myself grabbing it, turning it on him. But what would happen if he got to it first? He'd make good on his threat. That was what. Next, I pictured myself making a run for it, but I knew I'd never make it to the door in time.

Fighting him would only get me killed.

For me, there was only one way out of this mess.

"You don't have to do this, Seth. You can trust me," I pleaded.

"You betrayed me," he said harshly, wrapping tape around my wrists, so tight it hurt.

"I'm so sorry about that. I never thought... I...believed in you. I thought getting to the truth would help you. Prove you hadn't done what he said."

"Stand up," he said, ignoring my words.

Another rip of the tape.

I worked my jaw, knowing what he planned to do. "No, please, Seth. Don't put that over my mouth. I won't be able to breathe." I turned, my gaze meeting his.

He wasn't the same man I'd dated. This man was pure evil. I could see it in his eyes. But there was also a trace of the man he'd been. Somewhere deep inside, I could see him. And that was the man I had to reach.

"Please." This time I didn't fight against the tears. I let them come.

He blew out a loud breath, his gaze shifting back and forth. "Fine. But you have to keep quiet. One peep out of you and the deal's off. Got it?"

I nodded firmly.

Tears tickled my cheek; snot painted the tip of my nose. I wriggled it. The tears slid slowly down my skin. There was no way to wipe them. I felt so helpless and it made the tears come harder.

"Come on. Let's go." One of his hands slipped through the space between my arms, his fingers wrapping around one. In the other hand he held the gun. I felt the barrel as it brushed against my back. Where was he taking me? I should have tried to fight while I had the chance.

If I had, maybe I'd be free now.

Or maybe I'd be dead.

But what did it matter?

He was probably taking me somewhere to kill me, anyway. I'd watched enough Dateline to know that getting in the car is a bad idea. Nate hadn't moved. And I hadn't checked to see if he was breathing in a little while. I glanced down at him as Seth guided me out of the room and down the hall. I thought about what it looked like outside. The large field between Seth's house and his neighbor's. The creek behind his house that we'd walked along one sunny afternoon. The woods on the other side.

Once we got out of this house, I had to make a run for it. Going to the neighbors was probably the best choice. Once there, I could call for help.

But he didn't take me out the front door. He shoved me into the garage...where his car was parked. *Oh, God.*

No, no, no, I screamed in my head as he tugged me forward.

He flung open the passenger door. I desperately looked around the garage, my gaze skating over tools and boxes, a fridge, ice chests, a pair of muddy shoes. There was a door leading to the backyard, but it was on the other side of the car. A lawn mower blocked it. If I ran for it now, I might make it to the door leading into the house, but with my hands bound behind my back I'd never get the door open.

I was trapped.

"I'll be right back," he said after manhandling me into the passenger seat. After he closed the door, I heard all the locks click. Then he headed back inside. I felt a slight glimmer of hope. I was alone. Now was my chance. I had to take it.

I threw my arms up to where the lock buttons were. I pounded on the "unlock" one. It clicked. I exhaled. Then I lowered my arms to the handle, and despite them being bound, I was able to grip it, shove it downward. The door didn't budge.

I didn't understand.

Then it hit me.

He must have had the child locks on.

Dammit.

I turned toward the driver's side, but then the garage door popped open, Seth standing in the doorway, holding a limp Nate in his arms.

It was too late. I slumped forward in my seat, a frustrated sob spilling from my throat. Why had I listened to Nate? Why had I agreed to this stupid plan? I would be on my way to work now. Oh, God, what I wouldn't give to be there, cocooned with the familiar scent of wood and beer, pouring drinks and chatting up the regulars.

Wait. Work.

I sat up a little taller.

In the two years I'd worked there, I'd never been a no-call, no-show. *Surely, they'll know something's wrong when I don't show up.*

The trunk slammed closed.

I whirled around. Seth was storming up to the driver's side, gun in his hand, but no Nate. Did he put him in the trunk?

Better him than me.

I hated myself for thinking that, but it was true. I'd never survive in a tiny space like that. As Seth climbed into the driver's side, jaw set, eyes avoiding me, my chest expanded a little. Seth knew about my claustrophobia. It was a small mercy, him keeping me up here in the front seat, mouth free. But one I noticed.

The garage door rattled open. He started the car and backed out. We passed my car sitting idly in his driveway.

When my coworkers realized I was missing, they'd come looking for me and they'd find my car. Then they'd know I was with Seth. My breath was coming easier now. Until reality hit. No one would have any reason to come looking for me here.

I'd never told anyone about Seth. Not explicitly.

Jazzy knew I was dating someone. But I'd never told her his name. Certainly not where he lived. If I would've confided in anyone at work, it would've been her.

When I still lived at home, Dad got on me all the time about what he called my "serial dating."

"Are you dating just to date or are you looking for a relationship?" he'd ask.

"I'm just looking to hook up," I'd snap back, annoyed at the condescending question.

"Adrienne," Mom would admonish me with a weary shake of her head.

Mom and I were finally starting to connect, but I hadn't told her, either. I wish I had. I'd underestimated my mom for years, thinking she sided with Dad on all things. Now I knew that wasn't true. The problem was that I didn't know for sure what things they lined up on and what things they didn't. So I'd still been careful with what I told her.

I would've told Mara if she hadn't been so tied up with her own life. Her perfect little marriage and baby.

God, I was all alone, wasn't I?

Well, other than Nate, but he's locked in the trunk.

So yeah, alone.

I had to face up to the fact that no one was going to rescue me. I'd have to do it myself.

40

THE DAUGHTER

Past

We were no longer in Rio Villa. Seth had driven us deep into the national forest and he didn't seem to be slowing down. Did he bring Jane Dekker here, too? Was this where he killed her?

I shivered.

Seth had been quiet so far, angrily staring out the front window. It was hard to imagine that this was the same man in my bed only a week ago, stroking my hair and whispering gentle words in my ear.

"Seth," I said quietly now, desperate to find that man again. "I'm sorry."

"It's too late for that," he said, and I saw the muscles on his arm tighten. He didn't turn his head, instead keeping his gaze trained in front of him.

My lower lip trembled, and I stamped it down, but then thought better of it. I allowed it to shake, allowed my words to wobble. "Seth, I'm scared. Please don't do this to me. If you ever cared about me, please…"

"You think I wanted to do this?" he spit out, finally glancing briefly in my direction. "I never wanted to hurt you. I thought we could have a—" He shook his head. "It doesn't matter. I was wrong."

"No, you weren't." I shifted in my seat, wriggling my hands.

My shoulders and arms ached from being tied behind my back for so long. I'd been working on loosening the tape for the past ten minutes or so. I could now separate my wrists, so I was getting somewhere.

"That Nate is such an idiot," he muttered, ignoring my words. "He never could see that I was doing him a favor. Carolyn was cheating on him. She deserved what she got."

"So you hit on her and then got upset that she took you up on it?"

"I didn't hit on her. She came on to me," he said, then added, "So did Jane. She tried to hide her ring, slip it into her pocket, but I'd already seen it. Made me feel a little bad for what I was going to do, though. At least she'd tried. Anna wore her fucking ring when she went off with that dude. Didn't even respect me enough to pretend we weren't en- gaged. She flaunted it."

He was a psychopath. How had I not seen it before?

How had he fooled me for so long?

But I knew the answer to that. It was the same way he got these women to cheat on their fiancés. Seth was manipula- tive. He knew how to use his good looks and charm to get women to trust him, to want him. It saddened me that he'd played Carolyn this way. That he'd reeled her in. Taken away her chance at a future with a man who cared for her.

Nate's love for Carolyn ran deep. That was obvious. She'd thrown away everything…including her life…for one night with Seth. One night she probably didn't even get. There was nothing in any of the articles about Carolyn or Jane having sex with anyone the night they were killed.

How long were they with him before he strangled them

to death? How far did they have to go for him to consider it cheating? Worthy of a death sentence?

Was it swift?

Were they scared?

I continued discreetly sawing my arms up and down. I had to get out of these restraints. Out of this car, somehow. Away from Seth.

I wasn't going down the way those other girls had. It couldn't end this way for me. I'd have been over an hour late for work now. Was Jazzy worried? Wait… What day was it again? Wednesday. My mom! She came in on Wednesdays. Surely, she'd know something was off. My heart lifted a little. Yes, my mom would come through. She'd report me missing. She'd try to find me.

Feeling a rush of motivation, I fought harder against the restraints. Seth was back to staring out the front window, but I still had to be discreet. It made it a little harder. Darkness blanketed us as he drove, the car bumping along the dirt road. No one would be out here this late. I wasn't even sure anyone came this far into the woods during the day, let alone at night. We were way off the beaten path.

I tried not to panic, but instead kept working the tape. I had to focus on that. If I let my mind go to all the possibilities of what might be coming, I'd fall apart. And that wasn't an option. I had to stay strong. Be brave. It was the only way I had any hope of surviving.

Abruptly, the car stopped. I sucked in a breath.

"What's going on?" I asked, my gaze bouncing around. We were flanked by tall trees and shrouded in pitch-black. I couldn't even see the stars or moon from here.

"We're here." Smiling, he opened his door and stepped out.

Desperation clawed at me. When his back was momentarily turned, I let out a grunt and, using all my force, pulled my arms apart. To my shock, it worked. My arms were free. Oh, my God.

He was coming around to my side.

My pulse quickened.

You can do this, Adrienne.

My breathing was labored by the time he opened my door. I clasped my hands together, needing it to look like I was still bound. I kept my expression grim as he tugged on my arm, roughly prying me from the car. Once both feet were on the ground, I threw my body toward his, elbow out. His eyes widened in surprise as the weight of my body propelled his own toward the ground. While he stumbled, I shot to the left, running as fast as humanly possible away from him.

"You bitch!" he screamed, his footsteps crunching over brittle leaves and wood.

I didn't look, just kept running, pumping my arms like they taught me in gym class. Trees zipped past my head. They were so close, I worried I'd plow into one. But I kept going, the soles of my feet pounding against the ground.

"Adrienne! You stupid bitch. You're just making this worse. I'm gonna find you."

His voice was to my right. I slipped behind a tree and careened farther left.

"I see you!" he hollered, and my muscles constricted. But he was bluffing. His voice was too far away. No way did he see me. I zigzagged through trees, moving slower now. Stopping every once in a while, crouching down and hiding. Listening.

"Goddammit!" he cursed.

There was a snap a few feet away. I shoved off the tree I'd been hiding behind. A gunshot rang out. I leaped to the ground, heart clattering in my chest. Pressing my body into the earth, I breathed deeply. I hadn't been hit. I lay still. Leaves rustled. A twig broke. I detected the sound of footsteps, but they were going in the opposite direction. He was heading right. Was he following an animal?

I couldn't help the twitch of my lips at the thought of him being torn apart by some wild beast. A bear with sharp teeth and large claws. But then my stomach soured. If a wild animal could get to him, it could find me, too.

I had to keep moving. Find help.

Hoisting myself up, I whirled around to the left again and started running. As I made it farther along, I thought about Nate trapped in the trunk. If only I'd had time to get him out. But it was too risky. This was our best bet. I'd keep running until I found civilization.

I'd get us help, call the police. Hopefully, it wouldn't be too late.

41

THE FIANCÉ

Past

I dreamt I was on a boat, bobbing in the waves. My body lazily swayed back and forth. Wind blew over my sun-drenched skin and I shivered. Hugging myself, I attempted to roll over, but my shoulder hit something hard, unmoving.

My eyelids flew open. It was dark, and I blinked a few times. Panic mounted as I took in the small space. My bones rattled, my teeth chattering. There was a buzzing beneath me, tires on a rocky surface.

A trunk.

I was in a trunk.

Memories flooded me.

Seth catching me. Dragging me out from my hiding spot. Snatching my phone. Me, lunging at him. Pain, deep and searing in the back of my head. Darkness.

There was something sticky covering my mouth. Duct tape, probably. My wrists were bound together in front of me. I wriggled them around. It gave a little, pulling at my hairs. Also, duct tape. *Mother. Fucker.* The road got bumpier, my body being flung back and forth. Without my arms free, there was no way to stabilize myself. Mouth caged in, I bit my tongue, and a metallic taste filled my mouth. I gagged against it.

The road must've become less bumpy because my body steadied. Still, there was a buzzing sensation running through my muscles. Ignoring it, I focused on trying to get out of my restraints. I rubbed my wrists up and down, up and down, up and down. Cold sweat snaked down my back. My body continued to rattle around. But the tape wasn't budging. He had it on tight.

Panic stretched across my chest. I was having trouble breathing. I worked my jaw, attempting to loosen the tape over my mouth.

Giving myself a quick rest, I lay my neck back, breathing deeply through my nostrils.

God, I really did feel like a fucking joke now.

The car stopped so abruptly my body lurched forward and then back. I hit my head.

Great. That's what I need. More damage to my skull.

I heard a door pop open, footsteps outside. Then another door.

It was now or never.

Desperate, I rubbed my wrists up and down again while simultaneously trying to pry them apart. Several seconds passed before I felt movement. It was working. I used more force, creating a larger gap. Finally, there was a snap.

Reaching up, I tugged the tape off my mouth. It stung, and my eyes watered. But I didn't have time to worry about that. After tossing the tape aside, I felt around for a way to open the trunk. I kicked upward but only succeeded in causing pain to radiate through my calf.

Shuffling outside caught my attention.

"Adrienne!" I froze at the angry sound of Seth's voice. Had she gotten away? "Dammit!" Footsteps thundering. "You stupid bitch. You won't get away." His voice was getting farther away with each word.

A sense of urgency pressed on my chest.

My fingertips swept over the panel in front of me, feeling for a lever. I hadn't seen Seth's car. But I was praying it was less than twenty years old. When my fingertips brushed over something sharp and dangling, my pulse quick started. It couldn't be this easy, could it?

Gripping it, I tugged downward, and the trunk popped open.

No way.

A gunshot rang out.

I couldn't waste another second. Heart hammering, I climbed out, eyes frantically scanning my surroundings. Tall trees flanked me on all sides. My feet hit the ground, soles crunching on pine needles.

"Adrienne!" Seth's voice rang out from my right.

Had he shot her? Or was she safe?

I slammed the trunk closed and hurried away from the car. Let him believe I was still locked safely inside. He'd be back and I needed to buy myself some lead time. I turned in a circle, searching for the road, civilization, people. Anyone who could help us. But all I saw was trees and darkness. We were deep in the forest.

I needed to find Adrienne. I'm the one who'd roped her into this in the first place. And now she was in danger because of me. Nausea rose up inside me at the thought.

Shoving off a nearby tree, I jogged forward. To my right I heard a crunch. I ducked behind a tree. Held my breath. Waited.

After a few quiet seconds I emerged, jogging forward again. I made it past a few more trees, my eyes carefully tracking the area. I didn't see Seth. But I also didn't see Adrienne. I kept moving forward, arms out in front of me, fingertips occasionally brushing over a twig or tree trunk. A couple of times my toes hit something hard—a rock or bush, maybe. I'd teeter, but always right myself.

In the distance I heard an engine rumble.

Seth? Or someone else?

I wanted to yell out but swallowed the compulsion down.

If it wasn't Seth, he could be anywhere out here. With his gun.

I'd come so close to answers. It couldn't end now.

The ground sloped down beneath me, and I lost my balance for a moment, steadying myself with a nearby tree. It scraped at the tender flesh of my palms. I wiped them on the thighs of my jeans, but that only made it sting more. I bit the inside of my cheek. The air was bitterly cold as it whisked over my face, much colder than it should be in spring. But it was always cool out here in the woods. It was so dark I could hardly see. It wasn't a normal darkness. Not like the kind at home where there were streetlamps and homes to cut through the pitch-black of night. This was the kind that consumed you, swallowed you whole.

I landed wrong, my ankle twisting. Despite my best efforts, my body tumbled forward. It all happened so fast, I didn't have time to cushion my fall with my arms. There was a sensation like a knife stabbing me in the head and then I drifted off.

42

THE DAUGHTER

Past

I ran until my thigh muscles burned and my lungs were so tight it was difficult to draw in a breath. A layer of cold sweat coated my skin. I stopped and doubled over, hands on my knees as I breathed deeply, in and out, in and out. I was certain I'd lost Seth by now. I hadn't heard any noise from him in a while. Believing he'd been eaten by a wild animal was probably too good to be true. Surely, he was out there somewhere. He wouldn't give up until he found me, whether that was here in these woods or back in Rio Villa.

That was why I had to get somewhere safe so I could call the police.

If only I had been able to take the rings out of Nate's pocket. Or get the recording from his phone. No doubt Seth had gotten rid of our phones by now. And who knew if Nate was even alive. Still, there had to be a way to prove Seth had been the one to kill Anna, Carolyn and Jane. He'd clearly covered his tracks. Changed his name, moved towns.

But I knew the truth and, somehow, I had to get the police to see it, too.

The laptop.

It was still in my car. I'd brought it today, thinking we'd want to go straight to the police after Seth's. It was under the passenger seat. I prayed Seth wouldn't find it. And I kicked myself for not leaving it at my apartment.

God, what I wouldn't give to be back at my apartment where it was warm and safe. The inky-black air that circled me was icy, and I hugged myself. Thank God I was wearing a sweatshirt and tennis shoes, not a T-shirt and flip-flops like I often did. Even so, the sweatshirt felt too thin for this level of cold. I wished so badly I'd had on a jacket or better yet, a coat.

I stopped at the sound of rustling nearby.

It was nighttime in the middle of the forest. I may have been safe from Seth for the time being. But I wasn't safe.

Squinting, I scanned the perimeter around me, searching for any hint of light or marker that civilization was close. Not seeing any, I closed my eyes and listened intently for sounds of cars, people, water. Anything. But all I heard was stillness, the occasional creak or rustle. Animals. That was it.

I walked a little farther and then leaned against a tree for support. My hand slipped through it, and I almost fell. When I righted myself, I moved closer to the tree and peered through it. Much to my delight, I discovered it was hollowed out. A wave of relief washed over me at the realization that I'd found shelter for the night.

Mara and I had gotten lost in the woods once. We were thirteen. It was the middle of August during our week at Camp Grace. We went every summer. Camp Grace was located in the Redwood National Forest. Was that where I was now? Based on the route Seth took to get here, I'd guess so. But I wasn't sure where exactly I was in the forest in relation to the camp.

Mara and I loved going to camp. It was a glorious week away from our parents, swimming in the river and playing games, meeting new friends, talking to boys.

But that summer the camp counselor in charge of our cabin was a mean girl named Stella. I think she lived in Jenner. She was in her early twenties, and we were certain the only reason she was even at the camp was because her boyfriend was also a counselor. She snuck off to see him any chance she got. Whenever she was stuck with us, she acted like it was our fault she couldn't be with him. She did nothing to hide her boredom.

One afternoon she took our group on a hike in the woods. She was in a particularly sour mood, snapping at all of us the entire time and checking her phone incessantly. While she was distracted, I convinced Mara to join me as I set off on my own. I figured we'd have a lot more fun without her.

Quietly, the two of us had slipped away from the group, then we'd zigzagged through trees until we were far enough away. Until we couldn't see them anymore. Then we popped up, giggling. We traipsed around, talking about Mara's crush on a boy named Liam, while I went on and on about Quentin, the young worship leader with the long hair and brooding eyes, tats lining his right arm.

When the bright afternoon sun cut through the trees, we started heading back. We were hungry, anyway. I remember Mara's stomach had even growled and I teased her about it.

Giggling and talking, we went back the way we came. Or, at least, we thought we had. But after walking for what felt like an hour, we weren't coming across anything familiar. We didn't hear any sounds from the camp or the river, either. Had we gone farther into the woods?

"We're lost." Mara's lips quivered and her eyes filled with water.

"Don't cry. We'll find our way back," I said, knowing I had to be the strong one. It was my idea to leave the group. Out of the two of us, Mara was the rule follower. The safe one. I was the risk taker, the rebel.

"How?" Mara asked, her tone one of defeat.

And I understood. Outdoorsy, we were not. Grace Camp was more focused on teaching us about faith than it was about wilderness skills. But I was determined to get us back in one piece.

Unfortunately, I wasn't the one who got us back.

Stella had told the camp director who'd called the park ranger. He found us about an hour later and brought us back to camp. Mara was angry with me for the rest of the night, but she forgave me the next day when I got Isaac to talk to her—a peace offering.

Because of our little stunt, the following year the camp implemented a training on what to do if we got lost in the woods. The counselors walked all of us through it our first night. And it taught us how to find or build a shelter, what berries and bugs were safe to eat and how to find fresh water. I used to roll my eyes and make silly faces to Mara during it.

But now I was grateful for that stupid training, as I wedged my way into the hollow of the tree and hunkered down. It may have been the thing that would save my life.

My eyelids fluttered. I shifted, my butt damp, my body chilled. What? Where was I? I opened my eyes and groaned. *Oh, that's right. Lost in the middle of the goddamn forest.* Leaning my head back on the inside of the tree I was wedged inside, I blew out a breath.

I was a little surprised I'd been able to fall asleep. After climbing inside the tree, I'd spent the next hour scratching my head and neck, and the back of my legs, thinking for sure that there were bugs crawling all over me. I would've leaped out if I wasn't more afraid of bears and mountain lions than insects.

After ducking out of the tree, I wiped mud off the back

of my jeans. When I glanced around, I frowned. I'd hoped in the light of day, it wouldn't look so bleak. But it was just like that time I was lost with Mara. Nothing but trees as far as the eye could see.

It was early. So early the sun hadn't come up yet. The air was frigid. Well, frigid by my standards. I lived in Northern California, so it wasn't like it was officially freezing. Truth is, I was lucky to be in this situation in early spring, rather than summertime. The heat would kill me faster than the cold would. At least this way, I wouldn't get dehydrated as fast.

Didn't stop my head from pounding, though. I clutched it, thinking about how badly I needed a cup of coffee.

Birds chirped overhead; critters scuttled in the brush; insects buzzed. I walked a few steps forward, my gaze swinging to the left and right. In our little training at Camp Grace, the instructors always said to stay put. Wait for help. Don't try to find your way back because you might get more lost. Walk deeper into the woods.

It was too late for that now.

No one knew I was out here.

Well, no one except for Nate, and I was pretty sure he was dead.

Oh, God. I pressed my hand to my mouth, smothering a sob. *What a nightmare.*

What had I been thinking coming up with such a risky plan?

"You never think. You just do," Mara had said to me once in an argument.

She was right. And this time it may have cost someone their life. I couldn't let it cost me mine as well. I had to seek justice for Nate. For Carolyn. And for Jane and Anna, too.

I sniffed and wiped a hand down my face, then kept walking, listening carefully to the sounds around me. I wondered again about Camp Grace. Was it close by?

What about the road?

I'd seen a documentary once about a guy being lost in the woods. When he was finally found he'd only been a few feet from the road, just couldn't see it. Standing up as high as I could on my tiptoes, I peered out, hoping against all hope that that was the case. That the road was just beyond the trees.

Knowing my luck, I'd probably walk in the opposite way, though.

I picked a direction and went in a straight line. After a few minutes I saw something. A change in terrain up ahead. There was a clearing. Maybe it led to something. Adrenaline spiking, I accelerated. When I reached it, a large field of tall grass spread out before me, bookended by more trees. No street or summer camp or ranger office. More trees. *Awesome.*

I reached down, my fingertips brushing over the top of the dew, coating my skin in cold water. And then I paused.

Morning dew.

Fresh water.

I needed something to collect it.

I hurriedly tugged off my sweatshirt, revealing the Rolling Stones T-shirt I had on underneath. I'd always been a big fan of layering. I never knew when I might get cold, or I might get hot. I liked having options. Today I was grateful. My teeth were chattering by the time I got my T-shirt off, so I swiftly put my sweatshirt back on. Then I tied the T-shirt around my waist and walked through the tall, dew-covered grass.

When they taught us this at camp, we were supposed to use a clean rag or something. But my dirty, sweaty T-shirt would have to do. As I made my way across the field, I had no idea if I was doing this right or if it would be successful. But I knew I had to try.

Reaching the other side, I untied the wet T-shirt and held it up.

Now what?

At camp they'd said to wring it out into a cup or water bottle. I didn't have either of those. For several seconds I stared at the shirt. And then I shook my head. Oh, screw it. I had to get the water in my mouth. I'd just think of it as a can of whipped cream.

Craning my neck backward, I held up the shirt and wrung it into my mouth. Liquid splattered my face and chin, but some slid into my mouth. It tasted weird, like grass, and it grossed me out thinking about what I was ingesting, but it also felt so good, coating my parched tongue and throat.

"This is so lame," I used to say to Mara during the first night of camp. "Like I'm ever going to drink dew or eat plants."

Man, I couldn't wait to tell her about this. I hoped I would get the chance.

By late afternoon I was still walking, still surrounded by trees, still seemingly no closer to civilization. But I had run across a plant with berries. I studied it for a while, wishing I'd paid more attention to the pictures they'd shown us at camp. Were these berries safe to eat or were they poisonous? I mean, they looked yummy and safe. But I felt like this was something I should be more confident about.

My stomach churned. I was so hungry and so tired.

And where was the road? Or the water? Or the camp?

Frustration burned through me.

Fine. I angrily tore a few berries off the bush and shoved them into my mouth. They were sweet. Blackberries, I think. Those are safe, right?

Bushes nearby shook. I flinched. I'd spent an entire day wandering in the woods and now the sun would go down soon. I needed shelter again. Heat rushed to my eyes.

This can't be happening.

I can't still be lost.

Salty, warm tears flooded my eyes and spilled down my cheeks. If only I could drink them. But I knew that wouldn't help. The little bit of dew I'd had this morning wasn't going to sustain me forever. Was I going to die out here?

No, no, I couldn't.

Then Seth would win, and there was no way I'd let that happen.

When I no longer heard the rustling, I ate a few more berries. There was a trail of ants near my foot. I moved it back, away from them, and then followed the trail to see where it started. They were coming from a nearby tree. I shuddered, grateful that hadn't happened when I was sleeping in one last night.

As I continued on, a comforting sound rang out.

Water.

I picked up the pace, moving quickly toward it, and within minutes came upon a creek, water moving swiftly over rocks. It was so small I could step over it. I knew immediately that was good. The smaller the better, I heard in my head. Must've been something they'd taught us at camp. And it was running. I could see where it started coming from the ground.

My mouth was so dry I couldn't drum up moisture to swallow down.

I needed this.

Bending down, I scooped the water into my hands and lapped it up like a dog. It was so good, and I kept drinking. Once I'd satisfied my thirst, I sat back up, liquid dripping from my chin. I wiped at it with my hand.

I needed to build a shelter, so I started collecting large branches. Holding them over my shoulder, I walked. I felt like a contestant on *Survivor*. I'd always joked that I'd never make it on one of those shows but look at me now.

My arms trembled from the weight of the branches. It had been such a long day. I needed to rest. Releasing the branches, they tumbled to the ground. I tried propping them up on a tree to create a shelter for myself, but they kept toppling over like a row of dominoes. After multiple tries, I sank down onto the ground. A laugh bubbled from my throat.

Why had I thought I could do this?

I was pulling things from summer camp as a child from my memory bank and using it as some kind of nature guide. For all I knew, all of it had been wrong. I barely paid attention in those meetings.

I couldn't believe I'd eaten berries and drank water from the ground.

Dropping my head into my hands, I groaned. What if my stomach was filled with parasites? Or some deadly disease? What's the one with the G?—Giardi. No, that was a girl I went to high school with. Lauren Giardi. She was a disease, all right. But not the one I was referring to.

I didn't want to die like this. Not in the middle of a forest where animals would tear apart my carcass afterward. But I didn't know how much longer I could do this. I just wanted to go home. To change into clean clothes and eat real food. To slip under my covers and get warm.

The tears were coming again. I'd never cried so much in my life as I had today.

Fuck Nate for getting me in the middle of this.

And fuck my stupid plan that put me in this predicament.

And fuck Seth for driving me out into the middle of nowhere.

Yeah, fuck him.

Seth.

That was who I had to stay mad at. Not Nate and not me. Seth. He was the reason I was out in this godforsaken place.

At least my lifeless body wasn't floating downriver. I had to remember that. I was alive.

I needed to stay that way.

Standing, I wiped my face and blew out a breath, then

went in search of more branches. Maybe I needed larger ones. More stable or something. I zipped between trees, looking, and ended up finding one that looked like it might work. As I bent over to pick it up, my gaze caught on a hollowed-out tree. I gasped, unable to believe my good luck. That was two nights in a row.

I guess I didn't have to make the shelter, after all.

Smiling, I dropped the branch and then my heart sank.

Wait a minute. I hadn't found two hollowed-out trees. This was the same exact tree from last night.

I must have walked in a giant circle. Now I was right back where I'd started.

43

THE FIANCÉ

Past

"No, don't touch him," a male voice spoke in a muffled, garbled voice, almost like the person was talking under water.

Like when I was a child, sitting at the bottom of the local pool, talking to my best friend, Mark, bubbles escaping through our lips and traveling upward.

"Is he breathing?" another voice asked, this one a little clearer.

I fought to swim toward it, just like when Mark and I were running out of air. "Could you hear what I said?" I'd asked when we broke the surface, water dripping from our hair into our eyes.

My eyelids felt stuck as if glued together. With all my might, I strained to open them. They fluttered somewhat. Regaining control of my limbs, I opened my hand, my fingertips brushing over something sharp and hard. A twig maybe. My head ached.

"Stay still," the first man said. "Help is on the way."

Help?

Why? What happened?

My eyesight was blurry. But I could see branches, greenery, dancing overhead. Movement, like the fluttering of a butterfly. Carolyn's butterfly, perched on her slender finger. Her laugh tinkled in my mind, and my eyes started to close again, darkness filling my vision. The pull to fall back asleep, to stay with Carolyn and her infectious laugh, was so strong. Stronger than my desire to battle with my eyelids. To stay in the cold. It was cold, right? So cold.

Where am I?

Somewhere with branches. Greenery. Trees?

"Come on," the second voice said. "Stay with us."

"An ambulance is coming," the first man said.

They sounded so hopeful, I didn't want to let them down. I struggled once again with my eyes, wrestling them open.

It was dark. So dark. Past the tree branches was the inky, pitch-black sky. I couldn't see any stars. There were so many trees.

Two men stood over me. They wore backpacks, ponchos and hiking boots.

Hikers.

Am I in the woods?

How did I get here?

I tried to ask the men, but I couldn't make my lips move. It was like I'd eaten an entire tub of peanut butter and hadn't swallowed it yet. My tongue felt like it was spackled against the roof of my mouth.

Carolyn's face filled my mind. Her smile. Her sparkling eyes.

We were in bed, our hands woven together, her hair haloed around her head. She was talking, softly, slowly, in that calming lilt she had. And then it was quiet, and she was gone. The bed beside me empty.

My heart picked up speed.

But this wasn't now. Carolyn had been gone awhile.

Over a year.

I'd been trying to find her killer. Trying to find Seth. I'd come to Rio Villa for that reason.

Had I found him?

In the distance I heard sirens. The men were right. Help was on the way.

Exhaling slowly, I closed my eyes.

When I opened them again, a man was standing over me, but not the same man from the woods. This man wore a navy collared shirt and navy pants. Bright lights shone in my face. We were in motion. I blinked.

An ambulance.

I was riding in the ambulance.

I couldn't keep staring into the bright lights. It was too much.

The darkness was welcome when I closed my eyes.

The room was quiet, dimly lit.

Machines beeped.

A curtain blocked me from seeing past my bed.

The hospital.

Safe.

That was the word that came to mind.

Safe from what, I didn't know. But I was, and that was all that mattered.

44

THE DAUGHTER

Past

I was in hell.

Growing up, I'd been taught that hell was a place of eternal torture, fires hot and all-consuming, perpetually blazing. When I was five, I burned my finger by accidentally touching my mom's curling iron as it heated on the bathroom counter. My skin stung for hours despite the cold water and aloe vera Mom put on it. I couldn't imagine that kind of pain forever. I was certain I wouldn't endure it. I'd lie in bed at night in a cold sweat, afraid I might die in my sleep and end up in hell, fire eating through my skin for all eternity.

But now I knew what hell really was.

It was this.

This was hell.

It wasn't an underground morbid fireplace. It was being trapped in this goddam forest sleeping in a hollowed-out tree, eating berries, drinking from stream water and walking in circles.

Today felt like a repeat of yesterday. As far as I could tell,

I was no closer to civilization. But I was determined not to make a giant circle again. If I had seen that same hollowed-out tree I know I would've lost it.

I wondered if Mom was looking for me. I bet Dad wasn't. He was probably glad I was gone. He still had his beloved child. The one who was literally a carbon copy of him. He didn't need me. Kicking a rock in front of my toe, I let out a small laugh, thinking of Curtis out here. No way would Mr. Choirboy survive being lost in the woods.

When we were kids, we rarely saw each other at camp. Since he was so much older than I was, he was in a different area. But the times I did see him, he was reading or talking with his buddies in the cabins. I never saw him outside or doing anything adventurous. The times I did see him his clothes were clean, his hair combed. I doubt he ever went on a hike or out into nature. Curtis always preferred books and quiet time to going out and experiencing life.

Did he know I was missing?

Did he care?

Probably not.

I kicked another rock and watched as it scuttled on the path in front of me.

I bet Mara knew. She'd most likely be the first person Mom would reach out to. She'd care. Sure, we'd grown apart a little in the past few years, but we still loved each other. She'd always been like a sister to me. More of a sibling than Curtis ever was.

We're so different. Always have been. We want different things from life. Mara never judged me for that. I wish I could say the same. Deep down I judged her all the time. Her life now made me sad. At home all the time with her boring husband and whiney baby, cooking dinner, cleaning the house and going to church every Sunday morning like clockwork.

It was precisely the life I'd been running from. Why would anyone choose that?

Tripping over a hard boulder in my path, I threw my hands out. They scraped the boulder, my neck jerking forward. But at least I hadn't fallen face-first into it. *God, can you imagine?*

I pushed a strand of hair out of my face and looked around.

Where was the road? The water? People?

Surely, I was close.

How big was this stupid forest?

Maybe I should've been seeking out a quieter life. One more like Mara's. She was probably sitting in her immaculate living room reading to her child or watching TV, and look where I was? Whose life choices were looking bad now?

Her husband may be the most boring man I've ever met, but as far as I know he's never driven out to the middle of the woods with the intention of killing her and dumping her body in the river.

A hysterical laugh bubbled up from my throat. I laughed and laughed and laughed. I laughed until my throat was raw; until tears dampened my cheeks; until the muscles in my stomach spasmed.

It was golden hour. I stared up through the trees at the sun high in the sky, painting it with bright golden streaks. Once I'd dated a guy who was a photographer. Jeremy. He loved to take pictures of me during golden hour. We'd trek out to the river, and I'd dance on the shore to the soundtrack of his camera clicking. I really liked him, and I'd assumed it was mutual. He was attentive and had the best smile. But then I found out I wasn't the only girl he was taking pictures of at golden hour. He had a whole slew of us. If all he'd been doing was shooting photos that would be one thing, but he wasn't.

He'd since moved and last I heard he was in a serious relationship, so maybe he's settling down. I wasn't sure I'd ever be ready to settle down. The day I moved out of the house

I'd grown up in, I swore to myself I'd never let anyone control me again.

When Seth and I first started dating, I'd thought he was different from other guys. I thought maybe he was someone I could get serious with. He seemed so into me, and I'm not going to lie, I did think we would make some beautiful babies. But things quickly took a strange turn. And looking back, I think I always knew something was off.

The ironic thing is that he was the only person I knew for certain was out there looking for me.

It was a sad shelter, but it would have to do. I'd lucked out by finding two large boulders close together, so I'd laid branches and leaves on top. Huddled into it, I laid my head on the rough ground, pine needles poking me in the scalp. I felt defeated. I'd hoped to be out of here by now. There was no way I could spend another night out here.

At least today I hadn't walked in a circle. Or, at least, I didn't think I had. There was no sign of the hollowed-out tree.

But I was still in the woods. Still trapped. Still lost.

Tomorrow I had to find a way out.

I had no choice.

If not, I'd die out here.

Dark night sky sprayed into my makeshift shelter through the slivers in the branches. I stared up at it as desperate words tumbled from my mouth.

"God, if You're really out there and You can hear me… please don't let me die out here. Please…help…me."

They were the first words I'd uttered to God in years. It may have been stupid. I may have been speaking to no one at all. My words may have disintegrated into thin air. A waste of precious breath. But maybe, just maybe, there was someone out there. Some being greater than myself. Some higher power.

If there was, I knew He wasn't anything like the one I'd been taught about in church.

If there was, I believed He was good. I believed He was fair.

And I believed He was a lot more powerful than any of the religious men I'd known had made Him out to be.

I awoke to the sound of rain.

No, not rain.

The sky was clear, my body dry. I listened carefully.

Water running.

I was near the water. How had I not heard it last night? As I scrambled out from under the branches, I prayed it wasn't another tiny stream. Don't get me wrong, I could've used the sustenance. But a larger water source could've led me to civilization, and that was what I wanted more than anything.

My palms were scraped from my brief fall yesterday, and the edges of the cuts were filled with dirt. I wiped them on my jeans as I walked. The sound of water got louder. I broke into a run, unable to contain my excitement. Right past another grouping of trees, I found it.

It was a stream, but a much larger one than before and I couldn't see where it started or where it began. That had to be a good sign. The water flowed to the right, so that was the direction I walked. I hoped it would lead me to the river, which would in turn lead me to some sort of civilization.

PART THREE

45

THE DAUGHTER

Present

"Is that...?" I stop. Squint. Blink.

A few feet away is a building. Familiar forest green roof, chocolate-brown paint, wooden stairs leading up to the door.

My limbs are jelly, my head filled with cotton. I'm no longer human. I'm a child's art project.

I can no longer be sure that what I'm seeing is real.

Walking unsteadily forward, I blink again.

Still there.

I know that building. It's one of the cabins at Camp Grace.

My palms moistened, my heart rate spiking.

I made it to Camp Grace.

Head pounding, I move quickly toward it. The sky is darkening, and my movements are too fast. I lose my footing, my body hurling to the ground. My arm hits in an odd place, pain radiating through my elbow.

Shit.

Using my other arm, I push myself up to a seated position. I bring my hand up to my shoulder and then extend it. The elbow works. It's just scraped and sore. Blood oozes from it. I wipe it with my other palm and then try to stand. That's when I realize my arm is the least of my worries. I must've twisted my ankle or stretched a tendon or something in my right leg. It throbs as I attempt to put pressure on it.

Once I reach the office, I can call for help. I'm assuming the phones are kept on year-round. I glance up. I'm at the wrong end, though. The office and parking lot are on the opposite side of camp. I'm near the cabins at the back end. On a good day, it would take at least fifteen to twenty minutes to walk from here to the office. On a bum ankle, it will take double that.

Spots fill my vision and I sway on my feet.

I need water...and food.

The dining hall!

It's on this side of camp. Most summers Mara and I signed up to be snack helpers. It was the best job, mostly because we'd always pocket extra packets of fruit snacks and chips. Sometimes steal a soda or two and hide it in our cabin. In the kitchen there's a pantry in the back where they keep pallets of bottled waters and baskets of chips, fruit snacks, granola bars. What I wouldn't give for some of that now.

As I limp forward, I pray there will still be some left.

When I reach the front of the dining hall, it's locked up and dark inside. I move to the back where the kitchen door is. It's locked as well. Rocks and boulders are scattered around my feet. I palm one and launch it into the back door window. I half expect an alarm to go off. And I'm a little disappointed it doesn't. Save me a trip to the office. Alert the police that someone's broken in.

I fist my hand and pull my sweatshirt over it to protect it from broken glass. Then I carefully dip it through the broken window, barely missing the jagged shards before I press the button on the doorknob. I exhale with relief when the knob moves easily.

After hobbling inside, I flick on the wall switch. Bright fluorescent light fills the kitchen. Clutching the edge of the chrome prep stations, I slowly make my way to the pantry. To my delight, I find a few bottled waters and bags of chips. Sinking to my knees, I snatch up a water. My hands are weak, my palms wet, so it takes several frustrating tries to screw the top off. Once I do, I pour the glorious water down my throat, savoring each drop. Then I tear open a bag of Doritos and pop a salty chip into my mouth.

I eat and drink too swiftly and pretty soon my stomach cramps and spasms violently. Oh, shit.

Clutching my middle, I limp to the bathroom. After getting sick, I rest my head against the wall. My eyes sting with exhaustion. Craving relief, I close them. I need one second. That's all.

Just…one…second.

So much for one second. Judging by the crick in my neck, I slept much longer than that. Dragging my gaze up the wall, I locate the window near the ceiling. It's fully dark now.

My ankle throbs. I lift my pant leg. The skin is puffy and swollen, turning purple.

I groan. *Great.*

In the cabinet I find a first-aid kit. Inside it is a bandage that I pull out and wrap my ankle with as best I can. Exiting the bathroom, I glance to my left and spot an open supply closet. It's filled with buckets, mops and cleaning supplies. But on the far wall are several hooks, and dangling from one is a key ring filled with keys. I snatch it up. Letters are on each one: DH, A, C, GR and finally there is one marked O.

O for office.

Before leaving the kitchen, I take a few more careful sips of water. I'm not sure my stomach can handle any more chips, so I don't push it. After exiting the dining hall, I pass a row of cabins. On the opposite side is the volleyball and badminton court; beyond that the spot on the lake where I'd almost broken my neck being shot from the blob by Steve and Thomas Rutherford. They thought they were so funny.

The tall steeple of the chapel appears. When I get closer, I see the porch and the cross hanging over the front door. I envisioned Dad walking through the doors, Bible tucked under his arm. Often, he gave a message to the students on the last day of camp. He and Mom would come up early on the day they were supposed to pick me up. It was my least favorite day. Not only because I had to go home, but also because I knew I was being watched, scrutinized. It was no longer a place that felt like vacation—free and fun. It suddenly felt constricting, like a prison. Like home.

Dad's message was essentially the same each summer. Something about taking the passion from camp into our everyday lives, living out the principles of God. No sinning and all that…yada, yada, yada. It was so embarrassing.

Next to the chapel are more cabins. I picture Mara and me sitting on the steps, chatting and laughing. Finally, the office comes into view right past the auditorium, light shining like a beacon. Anxious, I force myself to walk a little faster. The bandage that seemed to keep my ankle steady at the beginning of the walk now feels loose, and my ankle throbs once again. A heartbeat in my foot.

But I can't afford to give up now. I'm almost there.

I yank the key ring out of my pocket and find the one marked with the O. I stick it in the lock and turn. The familiar scent of musty wood and pencil shavings fill me with nostalgia. I make a beeline for the front desk, finding the phone right where it's always been, wedged between the computer screen and a cup filled with pencils.

I pick up the phone and press it to my ear. But there's no dial tone.

What?

Did it come unplugged?

My gaze follows the cord from the phone to the wall.

No, it can't be.

I yank at it, staring at the severed edge. It's been cut. But who—?

Why was the light on?

Who had turned the light on?

I whirl around, and something on the floor catches my attention. A photo. I bend over. It's me, here at camp. I'm around fourteen. The last time I'd seen this picture it was tacked to the collage in my bedroom.

Oh, my God.

I slap my hand over my mouth, panic inching its way up my esophagus.

He's here somewhere.

He's found me.

46

THE MOTHER

Present

Grace Camp?

Why did he come here?

He drives into the parking lot, but I stay back, idling behind a tree. I can't see past it, but I know what's there. The main office, the cabins, the shore with its volleyball net and canoes pressed into the wet sand. Curtis and Adrienne loved coming here. They'd take a bus to get here, but then Shane and I would come up on the last day. Parents' Day. A chance for the kids to show their families what they'd been up to. We'd come up early in the morning and spend the day. Shane would speak. I'd chat with the other parents and explore the camp with the kids. There was always so much activity. Cars filling the lot. Kids shrieking. Parents talking. Balloons, tethered to the fences, swayed in the breeze like hands waving. Signs painted in cheery colors—reds and greens and yellows— welcomed us.

Tonight there is none of that.

It's quiet.

Dark.

The camp isn't running this time of year. They'll open back up in a month or so. No one's here.

We'd only just told Seth about the camp tonight. And he hadn't acted like he'd known about it prior. He'd asked a lot of questions. They'd seemed to be nothing more than curiosity at the time, but were they more than that?

And if so, what?

What is he hoping to find here?

I turn off my car. Staring out the dirty front windshield, I take a deep breath. My phone still isn't working, but I shove it into my pocket as I step out into the cool night air, closing the door quietly behind me. From what I remember, cell service is spotty, but there are places where you can find it.

I step lightly up to the bushy tree in front of me and peek around it. Seth's car is parked, empty, engine off. I scurry forward, gaze sweeping the area around me. Lights are on in the main office. Was I wrong? Are people here?

My skin is cold and clammy. My teeth chatter and I stamp my mouth shut to try to stop it, but they continue to knock together behind my lips.

Something doesn't feel right.

The soles of my shoes crunch over pine needles and leaves. I slow down a little, aware of each sound I'm making. I don't know where Seth went. Gaze aimed at the light, I squint. Is he in the main office? Bending over slightly and keeping close to the trees, I move closer to it.

A figure appears in the window, yellow light glowing behind her like a spotlight.

I draw in a breath.

Adrienne.

My feet speed up.

I open my mouth to call out her name when another figure appears. I close my mouth, swallowing the word whole.

Seth.

I stop, frozen, a block of ice. I'm not sure what's going on. Did he find her? Or was this always the plan?

My head spins. It's been spinning ever since Adrienne went missing.

All the information. All the clues. They've left me more confused. I know what I've seen. The photos of Adrienne and Seth. And he has so much knowledge about her. So many things that only someone close to her would know. And yet, there's been something about him that I can't quite put my finger on that has felt off somehow.

I look up again, studying my daughter. Seth is across the room. Her back is to him. She doesn't see him. Doesn't know he's there. I'm sure of it. I squint. Seth is holding something. Shiny. Metal. Is it a gun?

My heart pounds. Adrienne is reaching for the phone.

Then she's drenched in darkness. I stifle a scream.

I can't alert Seth that I'm here. He has a gun and he's alone in the dark with my daughter. My only hope of saving her is by staying quiet. Staying incognito.

Heat rushes to the surface of my skin as if I've just stepped out of a hot shower. I yank my phone out of my pocket, fingers stinging as I rake them over the rough denim fabric. With slick, shaky fingers I punch in the numbers 911. But it's no use. It won't go through.

I can't see anything in the office windows. No movement. Only darkness.

I've come so far. I can't give up now.

I race to my left, zipping behind a row of cabins that lead to the main office. Behind the cabins I hold the phone up in the air, silently praying for a signal. I move to the left and to the right, the phone in my hand like the glow from a lighthouse, its beam shining on the path before me. I'm grateful for it. There's a creek somewhere back here. I'd found Adrienne and Mara back here once throwing rocks into it.

I'm rounding on the last cabin when it happens.

A signal!

I don't dare move an inch. Carefully, I dial 911 and hold the phone up to my ear.

47

THE DAUGHTER

Present

"So this is where you spent your summers as a child?" Seth steps out from behind the shadows, spinning the gun in his hand. "Your mom told me all about it. She and I—we've been getting pretty close."

"What?" I blink. It's not what I expected him to say. "My mom? H-h-how did that happen?" I think about our Wednesday night tradition. Seth had known about that. Had he somehow used that to his advantage? But no, he was with me on Wednesday night. My head whirled.

"We were working together to find you. You know, since I'm your fiancé and all."

"You told my mom we're engaged?"

"No, one of your friends did." He steps a little closer. I back up.

Jazzy. It had to have been her. She'd referred to Seth as my fiancé one night and I hadn't corrected her.

Why hadn't I corrected her?

I should have.

"She's nice, your mom. A little too trusting, but…" Smiling, he shrugs. "Met your dad, too. Had dinner with them, actually."

My eyes widen. I feel like I might fall over from shock, or maybe just from how unstable my ankle is. He was with my parents?

Mom and I had been getting closer. Did she really believe I'd keep a fiancé from her? Although, I guess the truth is I had kept Seth from her. I wish now I could take that back. If only I'd told her about him. Every detail.

Then she'd know about his unsettling behavior. How I'd been a little scared of him.

That I'd broken up with him.

Maybe she'd even have suspected him when I went missing.

"Wait," I say, my chest loosening. "You said you'd been helping my mom. So she knows I'm missing. She's been looking for me."

I knew it. I'd been right.

"She's not looking for you," he says coldly. "Not tonight. Trust me."

My stomach drops. It's because of him. Because she thought he was my fiancé, and she trusted him. She knows I'm missing. She's worried about me like I'd hoped. But she doesn't suspect the one person she should.

She's not looking in the right place.

And it's my fault.

I wrap my arms together, wrists brushing the same way they had when they were tied with duct tape. I think about Nate in the trunk, and I briefly wonder if he made it out alive. I don't have a lot of hope that he did.

His words from a few seconds ago flash in my mind, sending a shiver up my spine. *She's not looking for you. Trust me.*

Is there a more sinister reason she's not looking for me?

"Where is she now? My mom?" The panicked words burst from my throat. "Is she safe?"

"She's fine."

Thank God. I sigh, my shoulders visibly sagging with relief.

He shakes his head. "Is that really what you think of me, Adrienne? You think I'm someone who would hurt your mom? He really brainwashed you, didn't he?"

"He didn't need to brainwash me. You tied—"

"Were you fucking him?"

His words are sharp like a blade as they cut through mine. I flinched. "No." The minute the word leaves my mouth, I know it's a mistake. It's too weak. Too unsure. He'll see right through it.

He exhales loudly. "You're a bad liar." Another step forward.

I'm running out of steps back, the wall almost at my spine. And, dear God, I want off this ankle.

"Nate's a liar, too. But you believed him over me."

"No," I say firmly. "I didn't... I... That's why I went to see you... I thought you'd prove him wrong."

"You tricked me once, Adrienne. I won't let you do it again." His tone is hard. Unforgiving.

My insides tremble. I'm not sure what to say. What to do. I glance around. There has to be an exit nearby. There's a window behind me, but it's closed, and most likely, locked up tight. I'll never be able to distract him long enough to unlock it and climb out, especially not with my ankle like this. I can't move fast enough. Picturing it almost causes an irrational laugh to bubble up. I swallow it down.

The door is on the other side of him. He's closer to it than I am.

So the exits are out.

What's plan B?

I chew the inside of my cheek.

A weapon. That's what I need.

I scan the desk to my right. Pencil holder? Pencil? Stapler? Paperweight? To use any of these, I have to be less than a foot from him. And there's not enough margin for error.

Then there's the issue of the gun.

He has one.

I don't.

None of these will work against a gun.

I'm trapped. Again.

I got out last time. Escaped the duct tape and his car. I can do it now, too. I have more of an advantage. I'm not tied up. And I know the camp better than he does.

I just have to keep him talking. Keep him engaged. Long enough to figure out a plan. A way out.

"Come on, Seth, please just put down the gun so we can talk."

"It's too late for that."

"It's not too late," I say, trying to catch his eyes. He'd said he loved me. I just need him to remember that. "Come on, it's me, Adrienne. We can work this out."

"Stop fuckin' lying!" he snarls and I jolt. "God, you're just like her. You're all like her."

"Anna?" I guess.

"No," he says darkly. "My mom."

He'd never told me anything about his mom before tonight. Or his dad. His family had always been a mystery to me. Anytime I'd tried to ask he'd skirt the question or change the subject.

"I caught her," he says, his eyes a little glazed over as if lost in his memories. A part of me wonders if now is the right time to try to escape, but his eyes and the gun are still directed at me. So I stay still, grateful that he's talking to me, at least. "The day she left Dad. I was coming down the stairs when she was heading out the front door. At first, I hadn't thought anything of it. Like, she was off to run errands or something. But then I saw the suitcase. I asked if she was leaving, and she told me she had to. I cried, begging her not to leave. And you know what she said?" His expression was hard. Angry. But there were tears in his eyes. "She said she loved me and that she'd be back to get me as soon as she could. God, what a fuckin' load of bullshit." His hand slammed down on the file cabinet. "She never came back. Started a whole new god-damn family, a new son and everything. She chose that other man over Dad, and then she chose their son over me." His gaze found mine then and the dark look he gave me caused a shiver to run through my body. "And you're all like her. Anna. Carolyn. Jane. You." He laughs bitterly. "I gave Anna everything, and she threw it all away for one night with some other asshole. Chose someone else just like my mom had."

"But Jane and Carolyn, they didn't cheat on you...they cheated *with* you."

"Yeah, but they betrayed the men who they'd promised to love, so they're no better than the rest."

"I never betrayed you, though," I say gently. "We weren't engaged. I hadn't even said I loved you, because I..." I pause, praying I'm playing this right. It's a risk, but I have to try. "I never wanted to lie to you. I wanted to always be honest."

"That's what I thought you were, Adrienne. Honest. It's why I fell for you. Why I fought for you. Because I thought you were different. And that's why this is so goddamn hard. You're worse than the rest," he grinds out.

"What? No, how am I worse?"

"You betrayed me with him. Nate. You tried to trick me."

Nate. "Where is he? Is he—is he okay?" The minute the words are out, I know they're wrong.

He lets out a bitter laugh and shakes his head. "I'm done talking." He presses his finger down on the trigger.

48

THE MOTHER

Present

I creep around the back of the main office building. It looms overhead, large and imposing. Scared, my heart clatters in my chest, my pulse so fast it's like a race car at a speedway. If only the police were here. But we're deep in the woods. It will take them a little while to find us.

Swallowing hard, I think of all the unanswered texts and calls from Shane. I wish I'd called him back sooner. Not ignored his calls when they first started coming in. If he were here, he'd know what to do.

I lean my back against the side of the building and exhale. Squeezing my eyes shut I say a silent prayer.

Eyelids flipping open, I think I hear a sound in the distance. Sirens?

No, it can't be.

I chomp down on my lower lip. There's no one here to help me. To consult with. To lean on. I'm all alone. My daughter's life is in my hands.

Come on, Tatum. You can do this. You don't need anyone else.

Gathering up all my strength and courage, I push off the wall, stand up straight. When I face the building, there is a window to my left. I lean over, peeking into it. I see a desk, a computer screen, a chair, some boxes on the ground, then movement. Holding my breath, I fling my head back behind the building and pray he didn't see me.

I don't know if I can do this.

I can't afford to mess up. I have to get Adrienne out of here.

After pulling in a few long, cleansing breaths, I peek back in. This time I find them right away. He's got a gun on her. She has her palms up as if warding off an attack. Her mouth is moving, and I detect a tremble to her lips. Her hands are shaky, too. I want to lunge inside and scoop her into my arms. Press her to my chest. Protect her the way I did when she was a child.

But it's not that simple.

Not tonight.

I'd met Seth less than a handful of times. But each time he was friendly, charming. His smile was affecting, just the right amount of kindness and concern. None of that is visible right now. His expression is hardened, his mouth a tight line, his eyes narrowed. The hand not holding the gun is fisted at his side and his jaw is clenched. Anger radiates off him like a heater on full blast.

I can see what Adrienne is trying to do. The way her mouth moves while her gaze repeatedly flickers down to the gun. She's trying to talk her way out of this. Maybe soften him a little.

Adrienne is smart. Street-smart. And savvy. Much more so than I am. But even Adrienne can't beat a gun.

And with how angry Seth appears, I'm not sure the conversation is working.

She needs my help. It's cold out here. Bitterly cold. It bites at my fingers as if I'm holding them up to a block of ice. I roll them into my palm and study the window in front of me. It's shut tight and locked. I move around to the other side of the building. There's a back entrance. I'm certain it's locked, too, but I try, anyway. My skin stings as I grip the handle. The door shocks me by swinging toward me. And that's when I notice the lock is broken, the door frame split on one side. This must be how Seth got in.

I swallow hard. It was so violent the way he broke in. As if he was taking his anger out on the door. If this is what he did to an inanimate object, what will he do when he gets his hands on my daughter? I don't want to find out.

With slow movements I open the door a sliver. It creaks a little and I wince. Stop. Wait. I hear voices.

"God, what a fuckin' load of bullshit," Seth says.

They hadn't heard me. Thank God. I push the door open a tiny bit more until I can slide my body through. It's not much warmer in here, but at least in here I'm shielded from the breeze. I wonder where Adrienne has been the past few days. Was she inside? Was she here at camp the entire time? It seems unlikely. If so, there would have been a way to reach us. But it's what I want to believe. That she's been here where she's had food and shelter.

I want to believe she was hiding out.

Not imprisoned.

But if that's the case, if she was hiding from Seth, then I'm to blame. I'm the one who led him here.

My mind is like the teacup ride at Disneyland. Adrienne loved that ride. I hated it. Always felt like I would puke. I'd clutch the sides and pray for it to be over. That's what I feel like now. I want this to be over. I want off the ride.

I want this to make sense.

But none of it does.

I'm confused about why Adrienne's here. Why Seth's here. What's going on?

I'm hidden behind a file cabinet. I sink down onto my knees, dare a peek around the side.

"I gave Anna everything, and she threw it all away for one night with some other asshole. Chose someone else just like my mom had."

"But Jane and Carolyn, they didn't cheat on you...they cheated with you."

"Yeah, but they betrayed the men who they'd promised to love, so they're no better than the rest."

"I never betrayed you, though," Adrienne is saying, forehead pinched together so severely it's like the skin is being held together by a safety pin. It's clear she's been through hell. The only light in here is from the moonlight shining in from the windows, so I can't get a good look at her. But her hair is messy, her eyes lacking their usual sparkle; her voice is weak and tired.

My heart pinches. I want to gather her into my arms. To make it all okay.

But I can't.

Not yet.

I recall the way she'd run to me when I picked her up from camp. The way she'd grin from ear to ear as I drew her to me.

"I never wanted to lie to you. I wanted to always be honest."

"That's what I thought you were, Adrienne. Honest. It's why I fell for you. Why I fought for you. Because I thought you were different. And that's why this is so goddamn hard. You're worse than the rest," he grinds out so forcefully I involuntarily jump. My head hits the file cabinet. Smarts. I reach up to touch it. I hold my breath, my fingers caressing my scalp.

"What? No, how am I worse?"

Now's the time to make my move. He's not that far from me. I just need something heavy. Something I can hit him in the head with. I can use the element of surprise. Once he's down, Adrienne and I can run. By that time, hopefully, the police will be here.

"You betrayed me with him. Nate. You tried to trick me."

I venture out from behind the file cabinet, crawling along the carpet on my hands and knees. The carpet is rough. The industrial kind and it repeatedly snags on my nails and the toes of my shoes. There is a desk in front of me.

"Where is he? Is he—is he okay?" Adrienne asks.

My time is up. I have to make my move now.

I hoist myself up, flinging my arm onto the desk, my hands fumbling with the contents. And then I find it. A paperweight.

"I'm done talking. I'm done with your bullshit," he's saying. "I'm done with you."

I grab it, step back. My heel hits something hard. Unmoving. A box? I pitch to the side. Flailing, I hold my hands out to catch my fall. They slam against the desk. I brace myself.

"Who's there?"

I freeze at Seth's question.

His neck swivels in my direction. I duck down, holding tight to the paperweight.

"Hello? I know you're there," he says again. I hear a footfall. Then another.

I aim my gaze at the back door, take a deep breath and lunge toward it.

"Stop now or I'll shoot!" Seth hollers.

I halt, glance over my shoulder.

But the gun is pointed at Adrienne, not me. Her hand is on the front doorknob. She must've been trying to use my distraction to her advantage. Her eyes meet mine, and they widen. I shake my head. He picks up on it and he looks toward me.

"Go!" I scream to Adrienne, but she doesn't. "Go!" I yell again and this time I hurl the paperweight in his direction. It's been so many years since I've played any kind of sport or thrown a ball. Curtis wasn't into sports much, and the few times he did want to play catch it was with his dad. I walked a lot but that doesn't require a lot of arm strength. I feel the lack of it now. The way my muscles scream from the sheer force. It's no use, anyway. The paperweight misses Seth completely, crashing instead onto the ground.

The gun goes off.

No!

I look to the door. It's wide open, swaying in the wind. But no Adrienne. She listened. Relief fills me. I whirl around, blindly running toward the back door. Another gunshot.

Pain. Hot, searing pain. It shoots down my arm.

I clutch it, stumbling out into the cold. I don't know how badly I'm hurt. But I just keep running.

49

THE DAUGHTER

Present

A gunshot rings out. My muscles tighten. Cold dread pulses through me.

Mom!

I shouldn't have left her.

Oh God oh God oh God.

Wind whips through the trees, leaves rustling. My nerves are frayed; every sound ratcheting up my panic. I hurry forward, zipping through the brush and tree trunks until I reach the side of the building. Mom bursts out in front of me. And I exhale.

"Oh, thank God," I say, rushing toward her with the urge to fall into her embrace. It's an urge I haven't had since I was a small child, and the emotion it brings forth surprises me. But then my feet falter, my ankle weakening. Adrenaline had momentarily masked the pain, but now it was back, ignited by the reality of Mom's situation.

She's not okay. Her arm is bleeding. The arm she holds close to her body. It hangs unnaturally, reminding me of the fabric dolls I carried around as a child.

"Mom, you're hurt," I say.

But she shakes her head, glancing over her shoulder. "He's coming," she whispers harshly. Her eyes are wild and her body shakes. Even in the moonlight I can tell how pale her face is. Despite how grateful I am that she's here, I also feel so much shame for putting her in this situation. I know she's had her health struggles. I never wanted to add to those.

"Let's go." I hear his footsteps crunching on the leaves and twigs as we run to the front of the building. Mom is moving slow. Her breathing is a little shallow. We won't make it far.

"I called them," she says quietly between labored breaths. "The police. They're coming."

I look around. We need to find a place to hide out. The cabins have first-aid kits. If we can get inside one, maybe we'll be safe until help arrives.

It's worth a shot.

We sprint to the other side of the nearest building and cut backward. Back to where we came from. Seth won't expect us to do that. At least, I hope he doesn't.

Who knows what's going on in his mind? He's not who I thought he was. I can't predict his movements. I can't predict anything.

But I can try.

Tugging on Mom's good arm, I run straight for the nearest cabin. I'd left the keys in the main office. Set them down when I reached for the phone. The one that was dead. But it doesn't matter, anyway. I didn't have any keys for the cabins. As our feet clomp over the dirt and leaves, I keep peeking over my shoulder, making sure he's not gaining on us. There's no sign of him, but an apprehensive prickle tingles up my spine, anyway. He could be anywhere.

We reach the cabin and I guide us around the back. Mom's teeth chatter. She's lost a lot of blood. I place both hands on her shoulders, look into her eyes. She's fading. My heart pinches.

"Stay here. I'm gonna get us inside, okay?"

She doesn't say a word, just slumps down, her butt hitting the hard ground. I've never seen my mom like this, and it scares me. I worry she's giving up. I can't let her.

"I'll be right back," I say. Adrenaline surging, I scour the area around me. A few feet away is a large rock. It worked before; it'll work again. I pick it up and head toward the window above the door. Then I launch the rock at it, smothering my head with my hands. The glass pops and shatters loudly into the silence. I pause for a moment, listening, but I hear nothing over the thumping of my heart and my intense breathing.

I crane my neck around the side of the building. Mom is still there, but her head is falling forward, her chin hitting her chest.

Oh, God, I've got to get us inside. If he finds us now, it's over.

It's still quiet. No sirens or other noises. Where are the police?

We're far from Rio Villa. It could be a while, and panic claws at my insides. I can't give in to it, though. I'm so tired and weak. But I have to stay strong. Fight, just a little bit longer.

As before, I pull my sweatshirt down over my hand and dip it inside, feeling around for the lock. A surge of relief runs through me like an electrical current when my fingers fold around it. I'm an old pro now. I turn it, then yank my arm back. Heat flies through my wrist. Shit. I got too cocky and now dark blood seeps through the fabric of my sweatshirt. I sniff. Breathe.

No time.

I turn the knob and swing open the door. Then hobble toward Mom.

"Come on." I bend down and wrap my arms around her body. Using all my strength, I hoist her up. It takes several tries. "You gotta help me, Mom." I've always thought of my mom as frail and small, but maybe that was how she made her-self appear. She's not that tiny in stature. And right now she feels like a ton of bricks. Then again, my strength is drained.

Grunting, I get her up to a standing position. Then I push her toward the door.

I've never been so relieved to be inside anywhere before. I feel the sense of it flow through me as I close the door firmly behind us. The window is broken so cool air spills inside, and it's not like we're protected. But the door faces the woods, not the main building or the inner part of the camp. If we're lucky, Seth will never venture over here.

Still, I silently pray again that the police come quickly. The smart thing to do would be to keep moving. Not stay in one place. But Mom's in no condition to run around the camp.

I lay her down on one of the lower bunks.

It's strange being in here after all these years. The place of fun and adventure where I spent my summers. Tonight it's like something out of a horror movie. An adventure for sure, but not the fun I remember.

Mom whimpers. I touch her face. It's warm.

"I'm gonna find the first-aid kit, okay?"

"The police. Where are they?" The words tumble from her mouth in a desperate rush.

"I'm sure they'll be here any minute." I pause, my hand pressed to her cheek, the same way she used to caress mine when I was sick as a child. She's always been there for me. I've never given her enough credit. I feel shame about it now. "Mom." My fingers sweep up into her hair. "Thank you for—"

A twig snaps outside. Leaves rustle.

I whirl around, hoping it's the wind and nothing more. Another snap. Another rustle. Each one causes my muscles to tighten. They're so tight, they're like a rubber band pulled past the point of return, about to break.

I stand up slowly, carefully, eyes pinned to the window. A gust of wind spills inside, rushes through the small space, a wave smothering the shoreline. My muscles soften somewhat. I limp toward the bathroom and once inside I lower down onto my knees and rummage in the cabinet under the sink. I can't see anything. I hadn't dared to turn on any lights.

My fingertips light on a plastic box and I scoot it out. I trail my fingers down the edges until they catch on a buckle. I loosen it, pry open the lid. Inside, I feel for bandages and rubbing alcohol. After filling up my palms with supplies, I stand, my knees cracking, my thighs on fire. For a moment dizziness overtakes me. I lean my head against the wall, waiting for it to subside.

A thump.

I flinch.

Another thump.

Only not a thump. A footstep.

Has Mom gotten up?

Cold dread slides down my spine. Shivering, I move away from the wall and into the doorway. My breath catches in my throat. Seth stands in the middle of the room, gun in hand. My gaze shoots to the bed. It's empty. The contents in my hand fall to the floor.

Where's Mom?

"I'm done playing games." He releases the safety.

The bathroom is windowless. There's nowhere to run. Nowhere to hide. I'm trapped. Even if I close the door, a bullet can penetrate that.

As his finger presses down, I squeeze my eyes shut, steeling myself.

I hear a bang, a grunt and then a thud. But no gunshot.

My eyelids fly open. Seth is on the ground. Mom stands over him, a canoe oar in hand. She's swaying unsteadily on her feet. She drops the oar and it clatters to the ground.

"Oh, my God, Mom." I go to her, take her into my arms. Her skin is hot. As the tears begin to fall down my face, I hear other sounds in the distance. Tires. Car doors. Voices.

Thank God help is here.

50

THE FIANCÉ

A month later

I stand at the water's edge, foam covering my toes. The sun is hot. The wave recedes and my feet sink into the shoreline. When it returns, the cold is shocking as water sprays my ankles and lower calves. I'm home. Or at least, back to the place I'd once thought of as home.

Where home really is, is up to me, I guess.

I'd thought it would be with Carolyn. When I proposed, I had planned to make a life, a home, wherever she did. Wherever she wanted. All I needed was her. Not a town or location. That's what I told her. It's how I got her to say yes the second time I proposed. I promised to take her wherever she wanted. Far from the town she wished to escape. I know now that she wasn't saying yes to me as much as she was saying no to them. Her family. Her town.

I'd given up everything to give her what she wanted. I'd borrowed money from my dad, more than I ever had before. It was humiliating. And he made sure I knew it. Told me I wouldn't be welcome if I came back. That I was an embarrassment. But I'd thought it was worth it. To have enough money to start a life with Carolyn. Buy her her dream house in her dream city.

After her death, I'd used that money to live off as I spent all my time investigating her murder.

Staring out at the familiar dark blue waters of the Beach Boardwalk, chatter and laughter swirling around me, I shove my right hand into my pocket. They're not the same pants I was wearing when the hikers found me. Today I'm in shorts and flip-flops, a T-shirt. The unofficial California-boy uniform. But I remember with clarity the moment I was given my things at the hospital and saw the engagement ring and butterfly necklace in the clear plastic bag.

"Where did that come from?" I asked.

"Your pocket," the nurse replied.

And that was when it all came flooding back to me. Breaking into Seth's, recording the conversation, stealing the ring and necklace. Being attacked. Hikers finding me.

The nurse called the police in for me. I told them everything. Gave them all the evidence, including the recording Seth thought he got rid of when he took our phones. As if I was stupid enough not to save it to the cloud.

Finally, after months and months of investigating and searching, I'd done it. I'd gotten justice for Carolyn.

For Jane.

For Anna.

For Adrienne.

And for me.

He's behind bars where he fucking belongs.

A shadow casts over me, a bird flying overhead. I think about that damn butterfly. The one that made Carolyn smile so brightly.

The one I had made into a necklace.

I'll never forget the moment I fastened the necklace to her

neck. How my thumb had caressed her soft skin, and it made her giggle. She'd touched the pendant with shiny, lacquered nails. *Red.* The same color she'd worn the night she'd gone out with Seth.

Stop. Stop, she'd pleaded, wiggling and clawing.

I blink. Swallow.

Touch the collar on my T-shirt, look at a kid walking past, listen to the waves, smell the ocean breeze. Try with all my might to engage all five senses. But it's no use.

The images continue to come.

Carolyn screaming and kicking, her red nails scratching. Scratching. Scratching. So hard they drew blood. And yet, not hard enough.

Her face red. Redder than her nails.

Her screams softening, her hands stilling, her eyes bulging.

I shake my head firmly as if to knock the images loose.

I thought once Seth was locked up, once I'd proven it was him, they'd vanish. Leave me alone, finally.

But it seems they're coming faster now. More frequently.

As if to be sure I can't outrun them.

If only I hadn't followed them that night. But I couldn't help it. I'd seen her with him. And I was angry.

She was mine.

We were going to be married. Be a family.

I was finally going to have the family I always wanted. The family I'd dreamt of.

But she was ruining that. She was throwing it all away... for him.

I wanted to be angrier with him than I was with her, but she was the one who betrayed me. And the anger I felt toward her was unlike any other I'd felt before. I'd lived my entire life with a quiet rage under my skin, flowing through my veins. Rage at my mom for force-feeding me flashcards and words and math problems. Rage at Dad for his disappointed head shakes and pointed fingers.

I'd kept it inside all these years—only allowing it to play out in my fantasies—I'd never unleashed it in real life.

But that night it unfurled like steam from a fire.

I didn't know what I planned to do. Only that I couldn't look the other way. So I followed them. Saw much more than I wanted to. Saw her kiss him and touch him. Saw him kiss her and start to touch her. The rage surfaced.

I saw myself tearing out of the car, running toward them. Shoving him off her and then grabbing her by the neck, squeezing the life out of her, the butterfly pendant crushing beneath the weight of my hands.

And then she was screaming, choking, flailing.

I released my hands, shot backward. But it had only been the steering wheel beneath my fingers. I wasn't the one with my hands around her neck.

It was him.

The hand he'd used to slide up her chest was now around her neck. And it was clear from her expression that it wasn't some type of sex move. He was hurting her.

At first, I was in shock. I closed my eyes and opened them again, certain I was hallucinating. It felt like a movie. Not like real life.

But then an odd calm fell over me.

She deserved it.

She had done this to herself.

Those were the horrible thoughts that went through my mind. To this day, I like to think it was the shock talking. It was all so surreal. Like an out-of-body experience. I can't be expected to explain my behavior. No one should ever have to experience something like that.

It only took a few moments before I snapped out of it. I was no longer angry. I just wanted to save her. But it was too late. She was limp in his arms. He was carrying her toward the water.

I should have stopped him, but I didn't.

Oh, God. I didn't stop him.

I could have done something, but I didn't.

What kind of monster am I?

Body trembling as if I was having a seizure, I reached for the door handle and pressed it open. Cool air spilled into the car, and I sucked it in. Dizziness swept over me.

I lurched forward and the acidic contents of my stomach spilled out of my mouth. Sitting up, I wiped my chin with the back of my hand.

I almost jumped out of the car then. Almost confronted him. But what good would that do? What kind of man kills a woman in the middle of the night, outside on the cliffs near the ocean? If he knew I saw, wouldn't he kill me, too? People die on these cliffs all the time. One push and it'd be over for me, and no one would ever know what had happened to her.

I securely closed my door and reached for my cell. I'd call the police, turn him in.

My finger punched 9-1...and then I stopped.

What would I say?

If I told them what I saw, was I an accessory?

Oh, God, there's no good answer here.

In the end, I went home. I waited.

Eventually, Carolyn's family and coworkers reported her missing. And then her body was found. I became a suspect, and my alibi sucked, especially since a neighbor had seen me drive off that night.

My only hope of putting this behind me and seeking justice for Carolyn was to make sure Seth went down for it.

It's not like I did anything wrong.

He's the monster.

He's the one who killed her...and so many other women.

The world is a safer place without him.

And I'm now free.

Free to make a life for myself.

Free to fall in love. And this time I'll be sure it's with the right person. Someone I can really trust.

51

THE MOTHER

"You okay, Mom?" Adrienne turns, her hair whipping around her face from the warm breeze.

I nod, breathing deeply. Sweat gathers under the bandage on my arm as we make our way up the sandy hill.

When we make it to the top, the beach comes into view. At this time of the morning there are only a smattering of people, brightly colored towels sprinkling the sand like seashells. Later today our towels will join them. We're planning to grab fish tacos for lunch and then spend the afternoon lying on the beach and splashing in the waves.

"It's so beautiful," Adrienne says, staring out at the water. "I never get tired of it."

We'd been in San Diego for two weeks now. The minute the doctors gave me the green light, Adrienne and I packed up and headed out. We needed a break. Time to recover. Time to heal. Physically and mentally.

After the police arrived at Camp Grace, they hauled all three of us to the hospital. Once I'd received medical care, I gave my statement. Adrienne had already given hers. Apparently, she'd been working with a guy—Nate—to bring Seth down. Nate. The guy Seth had told me about. The one from the bar.

It all makes sense now. Why Seth was so desperate to find Adrienne and Nate. They'd escaped from him. He wanted to finish what he'd started. It chilled me to the bone to think about it. To think about what might have happened.

How I could have lost her.

But I didn't.

She's here. She's safe. We're together.

When I reach her, I grab her hand, squeeze her cold fingers. The wind blows through us, but we are immovable, mother and daughter. Just like we were that night at Camp Grace. Images from that night play in a constant loop in my mind. From my vantage point on the bed, I'd seen Seth coming through the open window. I'd tried to alert Adrienne, but my throat was so scratchy and weak, my voice didn't carry into the bathroom. It was clear by his determined gait that he knew we were in there. No doubt the broken window gave us away. I was in pain, and tired. So tired. All I wanted to do was lie there. A part of me was ready to give in to my fate. But I couldn't do that to Adrienne.

My baby girl was in there. And she was counting on me.

My teeth chattered as I pushed myself up off the bed. I flung myself down onto the ground and crawled on my belly, using my elbows to propel me forward. An army-crawl. A canoe oar was propped against the opposite wall. I'd seen it when we first entered. I crawled past the door and made it to the oar. Then I forced myself to stand. After grabbing the oar, I held it to my chest and pressed my back into the wall. My arm ached, my head felt swimmy and my skin was freezing. I could barely stand, my legs trembling.

Breathing deeply, I waited.

I only had one shot to get it right.

His footsteps were getting closer, stomping over dirt and

leaves, a child storming off in anger. When he burst through the door, I was ready. I raised the oar over my head and then lowered it down onto the back of his head with all the force I could muster. My wounded shoulder cried out. I knew I'd damaged it further, but I had no choice. The relief I felt when his body slumped to the ground was like nothing I'd ever experienced before. My entire body sagged as if I'd turned into a rag doll, bones nothing more than fabric stitched together.

Now he was sitting behind bars, rotting away in a jail cell, where he belonged. Tony assured me that there was enough evidence to convict him. I hoped he spent the rest of his life in prison. Often, I thought about how he'd been in my home. How I'd served him a meal, chatted with him, hugged him, treated him like family. I felt like a fool.

But I don't talk about it much. I know Adrienne struggles with her own complicated feelings of shame, guilt and foolishness. It's why I brought her here, to the place she'd wanted to be for so long. I figured a change of scenery would do her good.

And it has.

It's been good for both of us.

My phone buzzes in my pocket. I yank it out, read the text.

Good morning.

"Is that Dad?" Adrienne asks, her head bobbing down to the cell in my hand. When she used to say the word *Dad* it came out sharply, bitter edges of broken glass. Now the edges have softened a bit.

I'd always thought it was anger that fueled Adrienne. Anger at her dad and me, at religion. But it wasn't. It was her desire to be seen. For who she truly is. For who she truly wants to be.

And I get that. We all want—need, even—to forge our own path in life.

"Yes," I answer as I type back the same words in response: Good morning.

I don't know what will happen with our marriage. What will happen with us. But he's giving me space right now, to breathe and think, and I'm grateful for that. I've been so angry. Have felt trapped and alone. I need some time to untangle my thoughts. To just be.

I don't have all the answers, and I probably never will.

But I do know one thing: Adrienne and I are okay. We're alive.

"I prayed out in those woods," Adrienne confessed to me the other night. "First time in years, and I don't know. I kinda felt like someone was listening."

I nodded, understanding. I'd prayed, too, that night at the camp.

And here we are. Survivors.

I stare out at the sea, at the waves crashing into the shore. I've always felt most at peace near the water. Nature has been the place where I feel God.

I feel Him now. I do believe, maybe in a different way than I did before, but I do.

With my daughter's hand in mine, and the salty sea air whipping around my head, I feel happy. Content. Free.

★ ★ ★ ★ ★

ACKNOWLEDGMENTS

A couple of years ago, I began a season of deconstructing the belief system that I'd clung to my entire life. Things that had always felt certain to me no longer were, and that left me untethered and confused. That was my frame of mind when I started writing this story. As I wrote, I slipped under Tatum's skin, becoming her…or probably more accurately, she became me. This is, by far, the most personal I've gotten in a novel. Not only does Tatum's journey of deconstruction line up closely with mine, but her health journey mirrors mine exactly, down to the day the world spun around me and never stopped. There are also a lot of differences. Our spouses, for instance. My husband is loving and empowering, nothing like Shane. Tatum's story is not really my story. Most of it is her own, but I'm woven in there in the mystery, in some of the doubt, and, certainly, in some of her conviction. I hope you've enjoyed her story. I appreciate you reading.

I'm always grateful to you, the reader, for supporting me and allowing me to live my dream.

This book never would've been possible without the following people:

Ellen Coughtrey, my amazing literary agent, who pores through every draft, spends countless hours brainstorming with me and keeps me on track. I can't thank you enough. And to Will Roberts, Rebecca Gardner, Anna Worrall, Nora Gonzalez and the entire Gernert Team, thank you for all you do for me and my books. It does not go unnoticed. I'm so grateful.

April Osborn, my editor, whose insight and feedback is so helpful. And to Leah and the entire team at Mira—I appreciate your support and belief in my books.

Megan Squires, my bestie. Your support, encouragement and writing days keep me going!

Andrew, none of this would be possible without your constant support of my writing and career. You believed in me before anyone else and your behind-the-scenes efforts made it all come to fruition.

Eli and Kayleen, my first and biggest fans. I love you so.

I'd also like to thank:

My film agent Dana Spector for her tireless work on my behalf.

All the bookstagrammars and booktokers who promote our work. You are the true rockstars in this business. A special shout out to Abby @crimebythebook, Sydney @Sydneyybooks, Sonica @thereadingbeauty, Jessica @thetoweringtbr.

To my author friends who have blurbed for me—Samantha Downing, Christina McDonald, Mindy Mejia, Karen Cleveland, Sandie Jones, Eliza Jane Brazier, Ashley Winstead, JT Ellison, Hannah Mary McKinnon, Amy Suitor Clarke—thank you! It means the world.

To two of my best friends—Angela Lee for designing and maintaining my website, but more than that for always cheering me on. And to Sarah Belda for all the graphic work and for always making me laugh.

To my entire extended family—your support and encouragement is always so appreciated.

And to God, may I always be okay to live in the mystery. To not always have the answers. But to believe there is something bigger than me out there.